# HOUSE

# HOUSE OF ANGELS

*Yvonne Strickland*

This book is a work of fiction.
In real life, make sure you practise safe sex.

First published in 1995 by
Nexus
332 Ladbroke Grove
London W10 5AH

Copyright © Yvonne Strickland 1995

Typeset by TW Typesetting, Plymouth, Devon
Printed and bound in Great Britain by
Cox & Wyman Ltd, Reading, Berks

ISBN 0 352 32995 5

*All characters in this publication are fictitious and any resemblance to real persons, living or dead, is purely coincidental.*

This book is sold subject to the condition that it shall not, by way of trade or otherwise, be lent, resold, hired out or otherwise circulated without the publisher's prior written consent in any form of binding or cover other than that in which it is published and without a similar condition including this condition being imposed on the subsequent purchaser.

# 1

# The Door Opens

A figure hurried across the wide, deserted road, head lowered against the pelting rain, a shoulder bag pinioned under one arm, the other clutching the lapels of her fawn raincoat. She hesitated and changed direction momentarily to avoid a long, dark, churning pool of rainwater lapping against the kerbstones. She gained the doorway of a boarded up shop and, once in the entrance, shook her coat and brushed the damp hair from her eyes. The doorway was strewn with litter and dead leaves; it smelt faintly of urine.

Karen stood facing the grey, concrete bus station at which she had a short time ago disembarked from the cheerless, creaking bus. Of the bus there was now no sign. There was no sign of anything much; just a few deserted shops with padlocked doors and shutters, the drab bus station with its peeling posters and broken fittings, and the rain.

She pulled the coat more tightly about her to exclude the chilling damp and glanced at her watch. Still a while to go yet, even if they were on time. Still time to think, time to consider or reconsider, time to stand alone and watch the rain falling.

Who were they? Karen was not entirely sure, though this was to be her face-to-face interview after several exchanges of letters and many questions, some of a personal nature. The job, as she understood it, seemed to involve relatively straightforward office and secretarial duties at a business in southern France, though oddly, knowledge of the language was not a requirement. But why a box number in England? She did not like box numbers. Why the secrecy?

All she had was a name – a name without the image of a person to give it meaning. Still, they had paid her expenses in advance; enough to more than cover her travel and to buy a lunch she had not had time to take. Was she taking a risk? Perhaps so, but recent events had induced a lack of caution to which she was not usually accustomed.

Karen was twenty-three years old. Her long, light brown hair fell straight about her shoulders and framed a soft, round face with brown eyes and full lips. At her age most girls, especially those blessed with her looks and figure, were married – happily or otherwise. She had experienced her share of male relationships, but all of them had involved eventual complications. The complications taking the form of Sandra, an old school friend, who was more than just a friend.

Their association Karen had always taken for granted; it had always influenced her routine and her future planning and in her mind seemed to possess a steadfastness and permanency of its own. More than just physical, it co-existed with her male relationships, as long as these were casual. Eventually, the two of them had taken on a small country cottage, each convincing the other that it was a good move and to the advantage of both – and so it seemed for a time.

Their time together came to an end when Sandra met Derek. He desired to have her entirely to himself and wanted to run their affairs in his own way. Sandra decided that she wanted that too, and really always had. Karen recalled only too well that day not so long ago, the day she had returned to the cottage from a visit to her parents earlier than expected. She had let herself in through the front door, quietly, as she always did; never suspecting, never intending to witness what was to be revealed. She had heard their voices and laughter first, coming from within the bedroom; the bedroom she and Sandra had always shared. She had not called out but walked slowly along the hallway and up to the bedroom door, which had been left ajar. Peering through the gap, she had seen what she was never meant to see and now, in her mind, in that bleak and unwelcoming doorway, the tableau passed before her eyes again.

Sandra and Derek were naked. He lay upon his back with Sandra positioned astride him and his hands gripping her waist. Their heads were hidden from view, as the bed was aligned with the doorway, but their most intimate parts were on full display to Karen. Sandra raised and lowered herself upon the flushed and glistening penis, her movements slow at first but quickening with their rasping breath as the seconds passed and she drove him deeper and harder into her eager sex. He moved his hands along to her buttocks, grasping them tightly and pulling her down hard as both of them lost control. Sandra's cries and his groans had persued Karen along the hallway as she hurried back to the front door, where she had let herself out as quietly as she had at first entered.

She had waited over an hour before returning to the cottage for the inevitable confrontation. The enduring relationship was broken. For Karen it was shattered.

The advertisement she saw that day, over a month ago, offered the chance of a way out; an escape from a meaningless byway. If only the advertisement was genuine.

A maroon car appeared from around the corner of a street to her right. Karen glanced down at her watch. It was almost three o'clock and three o'clock was the appointed time. She moved forward a little so as to be seen more easily, but at once felt anxious as the car drew closer. The driver, indistinct behind the rain splashed windscreen and swishing wiper blades, ignored her and the car continued by, washing up a small cascade of grey water from the bubbling pool in the roadway.

Karen felt an amalgam of disappointment and relief. Perhaps they were not going to come. She had checked the return times of the buses. A bus to take her back to the station would leave the depot and wait over the road in less than ten minutes. If no one came by then, she would be on it. She looked at her watch again. This time her hand was trembling a little. The doorway was cold.

Another car appeared, a fawn saloon moving slowly from the same direction as the first. This time she did not step forward.

The car, she saw it was a mini cab, pulled to a halt in front of her, swilling water up onto the pavement. The hiss and click of the wiper blades ticked away the seconds, the engine murmured, and then the door opened. The head and shoulders of a man appeared. He was balding and had prominent ears. The face split into a wide grin.

' 'Scuse me love,' he called above the sound of the car and the rain. 'You Miss Karen Williams?'

'Yes!' she answered dryly.

With a feeling of unease in the pit of her stomach, she clutched the shoulder bag tightly but still did not move. I can't do it, she thought. I'll tell him – oh, God! I'll say I've got to go back – I'll say it was a mistake!

The driver scampered around to the side of the car facing her, and wrenched open the door.

'Quickly, Miss, we'll all get soaked!'

Karen hurried forward, the rain spattering her face, her mind blank, and swung herself into the car. The driver slammed her door and within moments was back in his own seat.

'God 'elp us, Miss!' he grinned. 'Will it ever stop?'

His open, friendly manner she found reassuring, and inside the cab was warm. It was the first comfort and cheer she had experienced all day. She had no idea where they were going, but now it didn't seem to matter so much. It was better than standing in the doorway.

'How far away is it?' she asked.

'Oh, no more than twenty minutes, Miss. You going for a job?'

'Yes I am,' she replied. 'How did you guess?'

'Well,' he smiled, 'the lady always uses my firm. We take her to the airport and back, and sometimes people going for an interview like you.' They drove through the rain and she stared out of the window into the grey drabness, seeing nothing.

'What sort of company is it?' asked Karen, after a few minutes of introspective silence. She was almost afraid of what he might answer.

'Oh, I dunno, Miss,' he smiled. 'It's always the hotel I go to, that's where she interviews and where she stays herself when she's over here. Could be she runs an agency of some sort ... mind you, I've seen some expensive motors outside when she's had a visitor – they're not hotel guests, not in that part of the world, that's for sure.'

Karen found that his easy going, matter of fact tone enabled her to relax a little more. They had passed through the drab town centre, with its drab people trying to keep out of the soaking rain, and now passed along a main road flanked by sad trees.

The girl stood naked, her arms stretched up above her head, handcuffed to the steel chains suspended from the ceiling beam. Her legs ached, held apart by the steel cuffs bolted to the stone floor. In front of her stood an old wooden table with a single drawer. On the table, spread out in the dim light was the whip, its thin leather thongs hanging over the edge, where she could see it and contemplate the reason for its being there.

She had lost all sense of time in the still, grey silence. A silence broken only by her own heartbeat and the creaking of the metal links as she tried to adjust her position. She was grateful for the two small ceiling lamps. She was afraid of the dark. If Pauline had known about her fear of darkness she would have switched the two lights off.

She recalled what had happened. It had been something quite minor, or so she thought at the time. She had been cleaning Pauline's office, as she always did on a Friday afternoon, and had carelessly spilled a few bits of paper onto the floor whilst emptying the litter bin. It was easy enough to have these small accidents, for Pauline sometimes had her handcuffed for such duties in order to make her work more difficult. She was picking up the paper when something caught her eye. It was a note, written clumsily, in a hand she did not recognise. She stood up for a moment and looked at the small scrap of paper out of curiosity. She was still standing there when Pauline suddenly entered the room through the main door to her right. She should have thrown the piece of paper away immediately, she knew that as soon as Pauline looked at her, but she held it in her hand and stared at it for just a moment too long; and in that moment Pauline saw exactly what it was that she was holding. She was about to drop the scrap of paper into the white plastic bag when the hand shot out and snatched it from her.

'You prying little slut! I've caught you red handed!'

'No I wasn't ... I just dropped some ...'

She had never finished the sentence for a hand had struck her hard across the mouth and an angry voice had ordered, 'Shut up and stand still!'

She had stood still as Pauline hurried across the room and then returned a few seconds later to stand behind her.

She had felt the strap pass behind her elbows then tighten as her arms were pulled in against her waist, the handcuffs holding her wrists against her stomach. Next, she had tensed as one hand was placed against the back of her head and the other pressed the red rubber ball into her open mouth. It only took a moment for the strap to be fastened at the back of her neck then a hand had seized her by the arm and propelled her towards the door.

She had guessed where they were going but knew that any form of protest would have made no difference at all.

Once down there, Pauline had released her elbows and removed the handcuffs only for as long as it had taken for her to unzip the short black dress and to order her to remove her shoes and little briefs. When the handcuffs went back on, she had on nothing other than her black, garter top stockings. She had managed to suppress any sound when her arms were pulled up above her head and the padlock was snapped shut. She had remained silent even as her legs were pulled apart and the ankle cuffs clicked into place.

It was only when Pauline had gone that she had let out a muffled protest through the ball gag. A protest which rang about the empty chamber, returning to her from the stone walls because it had nowhere else to go. What if Pauline didn't come back? What if no one came to find her at all? She knew the passing minutes would become an eternity. She knew that in time she would begin to wish for the return of the person who had so recently instilled her with so much fear.

Something happened in the distance behind her, a noise perhaps.

Yes, there was something; a muffled rattle. Then footsteps, remote at first but approaching; getting louder. She twisted, trying to see over her shoulder, but she could not turn her head far enough. The footsteps drew close and, suddenly, she noticed another shadow cast along side her own from the lamp behind. Her gaze fell once more upon the black whip. She caught her breath and began to tremble.

'Will you give me a phone number?' asked Karen. 'I'll need to get back to the bus station after.'

'Don't worry, Miss,' the driver replied. 'The lady will call us when you're done. It'll probably be me picks you up again later.'

The cab slowed down and Karen found they were turning off the roadway and onto a gravel drive. The drive curved around in front of a large Victorian brick house and they crunched along slowly until they stopped beside the porch.

'Do I, er . . .' began Karen, reaching for the clasp of her shoulder bag.

'All paid for, Miss, don't worry!'

The driver got out and hurried around in the rain to open her door, but she was already half-way out.

'Don't get wet, Miss, and best o'luck!' he grinned then disappeared back into the vehicle.

Karen hurried the few steps into the gloomy brick and timber porch and turned briefly to watch the minicab crunch its way back to the main road. Above her, creaking in the chill wind, hung a wooden sign on which was carved in rustic letters, Southdowne Hotel. She tried the handle on the door and pushed. It opened silently into a dim hallway with a small reception counter. She released the heavy oak door and let it swing shut with a gasp of damp air and a soft click behind her.

The reception was furnished in dark, heavy Victorian style. There were chairs in impractical places, chairs upon which probably nobody ever sat. On the walls were yellowing prints in ebony frames, showing nineteenth-century rural scenes, and a couple of old oil paintings with crazed varnish. It smelled the way it looked – neglected. Somewhere, out of sight in the shadows, a clock ticked slowly.

A door behind the reception counter swung open and a pale, thin young man with mousey, swept back hair appeared.

'Miss Williams?' he asked nonchalantly. 'Here for the interview I suppose?'

'Er yes, I am.'

'This way, please.' He moved around the counter without looking at her directly, and turned through an opening onto the staircase. Karen followed.

The stairs, with their drab autumn carpet, brass rods and ochre floral wallpaper, turned once through ninety degrees and led them to a sombre, quiet landing with three doors along one side and a single door at the far end. The place had such an air of melancholy about it that Karen now wished the cab had never arrived. They passed along the landing and reached the far door. The youth knocked and, without waiting for a reply or taking even a fleeting glance at her, gestured with his free hand that Karen should now enter.

The room before her was brighter and altogether out of keeping with the general character of the hotel. Everything was lighter. The walls and woodwork pure white, the carpet plain oatmeal, the easy chairs in rich green leather, plush but boxy, and decidedly of this century rather than of the last one. It smelt better too, of newness and fresh flowers; for fresh flowers there were on a low coffee table amongst the green chairs. More than anything else, the room was reassuring.

'Karen, please come and sit down. Leave your coat on the stand.'

The voice came from behind a modern oak and steel office desk on the opposite side of the room. The figure, silhouetted in part against a large sash window with venetian blinds and white net curtains, stood up and waited for her to approach. She held out a slim, well manicured hand.

'How are you?' she smiled.

'Oh, I'm fine, er, you're Sonia?'

'Of course my dear, I hope you weren't expecting someone else.'

'No, I didn't mean ... no, of course not.' Karen was alarmed at her own nervousness.

Sonia had dark eyes with a hint of the orient about her face. Her black hair was swept back into an old-fashioned bun at the back of her head. In the few seconds she had been standing, Karen had noted the manner of her attire, quite different from her own plain, deep blue business suit with skirt cut just above the knees. Sonia wore a black leather biker's jacket. At her waist was a braided gold belt and below this, opaque black satin tights. She was slim, about the same build as Karen herself, though older, perhaps in her mid-thirties; it was difficult to tell.

On the desk lay a pale brown folder on which Karen observed her own name written carefully in blue ink.

'I hope you didn't get too wet on the way here,' remarked Sonia, opening the cover of the file and carefully spreading out some of its contents. Karen noticed amongst the papers, some of her own letters sent in reply over the weeks to the many questions she had been required to answer.

'It's an awful day,' replied Karen, 'it seems as though the sky will never clear.'

Sonia did not reply for some time but perused the letters and documents in the file before looking up.

'Well, you've come this far so I'm safe in assuming that

you are still interested in the position. As I have quite a lot of information from you, perhaps there are questions you would like to ask me. I haven't told you an awful lot, have I?'

'Yes right . . . I am interested but I still don't know much about your business do I?'

Sonia fixed her eyes on Karen as if trying to penetrate her inner thoughts.

'The questions you answered,' she said, 'especially those about discretion and moral attitudes, did they not prompt any thoughts in your mind as to what this might be all about?'

Karen moved her hands out of sight and down to her lap in order not to give away her nervousness.

'Er, well I – I wondered if it was some kind of club or villa – for male guests that is.'

'You mean a brothel?' asked Sonia, her expression unchanging.

Karen opened her mouth not having quite decided what to say.

'Oh, well not quite, no. I thought perhaps, more like some of those places they have in Nevada I've heard about.'

Sonia broke into a smile and leaned back into the soft green leather.

'I'm sorry my dear, this must be awful for you. I really am not trying to get you on edge, but I do have to play this very carefully. I have to be very sure about everybody with whom we have dealings. If I said that you were going roughly in the right direction, I then have to make it clear to you that now is a good time for you to say if you wish to continue this interview. If you do not I shall quite understand and I'll have the taxi here for you in a few minutes.'

'Oh please,' replied Karen. 'As long as the job I'm here for is nothing to do with . . . with . . .' She felt her cheeks reddening, she untwined her fingers under the table.

'No it isn't,' answered Sonia. 'It is exactly what I described it as. I need someone to help run the business side of things. Your involvement will be strictly as we have discussed and, as you know in my letters to you, I have offered certain safeguards with this position which means that should you wish to terminate your employment with me, you may do so at short notice, knowing that you have a little money in your own bank account. More than a little if you stay on a reasonable time.'

'All right, then please, go on.'

'Good,' continued Sonia. 'Well if this business is about anything at all, it's about exploitation of the weaker gender of our species – and I don't mean women.'

Sonia hesitated, pushing the paperwork back into the folder.

'We make movies, we are involved with publishing and at the house we cater for some of the more esoteric forms of sexual expression, very, very taboo in this country I might add.'

Karen bit her lip and asked, 'So why are you here? Why this office, in this hotel of all places?'

'Oh that's an easy one – some of our best customers are in this country. You will never see them and you will never know their names. Discretion is a vital ingredient in this business. But I can tell you this, the British establishment more than helps to pay my bills. We supply some of these people with the fantasy in private which they are only too ready to condemn in public.'

'You mean they come to the house?' asked Karen.

'No,' replied Sonia, 'never. You might say that "the house" goes to them. What we do inside the house is theatre, playacting if you like. It's like when you watch something on TV, they're only doing it for the money, but you're convinced it's all real. What we produce is marketed throughout Europe and the U.S. Some of my girls are in London regularly, on visits; some of them are actually based there. The wealthy and powerful have an insatiable appetite for our services. Sometimes the tabloid press catches them out, but that's their fault and their problem, not ours. Do you understand now?'

'Yes, but surely, going back to the videos and magazines, that's just pornography. You can get stuff like that in most parts of the world. Please excuse me putting it that way – I don't think I'm a prude, but there is more than enough of it about, especially in Europe, and a lot of it is pretty awful, at least the few examples of it that I've seen.'

'I agree,' replied Sonia, 'but it's all a matter of exploiting the right part of the market. There is room for refinement and quality, the participants, the locations, the recording techniques, presentation if you like. We sell fantasies, sometimes as images, sometimes for real, but it's quality, and we exploit the upper end of the market, people who want to experience the scene.'

She looked hard at Karen again. 'Do you know what "The Scene" is?'

Karen smiled slightly and nodded to indicate that she did, though her knowledge of the subject was rudimentary and entirely hypothetical.

'Well that is basically what we are involved in,' continued Sonia. 'Oh and some of the girls are sent to us, so they can see what it's all about. They have wealthy patrons, some in this country too, and they pay very generously like most of our clients – after all, they wouldn't want me falling onto hard times and having to write my memoirs!'

'But surely,' said Karen, 'girls like that are under someone else's control, and the others, what they do – isn't that exploitation?'

'You can look at it that way if you like,' replied Sonia, 'but I would suggest you compare it with what people do in so-called ordinary life. How many spend endless years in mundane, thankless jobs, just working to pay the bills? If circumstances allowed me to advertise for girls openly, I bet I'd have a queue a mile long outside this wretched hotel. Some of them would swap this work for their dull, miserable lives without a second thought. And the girls who work for me have the same terms I'm offering you – they can leave at any time and they have their earnings and bonuses. The fact that they do so well out of it helps to protect me from the media. It also introduces them to some very wealthy and influential people and they don't give that sort of chance up without a second thought. Incidentally, you might be interested to know that dismissal is my ultimate threat so far as they are concerned. And the longer they are with me, the more disagreeable the prospect of being shown the door becomes.'

'What about social life,' asked Karen. 'I mean male friends?'

Sonia's expression darkened. Karen wished she had not asked the question.

'I'm afraid my dear, that the house and grounds are not open to unauthorised visits by anyone – ever! Any of the girls found breaking that rule know what to expect and there are no, and I mean no, exceptions. What people do when they're away is something I have little control over, however. So far we have not had any problems. But I understand from your letters that you have no current male connections. That is so, is it not?'

'No, no, I haven't,' replied Karen, looking down at her hands.

'You understand, don't you,' continued Sonia, 'that the house is in a fairly remote area. There is no public transport and the nearest village is several kilometres away. It is possible to visit Béziers and Narbonne and there are some quite attractive little villages in the area, but Languedoc is not the Côte d'Azur, though I suspect it may well be developing in that direction.'

Sonia relaxed again a little.

'Look, if you're worried about having a boyfriend, you may be going to the wrong place. We do have a male resident – not at the house, he has a chalet. Unfortunately, he is needed for maintenance work on the house and the gardens. His role is strictly defined and it's not in his interest to cause me any problems, especially as he is wanted by the police in this country . . .'

'He's a criminal?' interrupted Karen.

'If you like,' Sonia went on, 'but it's tax fraud, he hasn't murdered anyone if that's what you're worried about – though over here what he's done is regarded as worse than murder! So there you are. Unless you get yourself a car, you don't have much of a choice I'm afraid – and there is the language of course.'

'Oh,' said Karen, 'I do speak a little French.'

Sonia smiled. 'I think you'll find the village people speak a style of French different from the French you were taught in school. But never mind, nearly all the girls are British, and the few who aren't still speak good English. Our male visitors are usually not British, interestingly enough, too risky for them I suppose. But that's not important really.'

'Would I have reasonable privacy?' asked Karen.

'Complete privacy,' assured Sonia. 'You would have your own apartment, self-contained with TV, hi-fi, whatever you need within reason, but no direct phone line. I have to be very careful you understand, though you will have the line in your own office if you really need it.'

Sonia raised her hands and exclaimed, 'Oh look! I'm making the place sound like a prison and it's not at all. There's a bar and restaurant where you'll meet all the others – you'll get on fine I'm sure. There's the library, beauty parlour and keep fit class; the gardens are quite extensive and lovely most of the year round, especially in the summer, and some of the girls have cars if you don't want to drive. We're located in an extensive wine growing region too; there are lots of vineyards in the area. Our male resident, Mike, has the pick-up. There's the pool of course, and tennis court. Then we . . .' she hesitated. 'How are you feeling about all this? I've been going on as if you've decided to accept, my dear, but maybe you're still not sure.'

Karen looked at Sonia, then from her to the window behind. It was not late, but the ragged grey sky was darkening and she became aware for the first time since entering the room that the wind and rain were buffeting the window.

'How about a cup of coffee?' offered Sonia. 'You can think more easily if you're relaxed.'

'Yes please, I would like a coffee, and, well yes, the job, if you think I would fit in, I would like to take it.'

Sonia looked at her with an odd, fleeting smile. 'No my dear, decide after coffee not before.' She rose from the chair. 'White? Sugar?'

'White please, no sugar.'

Karen watched her move across the room and noted her stiletto heeled ankle boots. She moved with a purposeful elegance to one of two doors to Karen's right and opened it slightly. She did not enter, but spoke to someone who was evidently just inside the room, then returned to her chair.

'I thought we were alone,' said Karen in a low voice, glancing at the door. 'I didn't realise that . . .'

The odd smile returned to Sonia's face. 'Oh, don't be concerned. I usually bring one of the girls with me. It helps make this place a little house from home.'

Karen thought how odd it was that this other person had remained so silent and out of sight, but considered it best not to remark on the subject. She was aware now of faint sounds from beyond the plain wooden door. Sonia was perusing the file again when the door across the room opened quietly.

Karen was aware of a figure entering the room, just outside the main field of her vision. Sonia did not look up from the file but remained silent, a silence which opened Karen's mind to lesser sounds, like the soft metallic 'chink, chink, chink,' as the figure approached. Karen turned, her mouth opened but the intended 'thank you' remained stillborn in her throat and her eyes froze wide.

The girl who neared the table was about Karen's age, perhaps a little younger, with silver-blonde hair gathered up in a clasp at the side of her head and sweeping down across her temple. Her eyes were a soft blue-grey and framed by high cheek bones; her complexion was fair but her lips were red and full, slightly parted to almost give her a look of mild surprise.

She was dressed in what Karen saw as the parody of a maid's uniform; black, with a subtle gleam, fitting her slim, shapely body like a smooth skin. The short, flounced sleeves were trimmed with white lace, as was the neck of her outfit, scooped wide and low so as to almost expose her squeezed breasts. A small, white, semi-circular cotton and lace apron was fastened high about her slim waist and the dress finished just below this, short and tight. Her legs were sheathed in sheer black nylon with an elusive, shimmering gloss and their length was accentuated by the patent leather, stiletto heeled, open sandals on her feet.

Karen momentarily thought that the short, careful steps she was taking were because she held at waist level the small tray bearing the coffee cups, and because the style of the dress would not have allowed any girl to move about too quickly without some risk to her modesty. The metallic sound, however, drew her eye to the real reason. The girl was wearing ankle cuffs. A smooth steel bracelet enclosed each of her slim ankles and these were connected by a steel chain some twenty or so centimetres in length.

Karen turned away quickly only to find herself fixed by Sonia's gaze, so she looked down at the desk, trying to express no reaction to what was happening.

'Thank you, Angela,' smiled Sonia as the girl lowered the small silver tray to the table.

'Is that all, Miss?' asked the girl dryly, avoiding eye contact with either of the two.

'That's all,' replied Sonia, her eyes still fixed on Karen's face.

With the tray set down, Karen could see that her wrists were manacled too, but with a shorter chain connecting them. The pungent odour of latex, warm and sensuous, invaded her nostrils, for the black, sleek material of the girl's dress was close to her face.

As the girl began to move away, with short measured steps, Karen attempted a belated, 'thank you' which emerged as a high pitched croak. She turned, intending to pick up her coffee cup, trying to effect a mask of indifference but her trembling hand gave her feelings away.

After what seemed an eternity, the kitchen door closed. Meanwhile, Karen thought desperately for some remark to offer until Sonia asked, 'How is your coffee?'

Karen cleared her throat, 'Oh, er ... it's just fine, yes, fine.' She took a small gulp and met Sonia's gaze. 'Does she, er, I mean do you ...'

Sonia raised her hands and smiled. 'Forgive the little trick my dear. I thought you coped rather well.'

'I don't understand.'

'Just a little game to test your reaction. I don't usually keep her like that – not here anyway.'

'Doesn't she object?' asked Karen.

'You can ask her if you wish. You'll meet her at the house, unless of course, this has changed your mind.'

Karen thought for a moment. 'But all that has nothing to do with me does it?'

'You may not be any part of it,' replied Sonia, 'but you ought to know what you will meet up with at times. So, well?'

She stared at Sonia for a second or so, feeling that the world was not quite real. 'Yes, I still accept,' she heard herself say.

The sight of Angela had shocked Karen at first, but now the image of her, dressed in the revealing latex dress and manacled hands and feet held an odd fascination she did not comprehend.

'Shall we discuss your arrangements, my dear?' Sonia smiled.

The girl was alone again in the dimly lit room of the cellar, now half standing, half hanging in the steel cuffs. Pauline had gone and the black thonged whip lay on the floor a short distance from her, where it had been carelessly thrown down.

She sobbed quietly, her long brown hair strewn about her shoulders, the tears streaming down her cheeks and forming glistening tracks over her breasts. She clutched the cold chain above her and wiped each side of her face against an arm, drying her cheeks and pushing the hair away from her eyes. Her breath came hot around the firmly placed rubber ball.

The flesh of her behind and around her thighs was crisscrossed with a myriad of pink streaks. Even her shoulders and breasts had not escaped the stinging anger of the whip, and the cries, 'Nosey little slut!' still rang in her ears as a distant mocking echo.

The lips of her sex were moist and inflamed. She urgently needed the attention and relief which she realised she could not have. She knew that was why Pauline had left her like that, chained up helpless, unable even to relieve herself. Pauline was too well aware how the whipping aroused her; how it made her burn intensely inside as well as out. If only her legs were not held apart. She twisted against the chains. If only . . .

It had taken less than a fortnight for Karen to put her affairs in order, during which time her travel documents and schedule had arrived in the post. With her property in the hands of an agent, there was little else to do. It was to be a complete break but if she still harboured any doubts, there were put to rest on the day the taxi arrived to take her to the airport. That day, like so many others before it, was dull and overcast with a fine drizzle sweeping down from the featureless grey sky.

The people in the streets appeared downcast and grey too, going about their uncommunicative business with dour complacency. Even the cab driver was despondent, complaining bitterly about the government, immigrants and taxation. Karen politely agreed with all of his sentiments, feeling relieved when they reached the airport and a little happier once inside the terminal building. At least, here, the lights were bright and the place was full of purposeful bustle.

She was to fly only as far as Paris, having opted to make the long journey south by train, wanting to see as much as possible of the countryside on her way. It was this final stage of her journey she found to be the greatest ordeal.

She did not sleep well on the train, and worse, found that her night school French was by no means as great an asset in aiding communication as she had hoped. She had nearly missed her connection at Lyon and, on the long second stage of the rail journey, suffered bouts of travel sickness for the first time since her childhood.

By the time she reached the small town where she was to disembark, Karen was exhausted. When she stepped out into the station forecourt with her two small cases, it was past seven o'clock in the evening. The air was calm, pleasantly warm and suffused with the perfume of flowers, though Karen was almost oblivious to it. Then a welcome voice from the figure emerging from a white Citroen nearby reached her ears.

'Hi! You're Karen, yes?'

'Yes,' she replied to the smiling face, open, honest and blue-eyed.

'I'm Kim. Let's get your stuff in the car and we'll get going!'

Karen did not recall much of their conversation, nor did she see much of the passing countryside, for she slept in the small car as she had not slept since leaving England.

'Wakey, wakey!' came the voice in her ear, and she opened her eyes to see Kim pulling on the handbrake.

It was dusk as she climbed from the car and looked about her. The house, a three-storey rambling old villa, rose in front of her, some of the windows already lighted. Karen had no idea where she was, and did not particularly care. If there was a cup of tea, a shower and a decent bed, she would be blissfully contented. The events of the past day were becoming a distant memory. The present had become a dream.

When she awoke, the morning sun was filtering through the venetian blind. She had deliberately left the powder blue curtains opened so to greet this first morning from her bed. The birds were singing in the distance and the clock radio at her bedside told her it was six-thirty. What day was it? That didn't matter, and it was at least an hour before she needed to think about getting up. She slid back under the smooth apricot sheets, not to sleep, but to think about the past, and the future.

# 2

# A Lesson in Submission

When Karen arrived in the main hallway at a little before nine o'clock, Sonia stood in conversation by the office door. Karen approached somewhat hesitantly, eyeing the girl who stood in discussion with Sonia, regarding her slim form. Many things rushed through her mind at the same time; she wondered if she ought to approach closer in case the subject of their conversation was of a private nature and not for her ears. The girl was about Karen's age and build, stunningly attractive with long, waved auburn hair pushed back over her shoulders. Seeing Karen approach, she turned and smiled. Sonia, following the direction of her gaze, turned also.

'Karen my dear, did you sleep well?'

'Yes, I did thanks,' she replied, feeling now that the time was right for her to move closer and join them. 'I don't remember going to bed.'

Sonia turned with a gesture of her hand to the girl and said, 'Karen, this is Annette.'

'Hello, Karen,' smiled Annette, holding out her hand. 'It's nice to meet you.'

'I'll talk to Karen this morning,' continued Sonia. 'We'll get a bite to eat, and then we can get down to the mundane details of our office routine.' Sonia glanced down at her watch then back to the vivacious Annette. 'Look, my side of things won't occupy a great deal of our time, perhaps you could be back here by lunchtime so you could take Karen to meet a few of the other girls in the restaurant, then she may as well be free for the rest of the day.'

'Of course I will,' replied Annette, turning to Karen. 'I'll call here for you at one o'clock then and after lunch, if you want, I'll show you around the grounds.'

'Sounds fine to me,' smiled the newly reassured Karen.

Annette turned and, with a small circular gesture of her hand, said, 'See you later!'

Karen followed Sonia, thinking that perhaps her imagination had been earlier working overtime, for here there was nothing untoward, nothing unusual about the place that she could see to cause her the slightest degree of apprehension.

Annette smiled to herself and glanced back at Karen as she pushed open the main doors.

Stepping from under the portico and into the soft morning air, she looked down and hesitated.

'Oh, Pancake, are you enjoying the sun today?'

The ginger cat rolled onto his back and Annette ran her fingers under his chin and over his chest. Everyone, even Pauline, liked Pancake and found time to fuss over him. He was Valerie's cat and Valerie had named him Pancake because, as she told everyone, 'The lazy little bugger spends all day flat out!'

Anyone seeing Annette leave the house and set out along the pathway that morning might have guessed she was on her way to the pool or to the tennis court, except that she carried neither towel nor tennis racket. She stopped again for a few minutes and chatted casually to a couple of the girls sitting enjoying the sun at the poolside, before continuing on her way past the tennis court and over the gentle rise towards the driveway which led out towards the main gate. Once out of sight of the house she made an abrupt left turn, heading now in the direction of the chalet, the intended goal of her excursion.

Mischief and deviousness were, as all those close to her were aware, almost synonymous with Annette. She was single-minded too and usually gained what she wanted, especially from men of financial means, with little discernible effort. Yet, this woman of the world was only in her mid-twenties, her youth belying what, to many people, might appear to be a lifetime's experience. She could boast an enviable list of clients, some of whom were in possession of considerable wealth and influence, most gained through her association with Sonia and the opportunities that had subsequently developed from it.

She had been familiar with the SM scene before meeting Sonia and her eager propensity to investigate this secret world further, together with its financial rewards, had made Annette one of Sonia's greatest assets.

She had met Sonia at a party – a very private party, in London. Sonia already knew about Annette, but of course Sonia made it her business to know about a lot of people; that was, after all, part of her business. Annette was fascinated by Sonia's little empire, she saw its potential immediately, and she was delighted when Sonia suggested that she might like to apply her abilities in the tailor-made surroundings and more congenial climate at the house in France.

Once established there, Annette had not been dilatory when it came to investigating the only two males on hand at the villa. Having a natural inclination for older men brought her first into contact with James. She had managed to contrive a visit to his daytime retreat at the annexe, and their first meeting dispelled any illusions she might have had as to his suitability as a lover.

James was a tall, slender, academic type, patient and modest in manner. His abundant white hair hung about pale blue eyes which gazed, disconcertingly magnified, through heavily framed spectacles. He walked with a stoop, though not through the passage of the years, for, after some consideration, she guessed his age to be no more than forty-five.

With his long limbs and extended, delicate, waxy fingers, he reminded Annette of a large, pale spider. Indeed, the analogy proved an appropriate one for James sat like a large, pale spider at the centre of an electronic web; a web of cables and optical fibres stretching through the appropriate parts of the house and terminating in little cameras concealed or otherwise in strategic places so as to capture and record, from all angles and in intimate detail, the charades and games for which the market saw no end of demand.

About his person stood a confusing array of consoles, monitors, video players and an editing unit of impressive complexity. Here all the images were brought together; stored, digitised, manipulated and modified before being transferred onto master discs and tapes. This, Annette had thought, was an empire within an empire, discrete but ever present, seeing but unseen. It gave her a degree of sensual satisfaction to know that on certain occasions he sat watching her and it did not concern her in the least.

The fact that James would see her on his screens, from several viewpoints, performing some of the most shameless and intimate of acts with both men and women did not appear to concern him either, a phenomenon which puzzled her greatly for a while. No man, she considered, could watch such goings on for long, without wanting a piece of the action unless, unless . . .

A simple question to one of the other girls confirmed her suspicion. It turned out that James lived with his French boyfriend in a small village some ten kilometres away. What was he, she then wondered, doing here? It transpired that even an electronics wizard might succumb to scandal, as had James at Cambridge, after his involvement with two young men under his tutelage and an affair with a prominent Church of England clergyman.

So that left Mike.

Annette had initially thought of Mike as being a little rustic, not at first knowing of his professional background in London, nor of his timely escape from England before his arrival at the house. Here was another individual for whom acquaintance with Sonia had proved an unexpected blessing.

The morning sun glistened on her long auburn hair and danced in her green eyes as she approached the door. She wore her black T-shirt, Mike admired the way it moulded to her breasts, and her tight blue denim mini-skirt. Mike liked that too.

Mike was slim with short fair hair and, in Annette's well practised estimation, a reasonably good physical specimen. She judged his age at thirty-two or thirty-three, on the younger side for her tastes but he represented a freer and more natural outlet for her sexual expression. He was both passionate and considerate, an ideal lover perhaps, for many women, but his desire to be in control during their lovemaking was not by any means in keeping with her inclinations.

Mike, for his part, regarded her as a challenge. He did not have to lure her into his home in the first instance, she came quite willingly. Nor was there any need to contrive matters so as to render her seduction easier. From the time of their first physical encounter, she was just as willing and forthright as he was. It troubled him slightly that she was so, for Mike had never felt entirely at ease with women he regarded as over confident. Nevertheless, her personality, her looks and her figure had always conspired, and succeeded, in rapidly overcoming his misgivings.

They both knew that such a liaison as theirs was forbidden and what the consequences for either of them might be if the ever alert Pauline, and thereby Sonia, was to find out. As for Pauline, the only occupant of the house who appeared to orbit outside the influence of that dark star was Cheryl, although her degree of influence over the other inhabitants of the house appeared to vary with their status.

Annette, however, often regarded other people's rules as an obstruction to be negotiated and she didn't doubt that Mike was worth the risk. Mike, on the other hand, stood to lose more than anyone if the worst should happen. Other men might only dream of being in a place like this, even if the money was not what he had long been accustomed to drawing whilst running his affairs in London. There was no need to spend much money here anyhow. The weather was good, the food and wine even better, and the outdoor work, healthy and worry free. Mike saw no reason to fall foul of Pauline, and if she ordered him to lick her boots, he just might! Others, it was rumoured, had.

Annette reached the white painted door and pressed the bell button, looking about to see if anyone else was in sight. The door opened part way and Mike's face appeared in the gap, his eyes darting about over her shoulder.

'Hi! Come in.'

She slipped quickly in and the door closed.

'Nobody about, I hope,' he said, taking her in his arms and kissing her.

'No, we're OK,' she answered, returning his kiss.

Mike had on his white bathrobe and smelled strongly of aftershave. She could see that he had made a nominal attempt at tidying the room, he always did before she arrived, but putting things behind chairs and arranging magazines into one large pile instead of several smaller ones did not, as far as Annette was concerned, constitute good housekeeping.

'Want a drink?' he grinned.

'Sure,' she replied, 'if you have any clean cups.'

'Ooo! Knife out already?' he responded with an exaggerated look of offence.

'Well, you're such an untidy sod despite all my efforts,' she remarked, 'but I'll have a coffee since you ask!'

After coffee, Mike said, 'How about we check out my bedroom, see if it's tidy enough?'

'All right,' she smiled, and both of them arose, he letting her go ahead of him, slipping off her sandals as she went.

The blinds were closed against the outside world but a gentle light filtered through and illuminated the room softly. They kissed, then Mike lifted the hem of her T-shirt, pullng it up over her head and raised arms, so that her naked breasts fell free and he could feel her warmth. Even before she had discarded the T-shirt he had cupped her breasts in his hands and begun to kiss her again; working down methodically from her soft neck until his lips closed about her nipples. She stood with her eyes lightly shut, feeling his hands move around her and his fingers close on the zip fastener at the rear of her skirt. The waistband loosened and the skirt slid over her thighs, with a little encouragement from him.

Annette reached for the belt about his waist. She had felt his arousal through the heavy material of the bathrobe and knew how it yearned to be freed. All she now wore was a sheer black bikini brief and as she released his bathrobe she felt the tips of his fingers, cool and firm, ease themselves under the elastic below her stomach. Their lips joined firmly as his fingers, held against her body by the briefs, slipped quickly between the warm folds of her sex and stroked gently, causing her to breathe in sharply.

At the same time as his bathrobe fell open, her cool hand closed about the firm heat of his erection and began to work it slowly back and forth, causing the fingers of his free hand to press hard into her back, before beginning to tug down at the rear of her briefs.

They disengaged from each other so that Annette could remove the briefs quickly, but having done so, she dropped to her knees in front of him and, taking the livid shaft in her hand once more, slid her lips over the head and down behind it, moving her hand back and underneath his testicles. His eyes closed tightly and he breathed in deeply, letting his fingers stray through her shining hair, willing her never to stop her voluptuous game with the focus of his senses. After a minute or so, she could feel the tension in his groin and knew that this could only last for a short time longer. With well judged timing, she slid off him, twirling her tongue about the head, making it, and his whole body, quiver. She raised herself up and made hurriedly for the nearby bed, he close behind her, letting slip and discarding the bathrobe as he went.

They played for a while on the edge of the bed, letting the intimate explorations of their fingers and tongues drive them beyond the bounds of urgency and into the realms of lustful abandon. They wrestled, laughing, into position, he pinning her down so that her thighs were pushed up and back, trapped under his armpits, with her knees over his shoulders. With his hands, he held her arms either side of the pillow, his weight keeping her firmly down, spread out and immobile. He entered her hard and deep, riding her vigorously until she gasped and cried out, gripping him hard and insistently with her legs, he groaning softly, until both their passions were exhausted.

It was now mid-morning and they lay in each other's arms, her auburn hair spread across his chest, her cheek resting on his shoulder. She lifted her head and gazed into his eyes, stroking her finger down over his lips.

'Next time . . .'

He waited for her to continue.

'Next time . . . why don't we get you into the house?'

'Now that's not a terribly good idea, much as I'd like to. I really would, believe me.'

'We could you know,' she pressed, 'the back door is usually locked at night so nobody uses the back stairs. I can easily get us in.'

Mike propped his head up on his hand. 'Look, if I'm seen anywhere in there apart from the bar and restaurant on the ground floor, I've had it – I've got nowhere else to go. It wouldn't matter so much if you got the push, you could go anywhere you liked.'

'So you don't want to bother?'

Mike tutted in exasperation, 'Well, yes, all right! I'd love to spend a bit of time in your place, you know I would, then I wouldn't have to tidy up in here – unless you think I haven't bothered!'

'Well, it is a bit of a tip,' she smiled, 'no place to bring a lady!'

He slapped her hard on the behind and as she jerked and let out a squeal said, 'I didn't exactly force you in through the door did I!'

'Cheeky sod!' Annette retorted. 'I took pity on you – nobody else would except Jackie, and you wouldn't have the benefit of my conversation, she's purely carnal.'

'Sorry,' grinned Mike, pulling her close and kissing her, 'I didn't mean it that way, honest. I'd really like to see you over there if you want to tell me when, but we would have to be so very, very careful – make it a night when we know Pauline is a long way away, preferably in a different country!'

'Tuesday's all right,' said Annette, nonchalantly. 'I think there must be something on TV she watches or somewhere she slopes off to; she's never about and Sonia very rarely goes upstairs that late in the day either. Even if they did, they wouldn't use the back stairs; with the door locked, there's no point, it's just a long way round.'

'OK,' he smiled, 'Tuesday. What time?'

'Nine o'clock,' she responded, 'and I want to do a deal with you.'

'A deal – what sort of deal?'

'Right, how many times have I been down here to see you, including now?'

'Er . . . four, no five times,' he answered. 'Why?'

'Well,' she went on, 'you always call the shots in here, yes? I mean it's your territory after all.'

'I've never quite thought about it that way,' he answered, 'but go on.'

'OK, well we'll be on my territory over there, so what I say goes – that's the deal; my rules on my patch, yes?'

'And what might your rules be?' he quizzed.

'I'll tell you when we're over there,' she teased.

'Be fair,' he objected with mock seriousness, 'how can you expect me to agree to something if I don't know what I'm supposed to be agreeing to?'

'Up to you,' she answered nonchalantly. 'I say we do things my way on my patch just as we do them your way on yours.'

Mike pulled himself up until his shoulders were resting against the padded headboard. He took her by the arms and said, 'I reckon you've been planning this for quite a while. I know you, you're up to something!'

Annette did not reply but narrowed her eyes at him, smiled and kissed him on the forehead.

'Tell you what,' he grinned, 'I'll go along with it, whatever it is, if we take turns, how's that for a deal? If it's something I won't mind, then you won't mind either.'

'Oh, Mike, you're being childish, it was just a . . . oh, all right, if you want.'

At a minute to nine, Annette left the small group at the bar and stepped into the foyer. As she did so, a pair of red lips and a figure in glistening black swept by and out through the open front doors, evidently without seeing her. It was Pauline.

'Where the hell's she off to I wonder,' Annette whispered to herself.

She watched the figure disappear hurriedly along the pathway and into the night, then turned along the ground floor corridor and passed first Sonia's office on her right, then the main stairs on her left. Carrying on to the rear of the house, she heard voices and laughter but saw nobody else as she reached the side entrance to the kitchen, then the smaller corridor, running off at a right angle to the back stairs, the cellars and the rear door.

Annette had two keys in the pocket of her jeans. One of these, a large old iron key, she pulled out as she reached the door. She drew back the two iron bolts, turned the key in the lock and swung the creaking wooden door inwards. The night air was pleasantly cool and the chirping of insects broke the silence as she peered into the darkness.

'I'm here!' came a voice from the shadows close to her left.

'Oh Christ!' she started. 'You'll give me a bloody heart attack jumping out like that!'

'Sorry,' he grinned, 'but I had to hide, it might not have been you.'

'Who d'you think it might have been,' she hissed, pulling him inside, 'the Archbishop of Canterbury?'

'No, Lyon,' he quipped.

'Didn't know they had one,' she responded, sliding the bolts shut and turning the key in the mortice lock.

Annette led the way up the narrow stairs with their ornate brass wall lights. They reached the small first floor landing where she hesitated. Mike started up the next flight of stairs.

'Come back!' she hissed, 'we're not going any further.'

He turned abruptly, his face showing apprehension in case she had heard someone approaching.

'This way, not up there.'

'I thought your room was on the top floor with the other girls,' he whispered.

'It is,' she replied, 'but we're not going to my room, we're going to a different one.'

They passed quietly down the corridor until they reached the second of three arched doorways on their left. Annette pulled the smaller key from her pocket, turned it in the lock and pushed down the ornate brass handle. They passed hurriedly inside and the door closed behind them with a reassuring click.

'How did you get the keys?' asked Mike.

'Never you mind,' she replied with a knowing smile. 'I just did, that's all.'

'Why have we come here?' he asked, looking around.

'Because I prefer it – what is this, the Spanish Inquisition?'

The room was dimly lit by a rose pink glow from the cornice lights. The plush maroon carpeting and the warm light gave it an intimate, inviting ambience; the still air was suffused with a sensual, undefined perfume. There were two doors to their left. One of these was closed and the other ajar with a pink light showing inside. He could make out sufficient detail to see that it was a bathroom.

'Where's that door lead to?' he asked, indicating towards the closed one.

'That's the kitchenette,' she replied, 'and I've got a bottle of dry white wine in the fridge for us you'll be delighted to know.'

The centre of the room was occupied by two modern style black leather easy chairs and a two seater, all arranged about a low coffee table. Annette led him over to the chairs and said, 'You sit down and behave yourself, I'll get the wine.'

He settled down into the soft leather and inhaled the odour of luxury.

On the far side of the room was a large, semi-circular arch, behind which hung a heavy black curtain. When Annette reappeared with the wine and sat down in the chair opposite, he asked, 'Is that the bedroom?'

'Well, not exactly,' she answered guardedly, and filled the glasses. 'Hope you like a decent Chablis, and, by the way, the door across the corridor from this one is Pauline's.'

Mike's eyes widened with consternation and the wine glass stopped just short of his lips.

'But don't worry,' she continued with an impish smile, 'I saw her go out earlier and anyway, she doesn't have a key to any of these rooms. She has to collect them from the main office whenever she needs access.'

'Phew! Right,' he breathed, drinking back his wine. 'So what are the rooms for?'

'Visitors and, er . . . special occasions,' she replied.

After pouring their third glass of wine, Annette pushed her long, flowing hair back over her shoulders, smiled knowingly at Mike and said, 'I'll finish this later. I'm going to get showered and changed, OK?'

'Sure thing,' he grinned, lifting his glass. 'I promise I won't go anywhere.'

He watched her slim form as she disappeared into the bathroom, pushing the door shut behind her. After a short time he heard the shower start up and the splashing of water. He put down his glass, arose from the chair and made his way over to the archway with its black drapes, curious about her reaction to his question, intent on knowing what lay hidden beyond the heavy black veil. He reached inside the archway and feeling the edge of the curtain, pulled it slowly aside.

He could see nothing, the room was in darkness.

Moving part way through, he slid his hand down the wall, hoping that the light switch would be on that side. It was. With a quiet click, the lights flooded the scene with the same soft, pink glow of the room behind so he could observe the interior of the chamber from end to end.

He stood in motionless wonder and let out a long, low whistle.

His first impression was of a collection of black leather and chrome furniture arranged randomly. Further examination revealed that it was not so, for this was no ordinary furniture. There were only six main pieces in the room, chairs and benches of different configurations and design, but all were fitted in one way or another with black leather straps or steel cuffs. At the far end stood, what appeared to be, an odd shaped bidet with a tall back and head rest and close by, a steel cage with various restraints fitted inside it.

Hanging along the wall opposite were assorted items of equipment. The purpose of some of this soon became evident, whilst that of other items did not. Groups of spotlights were positioned on metal tracks running across the ceiling and some of the lamps on tall stands looked to be intended for a photographic studio. He switched off the light and let the curtain fall back into place, then returned to his chair to finish off the remaining glass of wine. His hand was shaking. Surely she wasn't expecting to . . .

The sound of the shower stopped.

A short while later, Annette emerged from the shower room, momentarily silhouetted in the doorway, then walked slowly towards him. She was dressed in a pale coloured bathrobe belted about the waist, but she walked, and looked, somehow different. When she moved closer, and he could take in the full length of her form, he could see why.

On her feet were fastened high, stiletto heeled sandals, making her taller and accounting for her more deliberate and poised steps. The black leather gleamed softly in the rose pink light.

'Your turn now my lad!' she announced, her arm outstretched towards the bathroom.

Mike lifted himself from the soft chair. 'It's, er, OK, I took a shower before I came out.'

'Then go and take another!' she ordered.

'Oh, all right, but I can't see the point, I'm perfectly clean you know.'

He walked up to her and kissed her, running his hands through her hair and down her face, brushing her full and sensuous lips with his fingers. 'Won't be long,' he smiled, and turned towards the bathroom.

'And Michael!' she called after him. 'There's a bathrobe in there for you. Put it on, and what's in the pocket, put that on too!'

'You're the boss this time around,' he shrugged, and pushed the door shut behind him.

Some ten or so minutes had elapsed before Mike reappeared, now wearing a gown similar to hers but his feet were bare upon the soft, yielding carpet.

'God, this place would shame the Ritz,' he commented. 'It must cost Sonia a damn fortune.'

'I think it costs her clients a fortune actually,' replied Annette coolly, getting up from her chair and walking over to him.

There was soft music playing. She had switched on the hi-fi and he saw that the coffee table, minus glasses and bottle, was placed away from the chairs and over by the wall.

Annette smiled gently and put her arms about his neck, and Mike slipped his around her waist as she pressed her warm lips softly against his. She was perfumed, warm and very sensual, and she could feel his enthusiasm for her even through the heavy material of both their gowns.

Without speaking, she slipped her arms from him and gently eased his from her. He watched her hands move down to the belt about his gown and felt the knot loosen. The belt fell away and the gown slid open. Mike reached for her belt too but did not realise his intentions, for she gripped his arms and said, 'Not yet, wait!'

Her hands moved over to the lapels of his gown and she pulled these apart, easing them back over his shoulders so that the gown slid down his arms and fell into a heap on the carpet behind him.

She took her arms from him and moved back. 'Very good,' she whispered, looking him up and down so that he felt, for a moment, like a mannequin in a shop window display. She walked slowly around, running her finger lightly down his spine as she passed behind. She felt him tense as her soft fingers descended all the way down his back to the softness of his behind.

He was not quite naked but wore what she had left for him in the pocket of the gown. It was a g-string, held in place by a thin black cord, tied at each side of his waist, with another cord running down under his buttocks. The small elasticated pouch in fine, sheer nylon controlled rather than concealed his partly developed erection and made him feel even more naked in front of her than if he had worn nothing at all.

Annette walked over to the two seater and lifted something black up from it; something he had not seen until then because it was resting obscured against the blackness of the seat. She returned, smiling and held it open in front of him. It looked and smelled like a leather jacket but gave out a clinking metallic ring as she moved one side of it towards him.

'OK,' she said, 'put your arm in.'

He lifted his right arm but, looking closer, hesitated.

'What is this?' His eye focused on the straps and buckles hanging from each side of the garment. He quickly withdrew his arm.

'Now wait, you didn't say anything about . . .'

'You're not frightened are you?' she asked, eyeing him coolly. 'If you go back on your promise, the show's off – for good. I mean it!'

He hesitated, looking from her eyes to what she held out, then back again. 'Oh, come on then,' he muttered after some seconds, and slipped his right hand and arm into the leather sleeve which ran across the inside of the jacket.

'That's it, now the other, right inside.'

He slid his hand into the other end of the sleeve and pushed it through so that both arms crossed and were folded closely together inside it. Annette pulled the leather garment over his shoulders from behind so that it enclosed the upper part of his body from neck to waist, as well as cocooning his arms within the internal sleeve. The metal buckles chinked and rasped as she fastened the straps down the back, starting at the collar and working down to the waistband, then working back up to make final adjustments. When she was done, the straitjacket was firm and taut about his body.

'Well!' she proclaimed, moving around to face him, a mischievous smile breaking under her wide green eyes, 'that's got you both under control!'

She stepped back a pace and looked him up and down. 'How does it feel – do you think you can get out of it?'

He struggled for a few seconds, twisting from side to side, trying to move his arms appart but the tight enclosure of black leather was unyielding.

'God,' he muttered, still attempting to force apart his arms, 'I don't think Houdini could get out of this.'

'All right, now sit down,' she ordered.

He backed towards the chair, then, letting his knees bend, half sat, half fell onto the leather seat, which exhaled a soft whistle with the sudden compression. Annette loosened her belt and, with her eyes fixed on him, slid her own gown from her and let it fall to the floor on top of his.

'Phew!' let out Mike, squirming to adjust himself in the chair, his eyes assimilating this newly revealed image.

Annette stood before him with hands on hips. Her auburn hair tumbled down over a white chiffon blouse with long flounced sleeves and lace ruffle down the front. Even in the subdued light of the room, her firm breasts and nipples were barely veiled by the sheer fabric. Below the blouse she had on a tight, glossy black PVC mini skirt which stretched like a second skin across her thighs, although she stood with her legs only slightly parted. She turned about slowly, running her hands provocatively over her hips, letting him view her behind and the seams of her sheer black stockings, and her feet poised on the long stiletto heels.

'Nice?' she teased, turning to face him.

'Sensational!' he breathed.

'You're a naughty boy, Michael,' she remarked, looking at the flimsy, bulging pouch between his legs, 'you look as though you're trying to squeeze out of that!'

His arousal was obvious to both of them and he felt the cord pulling tight under his crotch, like a hand reaching between his legs from behind to cup his genitals.

Annette eased herself gently into the chair opposite and sat with her arms folded, watching him in silence, crossing and re-crossing her legs occasionally because she knew how it affected him. It amused her to watch him as he now and then adjusted his position to make his aching, swollen penis more comfortable.

Eventually she asked, 'Don't you feel a bit vulnerable like that? I mean, I could just leave you here if I felt like it. Anyone could come in if the door was left unlocked, the maids – Pauline maybe. You never know, she might fancy you and take you in for the night! I wonder what she would do with you.'

Mike did not reply, there was little point. He realised he was going to be wearing the straitjacket until she decided to undo him. So that was that, and if she was trying to torment him, she was succeeding very well. The muted light glistened in her eyes as she shook back her hair.

After a while, she stood up, adjusting and straightening the hem of the tight little skirt, then again smoothing it slowly and tantalisingly down with her splayed fingers.

'Get up!' she ordered.

He hesitated for a few moments, not being sure how to comply without the use of his arms. After a couple of failed attempts, twisting from side to side, he swung his body forward in the chair, using the momentum of this action to bring himself up to his feet.

'Well done,' smiled Annette, 'now, over here!'

She indicated the area of floor in front of where she stood. Mike stepped up to her, his eyes fixed on hers. She raised her hands up to the collar of her blouse, and without taking her green eyes from him, her fingers, with slow deliberation, followed the lace ruffle downwards, undoing the buttons one by one until the blouse fell open, not quite uncovering her breasts. She eased the hem of the blouse from under the waistband of the skirt before slipping it from her shoulders and arms, and draping it over the arm of her chair. She placed her arms about his neck and pressed her lips against his in a long and voluptuous kiss.

He felt her hands move down his back and over the straps until they reached the bare flesh at the base of his spine. Her fingers slipped under the thin cord, stroking where the cleavage of his behind began, aware of the electric tension passing through his body. She could feel too, his coiled erection straining to be free. Their kissing became more intense.

Suddenly, she moved back, and pointing down to the floor, said, 'Kneel!'

He hesitated before her wide-eyed expression, then lowered himself unsteadily, letting himself fall the last part of the way until his knees hit the soft carpet. He rested with his face close to her stomach, feeling the sensual warmth of her body. She turned around with her back to him, looked over her shoulder at him and ordered, 'Undo it!'

His eyes focused upon a small, bright metal ring shimmering at the waistband of her skirt. He leaned forward, almost losing his balance in attempting to grasp the ring in his teeth but without succeeding. He moved closer still and tried to lift the ring into position with his tongue. That worked. So now he held the ring firmly, his chin and nose pressing into the warm plastic covering her soft flesh. He pulled the ring, almost overbalancing himself and causing her to sway. Realising that he had to pull downwards and not out, he tried again, and was this time rewarded by the soft whirr of the zip fastener opening. The waistband and the black shiny fabric parted widely to each side, contracting away from the cleavage of her behind. The zipper ended half way down the skirt so he released the ring and brushed his lips against the exposed flesh before leaning back onto his heels.

Annette said nothing, but eased the skirt down with a whispering swish over her thighs and down to the floor where she kicked it away. Apart from the elasticated stockings and the high heeled sandals, she was naked. She walked around him and sat down on the two seater.

Her voice from behind him called softly, 'Over here.'

Mike turned around and shuffled towards her on his knees; it was easier than trying to struggle to his feet. She sat with her legs crossed and her hands at either side of her, resting her palms down on the cool leather. As he came closer, she uncrossed her legs, and leaning forwards, reached out and placed her hands on each side of his head. She pulled him on, parting her legs either side of him until he stopped with his face close to her breasts. She leaned forward further and kissed his forehead, at the same time reaching down between his legs and cupping her hand over the bulging organ held still in place by the smooth nylon skin.

'Still enthusiastic, I see,' she whispered in his ear.

The intake of breath and the sudden tremour of his body had already answered her question. Her fingers glided into the gap where the elasticated sides of the pouch were stretched away from his flesh and he held his breath expecting at any moment, that she would slip the knots on the cord about his waist, so releasing at least that part of his body from restraint.

She did not. Instead, Annette placed her hands about his shoulders and pulled him further forward, spreading her legs wider still and letting her body relax back into the soft leather.

He breathed the warm perfume of her body, suffused with the rich odour of leather. His lips touched the warm flesh of her breasts, then her hard nipples, moving from one to the other, holding them gently in his lips, teasing and circling them with his tongue. She closed her eyes and let her head fall back against the seat with her hands resting at either side of her legs. She knew he needed no further prompting.

He moved back a little, bending lower so that his lips and tongue could play their tingling game down the soft skin of her stomach, where he lingered some while. He felt her tense as his kisses passed downwards and his lips found the firmer, smooth shaven flesh above her vulva. Here he coursed back and forth, feeling her body twitch in anticipation. Even with the tight restraint about his arms, he was still going to make her wait until he decided to do what he knew she craved for. He heard her give a little cry as his tongue stroked between the moist, inflamed lips of her sex. It was a practice at which, with her encouragement and his enthusiasm, they both knew he had become an expert. She began to moan softly and lifted up her feet, crossing them behind his neck and resting her thighs on his shoulders, willing him, pushing him deeper into her.

His penis ached hard against the restraining nylon and he urgently wanted to release it. He wanted his arms free as well; to be able to rise up and push her back, to enter her at all cost. But his own lust was caged and he could only act as a slave to her desires, letting his tongue act out its intense drama in the theatre of her sex.

Annette moaned more loudly and her breathing shortened until sexual release took her body into gasping spasms of pleasure, her legs locking about him almost violently so that his mouth tasted her climax.

It took her several seconds to recover herself, then she slid her feet back onto the carpet, allowing Mike to straighten up and rest on his knees.

She leaned forward and kissed him, then with her arms on his shoulders, helped him to shuffle back away from the seat, at the same time sliding down onto her knees to face him. Their lips met again and he felt her hands glide down over the enveloping leather and onto the bare flesh below his waist.

Her finges played tantalisingly with the cord then she pulled smartly on the knot at each side. The cord suddenly gave and released the confining pouch. His shaft sprang as if released from a trap and he caught his breath hoarsely when her cool fingers slipped under and closed about it, working it gently whilst her other hand cupped his testicles. Every nerve in his body was concentrated on her actions. Had the door burst open upon them, he would not have been aware of it. His pelvis moved back and forth involuntarily and after a few moments she said, 'Lie down on the carpet.'

She moved around to help as he lowered his body and twisted to one side, guided by her but half rolling, half falling onto his back. He watched Annette climb astride then lower herself over his erection. At first she would not let him enter her but took the engorged shaft in her hand and positioned the glistening head against the lips of her sex, moving back and forth so that it stroked between the wet folds of her labia. His need was now so great that he felt he could lose control if she did not stop, but it was obvious that Annette was arousing herself once more by this action. At last, she let the head of his penis slip into her, then leaned forward over him, resting on her hands and quickly lowering her pelvis, so that he eagerly drove into her up to the root.

She worked him slowly at first, knowing how close he was to sexual release, until she felt her own currents of pleasure rising to a peak once more, then faster, both of them panting in unison. The tide of orgasm engulfed them together, she gasping and thrusting down onto him as hard as she could, he twisting against the straitjacket, finding it all the more intense because of the long, teasing prologue and his own helpless restraint.

After her breathing softened, she lifted herself from him, turned and picked up her gown from the carpet. Mike rolled over and twisted about, trying to get to his knees.

'God!' he breathed, 'that was almost too much.'

Annette, still in stockings and heels with the bathrobe

draped over her arm, stood smiling as he eventually, by wedging himself against the two seater, struggled upright. They stood facing each other for a few moments.

'Right,' he said 'you'd better undo me.'

'Undo you?' she responded whimsically. 'You were much better at it with that on – I must say, I haven't enjoyed it so much in months.'

'Come on!' he insisted. 'Don't mess around, I've got to get out of here!'

'Mmm, well,' she replied, 'I don't think you're in any position to be giving orders. Maybe I'll think about it whilst I'm in the bathroom – do behave yourself, Michael, won't you?'

She walked away and left him, closing the bathroom door behind her. He struggled uselessly for a few seconds then stood motionless with his eyes fixed on the point of her disappearance. He listened to the water running and splashing in the shower, then looked towards the archway with its heavy black drapes and said quietly to himself, 'Just you wait you little bitch, just you wait. It'll be my turn next.'

# 3

# Trick and Treat

Whatever misgivings Karen might have harboured between her interview and arrival at the house were dispelled by the time her first month had passed. Not least in her estimation, was the smiling warmth of the countryside, the clear, blue skies and embracing sun.

The rambling, Mediterranean style house was some two centuries old, and whilst the interior managed to retain much of its past elegance, it was in matters of lighting, furnishing and facilities in general, much a product of the late twentieth century.

Karen had an apartment on the second floor, as did most of the ten or so other girls who were more than just short-term visitors to the house. Her rooms had a view across the gardens and wooded region beyond; and if she stood close to the window and looked over to her left, she could see the gentle rise which just hid the long valley beyond the trees. Outside working hours, she could be as self contained here and as private as she desired.

Her office, off the main room on the ground floor suite, where Sonia held sway, was also modern, light and pleasant. Her view here was from the side of the house, over the curving driveway and beyond to the gateway and thin line of trees running along by the road. In between lay the swimming pool with its scattering of tables and coloured sunshades, and off to one side, the tennis court. So in an idle moment Karen could take note of comings and goings, seeing sometimes those she already knew, and sometimes visitors to the house who were strangers to her.

Her work routine had not taken long to establish and the work itself was not as absorbing as she might have wished, though that may be, she thought, due to her own inability to adjust to a more leisurely pace of life in her new environment.

It was odd, thought Karen, during those first few weeks, that Sonia's manner and attitude towards her never seemed to change. She was friendly and polite, even humorous at times, but it was the same Sonia as in the interview room. Karen watched her, sometimes, through her open door when one of the other girls came to see her, for whatever reason, and concluded that she alone was not exempt from some privileged circle of confidantes, but that Sonia was temperamentally insulated from them all. She was beginning to feel that Sonia was like a sunlit island, her aquaintances knowing every contour, defile and ridge, every peak and valley, but never seeing the greater part, which lay deep and hidden beneath the impenetrable waters.

With most of the other girls, Karen fared better. She enjoyed their company and conversation during the daytime and evenings in and out of the house. However, the nature of the activities carried on within the house were never alluded to when she was present. Was it just out of consideration for her, she wondered, or did they never discuss these things amongst themselves at all?

Anyway, if most of the girls occupied the centre of the behavioural spectrum when it came to relationships, two were aside from it but at opposite ends. The first, perhaps, from Karen's point of view only, was Angela; the second from everyone's point of view, undoubtedly, was Pauline.

Angela, the lovely Angela, with the coolly alluring greyblue eyes, who had put in a pre-arranged, if rather bizarre appearance at the interview on that dismal, rainy day in England, had become Karen's real friend; and if Angela too never discussed her 'work' at the house, she was otherwise open, sympathetic and perceptive. Angela was the only person with whom she had felt remotely inclined to discuss her own past and she knew that Angela understood.

Pauline was another matter. Nobody had ever suggested that the house might be haunted, though Angela remarked, on one occasion, that if there had ever been a spectre resident within the villa, it would have fled in terror on the day Pauline arrived.

Whilst Sonia, as head of the enterprise, elicited respect, the reaction to Pauline's appearance on the scene was one of lowered voices or superficiality of conversation which, it was felt, had to be sustained until she had moved out of range. Karen wondered why for a time, for Pauline was not lacking in jovial conversation and had a ready smile for everyone, with the exception of Karen herself.

It took some time for her to appreciate that Pauline's conversation was not always what it seemed to be, but contained references to events and occurrences which had meaning for those at whom it was directed, but not to an outsider like Karen. What was eventually obvious was that Pauline had a hold on some of the girls and felt that an oblique reminder in public to those under her influence was not out of order. Her purpose in the house was to ensure that the girls complied with rules and regulations when it came, in the case of a few of them, to housekeeping and kitchen duties, and perhaps, above all, to enforce the ban on unauthorised visitors to the house and its grounds as far as everyone was concerned.

Pauline had a suite of rooms on the first floor. It was on the first floor also that Karen learned there existed three of the 'guest rooms'; so called because of the use to which they were put when some of the visitors came to stay at the house. She supposed that Pauline had at least a supervisory role there too. Somehow she could not imagine Sonia ever being directly involved in any of it. Sonia was a producer, not an actress nor even a director.

Karen avoided the first floor. This was not difficult, for to do so she simply carried on down the main stairs and past the long corridor which ran from the front to the back of the house. There was that first occasion, the time when she had left the office and called back to her room in the middle of the afternoon, when she saw something unusual, and then only for a moment. Who it was, she did not know, for the girl was turned away from her and moving slowly down the corridor – slowly, because in that passing instant, Karen had perceived that she was attired and hobbled the way Angela had been at the interview. Other, more conventionally presented 'maids', she had become used to, for it seemed that the less assertive girls, including, of course, Angela, undertook these duties whereas others did not.

Karen was surprised that this was all she had seen in the way of sexual or fetishistic display, although when visitors were at the house, she sometimes stayed away from the bar and restaurant, though not the pool, or else, in the evenings, kept to her room and passed the time reading or watching one of the English Language TV channels. It was in the seclusion of her room too, that she found the sexual gratification she needed, ironically denied her through the unique circumstances, in this bastion of sensuality.

During normal social gatherings, few of the girls deliberately dressed to create an impression, even if Mike or male visitors were about, as they occasionally were at the bar. Annette sometimes wore a short skirt and high heels and young Jackie, always ready to go further, usually dressed as though the bar was a stage, with an audience full of men, waiting for her to make an appearence.

Pauline too was different in matters of presentation. She was, thought Karen, a very attractive woman, a sentiment confirmed on one occasion by Mike, who confessed to finding her sexy, but only when she wasn't looking directly at him! Pauline was, at most, in her early thirties, with blue eyes and straight, silver blonde hair with a fringe across her forehead. Her hair, thought Karen, couldn't really be that colour. She was, like all the women in the villa, in full possession of those characteristics which men, Sonia's 'lesser gender', find desirable. Her features were somewhat rounder than those of the others and she carried just a little more flesh on her bones. According to Mike, her legs were in a class of their own. But, Karen mused, that's men for you. Karen thought too, that had she seen Pauline only in a still photograph, she would not have thought butter would melt in her mouth.

In reality Pauline not only tried to sound intimidating, in the nicest possible way, but affected an appearance to reinforce it. Karen had often seen her in a long black dress, similar to an evening gown but very plain with squared, padded shoulders and high collar. It had reminded her of a priestess making her appearance upon the celebration of a human sacrifice, as someone had once commented. On other occasions, especially out of doors, she displayed outfits and bearing of almost military severity. Pauline obviously liked to create an impression as a forceful and dominant lady; an old battleaxe according to Annette.

Her attitude towards Karen was ambivalent. If they passed in the corridor or in the garden, Pauline might acknowledge her with a curt greeting and a forced smile; or else she would simply glance at her and say nothing, if she wasn't ignoring her completely. Karen felt that perhaps she posed a challenge to Pauline because of her position, and the fact that she had ready access to Sonia. If Pauline was slighted by her very presence, then the problem was Pauline's and not hers. Karen considered that she had, until recently, been burdened with enough problems of her own.

It was Wednesday and a warm June afternoon. Sonia was away for a few days and Karen had little to do, so she had switched on the telephone answering machine and locked up the office, first taking care to ensure the absence of the cat from beneath the various items of furniture.

She had eaten a salad at the bar and chatted to Annette for half an hour, before setting off into the warm summer air, along the pathway then over the wooded rise and out of sight of the house to the seat under the tree. The wooden seat had a fine view across the valley, beyond which lay the shimmering sea, some nine or ten kilometres distant. She wore a cobalt blue beach dress with white lace shoulder straps. The dress she had bought in Greece when on holiday with Sandra only a couple of years ago. This was the first time she had worn it since that time, but it was a perfect day with the scent of flowers and a hint of the sea carried on an amiable breeze and she thought it appropriate enough. The birds were singing in the trees close by, as though they sensed her presence and wished to share their secrets with her.

She had taken to meeting Angela at this place when both could get away at the same time. Sometimes Angela was here when she arrived but today there was nobody and the empty seat looked forlorn and sad. Karen pulled a packet of cigarettes and a lighter from her shoulder bag. She lit the cigarette and drew on it gratefully. Smoking was not allowed in the house, not even in her room. Reaching into her bag, she retrieved a paperback, also from two years ago, and never started. The dress and the paperback book were memories – memories of a time long passed, a time she wanted to release herself from. Now was as good a time as any to start and finish the book, and the memories with it. Perhaps, later, Angela would be free for a while and come to the seat so that she would have company.

Soon, Karen did have company.

'Good afternoon!' came a voice from behind. 'Isn't it beautiful up here?'

Karen looked up startled, letting the book fall shut.

'I'm ever so sorry to make you jump,' said Pauline.

'Oh, no, that's all right,' answered Karen. 'I was a bit preoccupied – er, did you want to sit down?'

Karen clutched her bag and moved over to make enough room for her unexpected visitor.

'I won't, thank you,' replied Pauline, affecting a reassuring smile. 'I'm taking my mandatory walk; at least two kilometres a day you know.'

'Er, no, I didn't,' said Karen, wondering if her appearance at this time and place was more than a mere coincidence. Pauline was not her usual intimidating self, but wore a light denim jacket with long, loose fitting skirt and flat-soled ankle boots. Quite out of character, thought

Karen. She could well have been taken at her word; out for a long stroll and nothing more.

'How are you finding things now that you've been with us for a few weeks – do you miss England?'

'Oh, fine, it's lovely ... I mean the house, the gardens, everything, and I really don't miss England at all I'm afraid. Er ... have you been over here very long yourself?'

'Quite a while now,' smiled Pauline, 'and I do miss England a little, sometimes. The odd rainy day never bothered me unduly; but too much sun isn't terribly good for the complexion you know, or so I'm told.' Her smile broadened as she continued to gaze down at Karen. 'But about yourself; it must be very different from anywhere you have worked in the past.'

'Yes, of course it's different isn't it?' responded Karen to so obvious a statement. 'I mean I'd never heard of anywhere like this before and I don't suppose many ordinary people have.'

'It doesn't cause you any problems then?' asked Pauline.

'No, I don't think so – and besides, I try not to be moralistic about these things and I'm not involved either, so why should I worry? Anyway, Sonia explained it all to me before I came, so I'm perfectly aware of what you all do.'

'Good,' smiled Pauline, 'but as you are a little aside from the others I thought you might get a bit lonely. I see you at the bar or the pool sometimes, or out walking; you're often on your own.'

'No,' answered Karen endeavouring to hide her growing unease, 'I'm really just fine and I'm not at all short of friends.'

'Oh well,' said Pauline, 'I was only a little concerned about you, that's all. I know we haven't spoken much between ourselves but, you understand, it's circumstances. I'm in a rather particular situation when it comes to most of the others as you are well aware.'

'That's all right,' replied Karen, trying not to sound as sceptical as she felt about this sudden and unexpected regard for her welfare after over a month at the house.

'You haven't been to the beauty parlour yet have you?' Pauline continued. 'Someone happened to mention it the other day.'

'Beauty parlour?' responded Karen. 'I usually manage to take care of myself, thanks.'

'Oh, I didn't mean that!' replied Pauline, her smile ever widening. 'No, they do a terrific massage in there, as well as all sorts of other things – you should try it, really; you'll feel like a million afterwards.'

'I didn't know about that,' answered Karen, 'nobody ever said anything to me.'

'Well they should have done. Why not try it, perhaps before dinner, I think they're free this afternoon but you can't always get in, it's ever so popular.'

Karen was beginning to wish, with no little impatience, that she would go away and so agreed, saying, 'Thanks, yes I'll go down a bit later.'

'Good,' said Pauline, turning at last to go. 'I'm off back to the house shortly – why don't I tell them to keep a time for you just in case. Six o'clock maybe, or a bit earlier if you prefer?'

'Yes,' replied Karen, 'all right, tell them six o'clock, I'll be down then.'

'Well I'll say goodbye for now,' beamed Pauline over her shoulder, 'and I'll tell them definitely to expect you at six!'

Karen breathed a sigh of relief, looked out towards the sea and picked out another cigarette. She didn't like the feeling of being pushed into any kind of situation by Pauline, but it seemed like a nice idea and something she ought to have taken advantage of.

Angela never appeared, so Karen returned to the house an hour earlier than she needed, intending to sit by the pool and chat to whoever might be there. The pool shimmered in the late afternoon sun, deserted. Beyond, there was a foursome on the tennis court. She could make out Mike and Annette but not the others because their backs were towards her. Oh well, she thought, maybe I'll go and read for a bit or watch TV.

She approached the house, entering through the swing doors under the portico. On her left lay the entrance to the bar, restaurant and conservatory, and a short way beyond, the turning to the main stairs. Opposite, was the familiar door to the offices. Past this point on the ground floor corridor Karen had never actually walked. She knew the kitchens and stores were further down on the left, then the back door and the rear stairs.

She carried on past the first door on the right after the office. This was plain and unmarked. The next door, panelled and painted in mid-blue was what she sought. A black and gold sign above the door announced 'Beauty Parlour.' Stuck to one of the panels was a piece of paper upon which someone with artistic leanings, and a liking for gothic script, had written, 'Dispare all ye who enter here'. This small work of creativity was some twelve centimetres square and covered, presumably to deter any additions, with a slightly larger piece of clear acetate.

Karen smiled to herself. This small example of visual humour was, if nothing else, a reassurance. Under the inscription was pinned a note which had partly folded over on itself. Karen reached up and flattened it out. In blue felt tip pen was neatly written, 'Prior appointments only this afternoon – Val & Kim'.

So they ran the parlour, thought Karen. She knew Valerie fairly well, had chatted to her often in the bar and by the pool. Kim had, of course, collected her at the station upon her arrival, but had not been much in evidence since, except on occasion serving at the bar.

She turned to make her way back to the stairs and found another figure approaching her from the direction of the main entrance; it was young Jackie. Everyone thought of her as young, not just because she was only eighteen, but with her long brown hair and large innocent brown eyes, she could almost have passed as a schoolgirl.

Her looks and figure, which she seldom took pains to conceal with any degree of conviction, made her according to rumour, a firm favourite with male visitors. On this occasion, she was dressed for tennis and swung her racket behind her as she smiled at Karen and said, 'Hi!'

'Oh, hello!' answered Karen, 'so it was you I saw on the court with Mike and Annette.'

'Yes, me and Kim; had a great game – were you looking for Val? I don't think she's in at the moment.'

'No, I was just looking to see where the beauty shop was, I'm coming down here at six o'clock.'

'Oh, for a hair-do?'

'No, I thought I'd give their massage a try. That's what I'm coming down for.'

'You are?' voiced Jackie, wide eyed and grinning.

'Yes, and I was wondering if I take a shower in my room first or not. Have you been before? Do you know if . . . ?'

'No, you have your shower and do everything in there,' cut in Jackie. 'It's real good fun, but you . . . I thought that you . . . er.'

'Thought I what?' asked Karen as they walked up the stairs together.

'Oh . . . nothing,' she giggled as they reached the first floor landing. Karen was about to press her further when Jackie veered off and started along the corridor.

'Where are you off to?' queried Karen.

'My room,' answered Jackie, turning about and playfully swinging the racket, 'it's down here next to Cheryl's; must hurry, I'm on bar duty in a bit. You'd better come down after your massage and I'll pour you a long, cool drink. You'll need it!'

Karen continued up, thinking that it had never occurred to her where some of the other appartements might have been. Now she knew. She wondered too, why Jackie found her planned visit to the beauty parlour so significant.

Just prior to six o'clock, Karen reappeared on the ground floor, dressed in a soft, rich, pink bathrobe and clutching her small white toilet bag. She came not from the direction of the main stairs, but from the narrow, less well lit stairs at the rear of the house. It was the first time she had been via that route, and although others were often seen walking about in housecoats or bathrobes, Karen had not, and did not care to be seen so doing in case anyone ventured to inquire as to her destination. Why this should be a cause for concern, she was not entirely sure, but her encounter with Jackie had made her a little wary about it, not to mention the fact that it had been instigated by Pauline. But she was under an obligation; she had agreed to the appointment and saw no logical reason to back out at this late hour.

She reached the blue door and saw that the note was still there, but held flat now with an extra pin. She reached down, turned the brass knob and pushed gently. The door did not move. Again she tried but with no more success. Next, she raised her finger to the small brass bell push. She heard the chime from within.

There was no sound but Karen waited with tense expectancy. Then, the door swung inwards to reveal a broad smile and flashing eyes.

'Hi, Karen, come inside!'

Valerie turned and Karen pushed in through the door, finding herself in a small, well lit hallway. No sooner had the door clicked shut behind her, than Valerie was through the next one and holding it open for her to pass inside.

The room she entered reminded her immediately of a top class hairdressing salon. To her left was a range of white cupboards, above which was a work surface and a couple of sinks, complete with shampoo sprays, combs and bottles of various shapes, colours and sizes. Two hairdryers peered down from their stands at the far end, and running the whole length of the cupboards was a range of fitted mirrors, rising up to the brass shaded spotlamps which stood out on their brackets less than half a metre below the ceiling cornice. Blue tiled walls contrasted with the rich, deep mauve carpet, all bathed in a warm, soft light from panels set into the ceiling, though there were small groups of spotlights set up above the room as well, presently switched off.

The whole room oozed comfort and luxury, and it soon gave Karen a feeling of ease and wellbeing. The various items of furniture were what might be expected, but the seats and stools were all of upholstered black leather and glistening chrome. Just beyond the middle of the room and set back from the sinks and mirrors, stood what she took to be a large, oddly shaped chair, but it soon became obvious that what she was seeing was a dark blue fabric cover draped over it in the manner of a dust sheet. She considered that odd shape for a few moments, but reached no conclusions.

To her right, but closer than the covered chair, a low bench under two metres long, and not more than half a metre from the floor, was spaced a short distance from the wall and ran at right angles from it into the centre of the room. This was covered with a rich pink fitted towelling, the fringes of which hung almost to the carpet.

'Posh isn't it?' grinned Valerie.

'Oh, yes,' answered Karen, a little awed. 'I really had no idea there was anything like this in the house.'

She looked down at her toilet bag and smiled sheepishly. The toilet bag was obviously going to be surplus to requirements.

Valerie, with her long, black hair and dark eyes, looked the latin type but spoke with the hint of a London accent. She was vivacious and outward going, unlike her assistant, Kim, who was fair haired and blue eyed with more rounded features and a pre-occupied expression.

In her late twenties, Valerie was the older of the two and a little taller. They struck Karen as a perfect team, each complementing the other in looks and manner. Blue was evidently the theme colour in this enclave of the house, as both wore satin tights in electric blue with pale blue sleeveless blouses and blue sandals. Both, thought Karen, looked thoroughly glamorous.

'Would Modom care to use the shower?' Valerie inquired with a sparkling smile, and both she and Kim stood aside.

'Thanks, yes, Modom would.'

The bathroom was straight ahead, where the dark blue

door stood slightly ajar. Karen made her way over, skirting about the low bench and the oddly draped chair. The shower room was equally luxurious with its deep blue wall tiles and matching fittings, some of which, especially the bidet, looked rather elaborate. She stepped across the thick, rose pink woollen rugs which covered the tiled floor, seeing a similarly coloured bath towel waiting for her on the rack outside the cubicle, and switched on the shower.

Standing in the hot, gushing water and bathed in the warm lights, Karen reflected on her situation. Some people paid a lot of money for luxury such as this. Now, if she had a lover waiting outside, that would be good. Mike, he was a nice guy; maybe she ought to try there a little. After all, the rules of the house didn't all apply to her. She slipped a soapy hand between her legs and closed her eyes, letting her fingers work gently about her sex. She could have stayed in that warm, enclosed, sensual little world until, until . . . but no, she mustn't, they would be wondering why she was taking so much time, and if she wanted to indulge herself, there was always the privacy of her own room.

Eventually, she emerged fresh, warm and glowing from the bathroom.

'Did you enjoy that?' asked Kim.

'Lovely, thanks,' she replied, 'I hope I wasn't too long – have you got anyone else booked in after me?'

'No dear,' smiled Valerie, 'just you.'

They showed her over to the low bench, and Valerie, helping her off with her housecoat said, 'Now just you make yourself nice and comfortable, we'll do your back first, OK?'

Karen smiled, standing quite naked and feeling a little self conscious in the warm light, 'Yes, OK.'

She settled face down onto the soft pink towelling. The bench was firm but comfortable and as she pressed her face into the covering material, the rich aroma of leather seeped through from underneath. She waited, utterly relaxed, her head resting on her arms. She was aware of Valerie and

Kim standing over by the basins and remained blissfully inert until a series of distinct snapping sounds caused her to open her eyes and turn her head so as to ascertain the cause.

The two girls stood facing each other, each had pulled on a pair of tight, translucent pink rubber gloves. Kim completed the adjustment of hers with a final sharp snap of latex against her wrist. Valerie was holding an elegant, fluted bottle in one hand and removing the glass stopper with the other. The bottle appeared to contain an amber oil. Karen turned her head downwards again but her eyes remained open. She had been to a massage once before and didn't recall the masseuse wearing rubber gloves. Perhaps they didn't want the oil on their hands.

Valerie and Kim returned to the bench, each pulling up one of the low chrome and leather stools and sitting one either side of her.

A hand settled softly on her right shoulder and Valerie's voice came, a short distance from her ear.

'Ready for a little oil?'

'Hope it's not too cold,' muttered Karen.

'Not at all, it's nice and warm,' smiled Valerie, and tilted the bottle over between her shoulder blades.

The pale amber liquid ran in a thin stream as the bottle was passed above and along her body, leaving a thin, but slowly spreading rivulet from just below her neck and down to the base of her spine, so that it trickled down the cleft between the smooth orbs of her buttocks. The sensation made her stiffen slightly before she relaxed again and closed her eyes.

She felt two pairs of hands, one pair around her shoulders, the other on her waist, gently spreading the oil and kneeding her flesh. The oil was developing a warm, pleasant burning sensation wherever it was spread over her and the soothing, sensual hands, plying their course over her, from shoulders to thighs, had her floating almost into a reverie.

After several minutes of drifting bliss, something began to distract her.

It was indefinable at first, but then became more insistent and of definite location. It was the oil between her legs. It had worked its way secretly down to the most intimate parts of her body, and what had started as a mild irritation was becoming a burning itch in need of urgent attention.

The two pairs of hands were down at the lower part of her body, working on her thighs and buttocks. The pressure on the latter, and the fact that she was able to squirm just a little and tighten the muscles about her anus and vagina, helped to alleviate the distracting sensation. Then two of the hands moved up to the tops of her legs, whilst the other two slid to the base of her spine. Both kneaded gently, dangerously close to where she knew they shouldn't go, but where the desire for relief was beginning to assert itself again. Her body stiffened.

Suddenly, the hands stopped their work and Valerie said, 'All right dear, shall we turn over?'

Karen eased herself up and began to turn. At the same time, Valerie pulled up the towelling where it hung over the end of the bench and folded it up onto the top so that turned onto her back, her head came down onto the extra layer. The act of turning over had dispelled the burning tenderness around her groin and she felt able to relax once more, closing her eyes against the soft glow from above.

'Let's have these out of the way,' said Kim with a smile, and Karen felt the soft, warm latex gloves close about her wrists and gently lift her arms up above her head, moving them inwards so that her wrists were parallel with each other. Karen assumed that this was part of her massage and remained still and at ease even when she felt a downward pressure exerted on her wrists and arms until they were in contact with the exposed leather near the edge of the bench. The hold on her arms relaxed for a moment. Then something slipped under her wrists and quickly caught around them, something cool and unyielding which instantly tightened and pulled them down hard against the leather.

Karen opened her eyes and immediately jerked her arms,

but it was too late. Valerie had passed the leather strap under and over her wrists and through a metal slot at the edge, enclosing them in a tight loop. The far end of the strap was fed into a buckle just under the bench and fixed well out of Karen's reach.

'Hey! What are you doing?' she gasped, looking wide eyed from Valerie to Kim and pulling up her legs in an attempt to lever herself free.

Neither of the girls spoke and simply ignored Karen's protests.

They moved along the bench and knelt down at the sides, each taking hold of one of her ankles and pulling them over and under the edges. Once her lower legs were under the bench, she again felt the cool grip of leather. This time a strap passed around, then tightened on each of her ankles, pulling them inwards and upwards against the underside. The metallic rasp of the buckles sounded out in final confirmation of her plight, fastened now as she was with her thighs held wide apart by the width of the bench, totally immobile and with the most intimate parts of her body exposed.

'Please!' she begged. 'Why are you doing this?'

'Shush,' answered Valerie smiling down at her, 'it's all part of your treatment.'

'Yes,' added Kim with a mischievous grin, 'all part of the service! Now, just you relax and behave yourself.'

Karen did not have any choice and was not only aware of the tension in the muscles of her shoulders and thighs, but the vague return of the prickling sensation between her legs.

Valerie sat on the low stool next to the bench adjusting her pink gloves, whilst Kim had gone over to the sinks and was removing something from one of the cupboards underneath. Then she returned to the stool opposite to Valerie, holding a black object in her hand. Karen suspected what it was and her suspicion was confirmed as the object buzzed into life in Kim's hand.

Valerie placed a warm latex hand firmly on the base of

Karen's stomach and Kim began her work with the cordless razor. Karen tensed as the cool metal cutters plied back and forth over the firmer flesh above her vulva. She said nothing and voiced no protest. She suspected that it would make no difference, but would only serve to compromise her dignity further.

After a few minutes, with most of the pubic hair removed, Kim let the foil head glide over her mons venera until it was entirely smooth.

'There we are,' announced Kim, switching off the razor, 'like a new born babe!'

She returned the razor to the wall unit whilst Valerie picked up the bottle of oil and once again removed the stopper. Karen watched helpless as the thin, glistening stream of pale amber progressed down from her neck, between her breasts and over her stomach, faltering and ending in the last few drops as it coursed over her newly shaven pubic area. She tensed against the straps as those last few drops spread remorselessly down over her sex and between her buttocks again, cool at first but then beginning to tingle and inflame.

Valerie put the bottle aside and began to massage the oil into Karen's neck and shoulders. Kim, back in position on the other side, did likewise about her stomach, spreading the thin film down the sides and onto the tops of her thighs. For a while, the hands moving over her distracted her from the growing itch between her legs, especially when Valerie's hands cupped her breasts and her fingers began to circle and pinch about the nipples.

She knew they were not going to harm her but they shouldn't be doing this. She ought to shout, to tell them to stop and let her go or she would ... would what? But it felt so good, good because she was so helpless to prevent them. Being helpless meant she had the perfect excuse to let it go on. But the itching; if only something would stop it, anything!

Karen closed her eyes. Her body was warm and tingling with the oil and the play of the hands. She felt a mixture of outrage and ecstasy over what they were doing to her but it had gone too far and it must not stop.

The hands, slithering snake-like all over her, were carrying her along like a roller coaster, driving her inexorably upwards towards the apex where she would hesitate above the void before the final screaming plunge. Valerie concentrated on her breasts so that the teats stood firm and swollen, whilst Kim's fingers played their game about the base of her abdomen and the firmer shaven skin just below.

The irritation between her legs was now a torment approaching unbearable intensity. She jerked her head from side to side and moaned feebly. Suddenly she tensed hard against the straps as a latex-skinned finger slid down and between the moist, burning lips of her sex. Her breath came in gasps as the finger stroked deeper into her, making her wish it would go further still. The roller coaster crested the rise and the currents began to course through her, uncontrollably.

Karen didn't care about her shame and indignation any more.

Her moans and gasps became louder and shorter. Then she felt Kim's other hand pass below its companion and a finger, at first stroking, then pressing insistently against her anus. She involuntarily resisted this second invasion of her body, but the lubricated finger entered her there too, cool and hard, pushing ever deeper so that she silently begged and willed them to go on and on into her.

The roller coaster gathered speed, careering out of control into headlong plunge until she quivered and cried out loudly and repeatedly, her back arching against the steadfast restraints in shameful ecstasy.

It was many seconds before Karen recovered her senses fully and realised that the hands were gone from her. She opened her eyes slightly, for now even the soft lights above seemed too bright for comfort. She could see Valerie and Kim easing off the rubber gloves near the sides and she heard herself mutter, 'God, I've not come like that in years.'

Valerie was then at her head, unfastening the wrist straps whilst Kim reached under the bench to release her ankles.

They helped her gently up off her back and turned her around so that she was sitting on the edge of the bench with Valerie and Kim seated on either side of her. Kim placed her arm about Karen's shoulder and Valerie kissed her on the cheek saying, 'You'll feel better now dear, all your tensions gone. You'll feel a bit stiff too – but don't worry, it'll all go when you have another quick shower.'

'And while you're in there,' smiled Kim, 'we'll put the coffee on.'

Karen smiled, glancing only momentarily at them both before making her way stiffly to the bathroom.

Afterwards, over coffee, Karen was quiet and pensive; then Val said, 'Look love, nearly everyone visits us from time to time and it's usually for more than just a shampoo and set. We're all girls together in here, it's just good fun.' Valerie and Kim looked at each other then back to Karen.

'Didn't you realise . . . ?' asked Kim. 'I mean, what it's all about, even in here?'

'Well, no,' replied Karen over her coffee cup, 'I didn't – I just thought that . . .'

Kim turned to Valerie again.

'But Pauline said . . .'

'Yes!' interrupted Valerie. 'I know what bloody Pauline said!' Her voice softened and she turned back to Karen.

'Please, understand, if we'd known, we would never have . . .'

'Wait,' interrupted Karen. 'Look both of you, I'm not blaming you – I'm not really an old maid you know, and I appreciate you were here to give me a good time. I just don't appreciate being tricked by someone else, that's all!'

'Yes, it was unfair,' responded Valerie.

Kim looked at them both and said, 'That old cow's got it coming to her you know, and when it does, I only hope I'm there to enjoy it!'

'Yes,' agreed Valerie, 'I think you could say that for both of us.'

'No,' added Karen, getting up and tightening the belt around her housecoat, 'you can say it for me too. She'll slip up one day, you'll see!'

# 4

# The Demon Stirs

'Isn't that breeze gorgeous?' mused Angela.

'It certainly is,' sighed Karen, feeling the glow of the afternoon sun on her face and body.

'You know,' said Karen, glancing up at the cloudless blue sky, 'everytime I start to take this for granted, I think of what a bad time of it I was having in England and how lovely it is here.'

'You've settled in rather well under the circumstances haven't you?'

Karen shaded her eyes and turned to Angela.

'I'm still the odd one out, except for Mike of course, but it's different for him anyway.'

Angela turned over to let the sun caress her back.

'I'm surprised you haven't hit it off with Mike for that very reason. You have more scope than we do in that respect – I don't suppose Sonia would mind if you moved in with him.'

Karen smiled, 'Oh, I don't know about that really, I've been out with him a few times in the pick-up. Usually to the village market for fruit and vegetables. He's a sweet guy but he's never shown much interest in me. I get the impression he already has a relationship with one of the others but he's never let on as to who it might be.'

'I think he'd better be careful if he has,' observed Angela. 'Sonia definitely wouldn't approve. The odd liaison she might turn a blind eye to, but anything more and, well . . .' Angela propped her head up on her hands and said, 'But don't you feel the need for some kind of relationship? I would if I were in your situation.'

'Oh, I don't know,' sighed Karen. 'I had enough of relationships back home. It all got too complicated.

Anyhow, I've always got you to talk to, and everyone has been nice to me here, except for you know who.'

Karen blushed slightly when she recalled the visit to the beauty parlour which Pauline had contrived. She had, nevertheless and in spite of herself, considered how wickedly exciting it would be to go back again and be treated like a captive goddess. To lie a prisoner but to be served voluptuously by those who were determined and able to please her.

She wanted Valerie and Kim to ask, just to drop the merest hint. But they never did, perhaps they thought it might cause her embarrassment and Karen felt too much shame and guilt to suggest it herself.

'What do you do when we have visitors?' asked Angela. 'I don't often see you about after office hours.'

'No,' answered Karen, 'you're not the first to mention that. The thing is, everyone goes out of their way to look so glamorous and sexy when there are people here. I mean you, Annette and Val, not to mention Jackie . . .'

'Oh yes!' laughed Angela. 'She's quite outrageous sometimes, but it's good for business as far as Sonia is concerned, I'm sure.'

'Well,' continued Karen, 'if I'm not working, I go for a long walk if it's light, or just stay and watch a movie, or just sit and read. I don't mind all that much. Anyway, they don't usually stay more than a couple of days.'

Karen sat up and reached for the suntan cream. Squeezing a little out onto her hands, she began to smooth it over her shoulders and breasts. She occasionally swam and sunbathed topless now, like the rest of the girls. At first she had not done so at all, but had quickly began to feel out of place if there were others present around the pool.

A large butterfly sped erratically by, its wings catching the sun, iridescent blue as it coursed across the pool and disappeared into the bushes.

'I feel a bit sorry for you sometimes, Angie,' she said as she again squeezed the plastic tube.

'For me – why?'

'Well, not just you, I mean the others as well who do

room duty under Pauline. I've passed you on the stairs, you see me and I know you daren't say anything in case she hears you. I don't know how you put up with it.'

'Oh, I wouldn't worry,' sighed Angela. 'I must say I do feel awkward having to ignore people but everyone understands, it's all part of the playacting – she loves to keep that up.'

'Well, I'm not sure I understand,' replied Karen, smoothing the cream onto her stomach and thighs. 'I know she's supposed to be a nasty bitch but I can't see what she has over you, Kim and the others. Surely Sonia . . .'

'Sonia is too occupied with other things to know half of what she's up to,' interrupted Angela. 'She just leaves her to it.'

'All right, but if ever you want me to have a word with Sonia, you only have to say.'

'Really,' smiled Angela, 'don't let it bother you, it's not your problem.'

Karen could see Angela in her mind's eye, going about her duties, sometimes in the latex outfit, sometimes manacled. No doubt Pauline expected her and the others to do all their work like that as some kind of humiliation and punishment. Karen wondered what it would be like to work for hours on end with only limited freedom of movement and dressed as they did. She found it darkly fascinating. She would never have dared put it into words, even to Angela.

Angela's voice cut across her thoughts.

'What's Sonia like to work with? You're with her much more than anyone else.'

'Oh, Sonia's OK,' answered Karen, recapping and putting aside the tube of suntan cream. 'I found her a bit too correct at first, but it's different once you get to know her.'

'Mm, well you're probably the only one who does, but it must be a good thing.'

Angela propped herself up and glanced at the shimmering blue pool.

'I'm going for a quick dip,' she smiled. 'Coming in?'

\* \* \*

The fact was that Karen's relationship with Sonia had changed over the weeks. It was not a situation Karen would have expected in the early days for she regarded Sonia as rather hard and unsentimental, the way she now regarded Pauline. She often wondered if people were all they seemed to be, though with Angela she did feel that she was talking to the real person and not a contrived image. With Sonia, people were impressed straight away with what they saw. In her black leather jacket, black leggings and high heeled ankle boots she could appear intimidating to some, though she would not have looked out of place in any busy town street. She could never imagine Sonia in anything as ordinary as a summer dress.

Was she becoming a friend as well as an employer? Karen thought so. She was usually greeted with a smile in the mornings now. And Sonia, instead of ordering coffee to be brought in, or waiting for Karen to get up and make it, took her turn to do it as often as not.

More recently, Sonia had kissed her. At first it had been an affectionate kiss on the cheek when Karen had finished her work in the late afternoon. It made Karen feel good. It made her feel appreciated and, more importantly, understood.

Yesterday, Sonia had kissed her full on the lips.

Karen could easily have moved her head a little and taken the kiss on her cheek, but she did not. The kiss had made her body tingle. It had frightened her. She was now sure there existed a darker side to Sonia and wondered how far she should allow herself to be drawn into it.

One day, it was a Friday, Karen was feeling low. Sonia had been away from the house since early morning and did not appear until four o'clock. Karen had looked up and affected a smile but it was not, apparently, very convincing.

'Is everything all right my dear?' asked Sonia, standing in the doorway of Karen's office 'You look a little downcast.'

'Oh! It's nothing serious really. I think it's because I've

hardly spoken to anyone all day – even the cat hasn't been around to be fussed over.'

'Poor Karen,' smiled Sonia, approaching the desk and gently stroking her hair. 'Don't do anymore now – it will wait until Monday – go and sit in there while I put on the coffee.'

'By the way,' said Karen, following her into the main office, 'those boxes arrived from England this morning. I checked them in of course – I, er, have no idea what they are.'

Sonia looked at the three white boxes placed one on top of the other by her desk, then back to Karen.

'Don't worry my dear, I don't expect they contain anything too dangerous!'

Karen felt slightly foolish. Boxes arrived every week or so. Sonia, never, as far as she knew, opened them whilst anyone was present, which added to the fascination as to what they might contain.

Through the windows, the gardens were bathed in the golden afternoon sun. When they sat down in the green leather chairs, with the tray of coffee cups and cream between them, Sonia looked at Karen with her dark eyes and said, 'If you're at a loose end this evening, you're welcome to come and have a drink with me.'

'Why . . . yes, I wasn't doing anything especially, I'd like to.'

'Good,' replied Sonia, 'you know I seldom go into the bar, it makes them feel uncomfortable if the boss pokes her nose in. I'll be down here, if that's all right with you.'

Karen watched TV in her room for a while before she showered and changed. Why should she bother to change? She was only going back down to the office after all. But Sonia was treating her as a friend, so it was special. Special enough for her to make the effort and look good.

She stood naked before the long mirror, gazing at herself and slowly brushing her hair so that it hung straight and glistening over her shoulders. Since that episode in the beauty parlour, she had kept her pubic area shaved, although at times it caused her some discomfort. Occasionally, if they knew Mike was away from the house, some of the others went naked in the pool and she knew they were shaved too. It seemed the right thing to do and it looked good. She regarded her body, slim, firm and sensual. She ran her fingers over her breasts and down her stomach and whispered to herself, 'Bet I could make it as well as any of them here if I wanted.'

She pulled on a small, transparent black bikini brief then eased her legs into sheer black stockings with elasticated tops which held up on their own. The dress she chose was plain, deep pink and close fitting. It was sleeveless, low cut but not too short à la Jackie or Annette, and certainly not see-through. About her waist she fixed a gold belt and on her feet she fastened open pink sandals to match the dress. The sandals were elegant, high heeled but not exaggerated.

On the way down the main stairs, she encountered Pauline.

Pauline was, as usual, dressed to intimidate or to impress, depending on one's point of view. Karen had intended to pass by and ignore her, but Pauline stopped and with a broad, almost malicious grin said, 'Karen dear, we're not off for another massage are we?'

Karen spun around and fixed her straight in the eye but the sudden anger writhing inside her did not resolve itself as verbal abuse, it was not her style.

'Oh, what's the point!' she breathed, and continued on to the ground floor.

In the restaurant, she relaxed with a tuna fish salad and diet orange juice, sitting by the doorway and declining the company of others even when Valerie called and waved for her to join the small group at the bar. It was getting dark outside when she returned to the office. Sonia was at her desk and the only illumination in the room was her brass desk lamp with its green glass shade. She got up as Karen shut the door and smiled, indicating for Karen to sit down in one of the green leather easy chairs set about a small table.

'What can I get you to drink my dear?'

'I wouldn't mind a scotch,' said Karen.

'With . . . ?' asked Sonia, opening the drinks cabinet by her desk.

'Nothing thanks . . . not even ice, I prefer it on its own.'

'Ooooh!' smiled Sonia, 'madam does have the odd little weakness, does she?'

Sonia poured herself a vodka and tonic and the scotch for Karen, both of them generous measures. She had changed too but only when she left her desk did Karen make out any detail of her attire. Sonia wore a black leather cat suit with zippers at the sleeve cuffs, neck and various other places and long, lace-up black leather boots with heels which looked to be about ten centimetres high. The outfit was the most flattering, and threatening, Karen had seen her in.

'Like it?' smiled Sonia, putting down the drinks and easing herself into the chair opposite.

'Gosh . . . yes, I mean, it's quite striking . . . really suits you.'

'Thanks,' replied Sonia, 'it's one of my favourites . . . cheers!'

'Cheers!' replied Karen.

'You're wasting yourself my dear, you know that,' said Sonia after a time.

'Why?'

'Your looks, your figure, you have more than enough going for you . . . more than some of the girls who visit us here.'

'But what are you suggesting?' asked Karen with some apprehension. 'If it's what the others do, I don't think that I . . .'

'No, no. I'm not trying to push you into that. What I had in mind was modelling, glamour, yes, but nothing too strong. We could, as they say, market you. I have plenty of connections, as you know well enough.'

They discussed this prospect at considerable length. Karen found the idea quite appealing. It was not the first time it had been suggested to her but at least here there were all the facilities and all the time she needed to think about it. Sonia poured them both another drink.

'Surely,' she asked, 'you must have wanted to try some of the outfits you see the girls here wearing? They make you into something special, they give you an exciting image, they make you feel good.'

'I suppose so,' Karen answered, 'but what is the point, I'm not involved with other people in the way they are, am I?'

She had thought about it quite a lot. She was perfectly aware of the effect the way a female dressed could have on men, and on the wearer. And it was often said that women dressed, as much as anything else, to impress other women.

'The trouble with you, my dear, is that you have never had enough motivation to exploit your potential.'

'We can't all go around from one glamour assignment to another,' said Karen.

'No, but then most people never see the opportunity. Look, I can walk down the main street in almost any European town and see girls who could really make something out of themselves if they thought about it. But they either never get the chance or they don't see it even when it's there.'

'Maybe they don't want to,' replied Karen. 'Some people just prefer an ordinary quiet life.'

This line of discussion went on through a third drink, by which time Karen had begun to feel herself much less inhibited.

'OK,' she agreed eventually, 'I'll have a go, really, I've often wanted to but it never seemed right at the time.'

'Look,' said Sonia, 'some stuff came today from the manufacturers, in the boxes you took. None of the others will have seen these designs yet. Want to have a look?'

'Yes, all right.'

A sensual warmth had come over her, the effect of the drink? Perhaps, or was it the thought of what the boxes contained? Boxes were always vaguely interesting if you didn't know what was in them, but only vaguely unless they were addressed to you. Now these boxes were suddenly special. Whatever they contained, she might find herself wearing something glamorous or sensual, something to make her very desirable, something outrageous.

Karen noticed that the seals on the boxes were already broken. Sonia pulled up the lids, pushed back the tissue paper and exposed the contents. Obviously she had already examined them but Karen, still seated, couldn't see into any of the packaging.

'Now look at this,' said Sonia, holding up the first item to be revealed. 'What do you think? Do you like it?'

It was a short, silver dress made out of stretch material woven with metallic threads. It glistened in the soft light. Karen put down her glass and stepped over to examine it. She felt decidedly unsteady.

'Yes, it's nice, I like it.'

'See what it looks like on,' suggested Sonia.

'What now? I thought we were talking about a studio set-up.'

'Go on,' said Sonia, 'we'll sort out what you like now and bother about that later.'

Karen turned and went into her own office to change, pushing the door shut behind her.

Minutes later she emerged wearing the dress. It fitted her perfectly and clung to every curve. It was not very different in style to her own pink dress, sleeveless but with a lower cut neck, more revealing and tighter fitting. It was also shorter, but she had expected that. She felt good wearing it.

Angela had switched on the pink cornice lights.

'How do I look?' asked Karen.

'Wonderful!' replied Sonia. 'Walk up and down.'

Karen did as she was asked.

'The shoes are wrong,' said Sonia, 'wait a moment.'

She went over to a cupboard and produced a pair of sandals.

'Sit down,' she requested, 'let's try these, I'm sure they are your size.'

She knelt down at Karen's feet, unfastened and slipped off her pink shoes. The new ones were rather different from hers. They were black leather sandals which fastened about the ankles with thin straps. Nothing unusual thought Karen until she tried to stand up. The heels were about fifteen or sixteen centimetres, so that when she tried to walk, she almost stumbled; the effects of the drink also playing no small a part.

'Steady,' said Sonia, holding her arm. 'Once you get used to them, you'll see they do wonders for your legs.' She stroked Karen's hair. 'Try again, my dear.'

She walked awkwardly away from Sonia, turned, stopped for a few moments, then walked back with more confidence to where Sonia waited.

'You look sensational,' smiled Sonia and kissed her on the lips.

'Now,' said Sonia returning to the boxes, 'let's put on a couple of things you may well not be familiar with at all.'

She turned her back to Karen.

'I've poured us another drink by the way.'

Sonia returned to where Karen stood by the table, glass in hand. She was carrying something, wrapped in tissue paper. She placed the item onto one of the green chairs and picked up her own glass.

'Cheers!'

'Cheers!' giggled Karen, who now became vaguely aware of an unfamiliar but subtle odour in the air, which mingled with the smell and taste of the scotch. 'I shouldn't have drunk so much, you know,' she murmured, emptying her glass. 'I'll never walk straight wearing these shoes! What have we got next?'

Sonia parted the sheets of tissue wrapping and lifted up one of the garments.

'Something different; unless you have worn latex clothes before.'

'No . . . no, I haven't. I've never gone in for that sort of thing.'

She recalled Angela at the hotel in England, and she

had, of course, seen such attire being worn at the house occasionally, and so was quite sure she knew what it would be like.

Sonia handed it to her smiling.

'Here's the skirt, my dear.'

Karen took it in her hands to look closer. The rubber was quite thick and looked a heavier material than she had expected. A heavy metal zipper ran all the way down it and glistened against the black latex.

'The top?' queried Karen, looking at the bundle on the chair.

'Yes, it's here,' said Sonia, 'but you'll need help to put it on – the skirt won't be easy if you're not used to it but I think you'll manage.'

Sonia's eyes were fixed on her – waiting.

'Right, I'll get this on first,' said Karen, steadying herself on the back of a chair.

'Look,' said Sonia moving closer and running her hand over the skirt, 'don't pull the zip right down, only about half way, then pull the skirt on. It will be easier to do the rest of the zip up if you do it that way. It will be fairly tight but it's powdered inside. Call me if you get stuck.'

Karen, in her office, took off the silver dress and wondered, 'Surely it can't be that difficult to put a skirt on.' It was.

With the top half of it unzipped, Karen eased the cool, soft rubber up her legs, finding she had to pull quite hard, taking care not to damage her stockings, when she got it as far as her thighs and buttocks. Even half undone the skirt was tight when she got it into place. Her head was not too clear either; she felt herself swaying and constantly had difficulty keeping her balance. Pulling on the metal tab at the back would not shift the zip up any higher. She had to reach behind her with both hands and pull the two halves of the skirt together, then grasp them with one hand whilst the other pulled up the zip. Despite her instability, it worked. The rubber slid and moulded to her body from her trim waist down to around ten centimetres above her knees, a tight sheath of clinging latex. She put her arm modestly across her bare breasts as she opend the door. The tight rubber held her legs together and though it gave a little, could not be stretched enough for her to take other than small controlled steps; something she was not presently at her best to accomplish. All the same, it was quite sensual, the way it squeezed her behind and her legs together.

'Well done my dear,' smiled Sonia, and pulled over a square stool, finished in green leather like the chairs. 'Better if you sit down now I think.'

Karen did so, saying, 'God, I know I'm a bit pissed but how could anybody walk properly in this?'

'You're not supposed to, it's a hobble skirt,' smiled Sonia. 'So now, lets see how you look in the complete outfit.'

She walked behind holding the garment in her left hand and passed it around Karen's front. Then taking her right arm away from over her breasts, she began to dress Karen in what looked like a sleeve of heavy latex, guiding her right arm in first.

'Please bear with me a minute, my dear,' said Sonia. 'It's a bit of a struggle to get this on.'

Karen, her mind in a haze, didn't quite know what to make of it, so said nothing and let her continue. The jacket, for that is what Karen took it to be, was now over her right shoulder and Sonia lifted and guided her left arm into the other end of the sleeve before pulling it hard over that side too, bringing the two sides around her back.

Karen turned her head, wide eyed.

'Hey! I think this thing is inside out and you've got me stuck in the same sleeve ... Ooh! Help me out, my arms are stuck!'

'I said it would be awkward, just give me a few more seconds,' replied Sonia, now pulling as hard as she was able to join the two halves of the metal zipper at the waist.

Karen felt her arms forced past each other inside the rubber sleeve and held tightly together, folded, with her fingers around her elbows.

'Sonia!' she pleaded, 'I can't move at all now! What are you doing?'

There was no reply for the moment but Sonia had engaged the zipper and pulled it part way up Karen's back. She now had the same problem as Karen had with the skirt but, with the advantage of being on the right side of the operation and of knowing exactly what the garment was intended to do.

As the zipper climbed inexhorably upwards and the jacket tightened further about her upper body and shoulders, Karen tried to push her arms out and get up off the stool. But it was too late. The zipper drew home and the heavy rubber neck collar asserted itself about her flesh as Sonia pushed the metal tab down into its channel.

'Phew! That was a hard job wasn't it?' Sonia remarked, standing back to admire the result. 'How does it feel – shall I help you up?'

'Sonia!' said Karen, confused, indignant and letting out a small hiccup. 'You tricked me – this is some kind of bloody straitjacket!'

She attempted to stand, at the same time twisting from side to side in a futile attempt to release herself, then fell back down onto the seat.

'Sonia!' she protested again, and let out another hiccup followed by a giggle.

'There my dear,' consoled Sonia, 'it's just another outfit for you to try, only this one is for naughty girls. Let me help you up – walk up and down a little as you did before, carefully though.'

Karen still gazed wide eyed at her as Sonia helped her onto her feet and moved to her side as she tried to balance. Karen tried hard, but managed only a few steps at a time before faltering.

'You need practice,' mused Sonia, 'a few sessions and you'll have no trouble at all.'

'A few sessions!' protested Karen. 'You'll have to undo me now! I can't walk with all this on ... are you going to undo me?' Then she tottered and began to giggle again.

'Let's make it easier,' said Sonia, putting her arm on Karen's shoulder and reaching behind her. Karen held still and heard the zipper start to move. But it was the tight rubber of the skirt which gave way and soon the zip ran all the way to the hem so that Sonia pulled it away from her legs within moments.

'There! Now you can walk!'

Karen stood swaying and looking at the floor. When she had been tricked into taking the massage by Pauline, strapped down and brought to a climax by Valerie and Kim, she had experienced physical sensuality and animal pleasure, and could now see the lighter side of it all despite a vow to get even with the instigator. This situation was different, instead of cresting a roller coaster to experience the uncontrollable thrill of descent, Karen now stood at the edge of an abyss. What Valerie and Kim had done was just fun and games to them, whereas Sonia was devious and manipulative, and seemed to have intentions beyond Karen's understanding. Sonia waited and watched for a few moments before putting her arm about Karen's shoulder. Karen shivered slightly and their eyes met. Sonia came closer and with her fingers, moved the hair away from Karen's eyes, gently and slowly, then whispered into her ear, 'My darling, you look very sweet.'

'How long are you going to keep me like this?' asked Karen hoarsely, feeling her head swimming and gazing into Sonia's black eyes.

Sonia kissed her on the forehead, then on the nose, whispering. 'You really do look very sweet.'

Then Sonia's lips met hers and Karen felt drawn into a velvet whirlpool of darkness.

Her lips against Sonia's burned and tingled, her eyes closed and she opened her mouth wider. A burning surged through her loins and stomach and she half imagined, half felt the snaking fingers which eased themselves under the elastic of her flimsy black briefs and began gently to spread and stroke between the lips of her sex.

'Oh no!' moaned Karen, 'Sonia, please no!'

But the dark fire was spreading through her, out of control.

Sonia's open mouth pressed upon hers again, enclosing her, burning her, pushing her over the edge and into the abyss. The invading fingers rioted within her sex so she wanted to spread herself wide, to become an outrageous slut, to do and to have done to herself whatever Sonia desired.

She gasped, heaved and almost screamed, 'Oh Christ, Sonia ... Sonia ... I'm going to ...!'

Sonia held her very tightly as she writhed and trembled against her in spasm after spasm.

Karen buried her head against Sonia's neck and face, moaning, weeping, exhausted.

'Oh my dear,' breathed Sonia, 'I think we both know how much you needed that.'

She kissed Karen again, gently on the cheek, and Karen opened her eyes, and with brimming tears, looked into Sonia's gently smiling face and breathed, 'Oh God! What am I bloody well doing?'

Sonia held her by the shoulders, searching hard into her eyes, into her soul.

'You really are a sweet, sweet girl. I've known you for so long, but I don't know you at all and you don't know me, do you?'

'Sonia, I want to go back to my room, please, I want to go!'

'Yes, yes, let me undo you.'

The zipper sped down and the restraining latex pulled away from Karen's body, leaving her cool and damp. Sonia watched her silently as she pulled on her dress and shoes, her eyes fixed downwards so that their gaze should not meet for the moment.

Once dressed, Karen hesitated and looked straight at Sonia saying, 'I don't know what I'm doing here anymore, I really don't.'

Sonia moved forward and took her by the arm.

'Karen, I just wanted to ... look, you must understand me!'

She turned her head aside then fixed her eyes back on Karen's.

'I want you to understand and say you will forgive me if I have hurt you. I really do not want you to be hurt!'

Karen gazed back at her for a few seconds then said, 'Look, Sonia, we just ... shouldn't ... look ... I feel completely pissed.'

'Yes, we've both had rather a lot to drink haven't we?' replied Sonia.

Karen opened the door to leave but turned momentarily to look at her. She wanted to say something but could not bring together the words. Eventually, she managed a hoarse, 'G ... goodnight, Sonia', before departing and walking, as if in an unreal world, up the main stairs and back to her room.

Sonia pushed the door to with a soft click. For a long time she had felt neither loneliness nor guilt about anything, but that evening she was to feel both in no small measure.

# 5

# In the Chair

Karen entered the office, brimming with apprehension. Sonia, not at her desk as Karen would have expected at that time, stood by the window looking out at the early morning sun on the trees. She did not turn, nor did she offer any greeting as Karen passed through to her own room. Karen glanced at her and pulled her door so that it stood slightly ajar.

She began to lay things out upon her desk, realising that concentration would be impossible until one of them spoke to the other. She did not hear the door opening but Sonia appeared, almost as though not wishing to be seen at all. Karen got up and they stood facing each other.

'My dear,' said Sonia, 'I . . . well, I've treated you most unfairly. I will understand if you no longer wish to remain with me.'

Her face bore an expression Karen had not seen before. Sonia appeared subdued, almost hurt. For a while, for once and once only, Karen felt she held Sonia at a disadvantage. The prey was down and the huntress could strike at her leisure. But Karen had no desire to strike, for she felt no anger, nor could she admit to herself any feeling of regret.

'Look, Sonia . . .' she began, then realised that she had no idea what she wanted to say. Sonia sighed, her eyes glancing from Karen to the floor, awaiting the blow she felt was bound to come. Karen walked over to her and placed a hand on her arm.

'Sonia, please, I don't want to leave. We were both pissed and I – I, well, it doesn't matter – I'm not angry – I know you never meant to upset me.'

Sonia placed her hand on Karen's; Karen leaned forward and kissed her on the side of her mouth. Her lips were warm and soft. Karen wanted to kiss her again and felt certain that Sonia was waiting for her to do so, but she considered that perhaps this was not quite the time. Maybe it would be better to leave her with at least a small degree of uncertainty.

'You've made me very happy,' replied Sonia. 'I do so want our friendship to last.'

'I too,' she replied with a gentle smile, 'I ... I'm very fond of you Sonia; you know that.'

Sonia looked into her eyes. Her smile in return told Karen that she understood.

'Look,' said Sonia, 'there's not a great deal of work for either of us to do today and the weather is lovely. Why don't you go along with Annette to Béziers and have lunch there. She's going to buy a few odds and ends but it's not going to take her long I don't suppose, so you'll have plenty of free time to admire the gothic architecture if you're in to that sort of thing.'

'Yes, I'd love to. I've never been there.'

'Well you should get out and about a bit more, there are lots of places to visit. If you had a car of your own you could go where you wanted.'

'Yes,' answered Karen. 'I dare say I could but it's so lovely around the gardens here I don't feel the need to get away.'

'Well, do so today and you can let me know what you think of the town when you get back.'

They had arrived at Béziers by ten-thirty and parked by the Musée des Vieux Biterrois. Apart from buying a number of mundane household items, Annette was concerned more with browsing around some of the small boutiques. The air was warm and still, the town busy but not too crowded.

'They're not just for the tourists,' Annette pointed out as they stopped before a small colourful shop which displayed sports and beach clothes in its window. 'They've got some nice things in here; the girls who run it are friends of Sonia's,' continued Annette. 'I shop at this place myself sometimes.'

'Yes,' agreed Karen, 'it's very chic and attractive.'

'You never buy anything for yourself do you?' commented Annette, glancing at Karen's Greek beach dress. 'Why don't you splash out now and then, you can't be short of money.'

'I don't go anywhere to warrant it. I have what I need back at the house.'

'Oh, come on! If you had a few more things to wear you might want to go out more.'

'I wouldn't mind shopping in Paris,' smiled Karen.

'Well dear, we're not in Paris at the moment. Look, why don't you get something a bit more modern for the poolside instead of that old department store bikini of yours? There's some really nice stuff in this shop.'

They moved closer to the window and shaded their eyes against the bright sunlight reflected in the glass. A selection of colourful and exotic beachwear adorned the display at one end of the window.

'See,' remarked Annette, 'that's the style I mean, the ones with the fine stripes.'

'God, they're no more than backless g-strings, Annette. They'll cover hardly anything at all. I can't wear anything like that, I'd be arrested in England!'

'Of course you can, this is France! Anyway, we all wear them around the pool. Nobody worries about it and you'll get a lovely all over tan, almost.'

'Not everyone wears that sort of thing,' countered Karen. 'Pauline doesn't.'

'Oh, bugger Pauline!' voiced Annette. 'Look, Karen, if you don't come into the shop now, I'm going to scream!'

After the bright daylight, the interior of the shop appeared dim and subdued. Racks of dresses, tops, skirts and beachwear crowded in on them and on the walls was displayed yet more clothing, interspaced with posters depicting exotic locations and smiling, suntanned bodies. A curtain moved aside at the rear of the shop and a figure appeared.

'Bonjour madame, ce que ... oh! mademoiselle Annette – how are you? It is good to see you again!'

The girl, in her mid to late twenties, had straight, straw coloured hair down to her shoulders. Her form was slim and her features angular with large blue eyes. She turned back to the curtain, pulled it aside and called, 'Marielle, oh, Marielle!'

Another face appeared, with features not unlike her own. They were obviously twins, though not close enough in looks to be regarded as identical. Both were dressed in blue jeans and white T-shirts.

'Louise, Marielle,' smiled Annette, 'I'd like you both to meet Karen. She's working for Sonia as our secretary and badly needs to have a look at some of your lovely things.'

The two sisters smiled widely and moved forwards to greet Karen and Annette, each squeezing them in turn by the arms and kissing them lightly on the cheek.

'Mademoiselle Karen is most welcome to our shop,' smiled Louise. 'She must have a good look around here and upstairs. We have not so much room down here but upstairs is a lot more for you to see and space to try things on.'

'Oh, now look,' said Karen, glancing from the two girls to Annette. 'I didn't bring much cash with me and I don't have a credit card – I wasn't intending to spend ...'

'No excuses!' cut in Annette. 'It goes on the house account and you can pay Sonia. We all do it that way.'

'Yes, that is so,' added Marielle, 'and we give you the, er, the discount, for everything you buy. Also, you have no need to take the things with you if you do not want to carry. We can bring around to you in two or three days at the house.'

'There you are, dear,' beamed Annette, 'what more could you want?'

'Well I ... oh, all right, I'll have a look and see if there's anything. How much time do we have?'

'You've got plenty,' replied Annette, turning towards the door. 'I'm going to see Renée at the antiques gallery. I'll be about an hour, then we can go and see a bit more of the town. If you're out of here sooner, go back the way we came and take the first turning on the left – you'll see the gallery almost in front of you. OK?'

Annette swung open the door, letting the light flood inside for a moment before she disappeared from view past the window.

'Em, yes,' said Karen to the pair of waiting, attentive faces, 'swimwear, I suppose, like the ones in the window.'

'Ah, please,' smiled Louise, 'we show you upstairs and you can try on after the little douche, yes?'

Karen followed her up the narrow stairs, turning twice until the room opened out before them. There were two small windows with slatted blinds at the nearest end, keeping the room private but allowing in sufficient light. One wall was partly occupied with a panoramic view of a tropical beach, complete with palm trees and bougainvilias. Opposite to it was a large mirror.

'You look into this,' smiled Louise, 'and you see yourself at the beach, yes?'

Either side of these, and beyond them, were displayed more clothes and beachwear, and further still, a curtained off area towards which Louise walked. Karen followed. Louise tugged the curtain aside to reveal a modestly sized room equipped with wash basin, toilet bowl and bidet. 'Please, you use,' she said, indicating the bidet, 'and then try on anything you like.'

As the curtain was only part drawn aside, it was obvious that something else lay behind it to the right of the changing room. More clothes perhaps. But Karen, feeling unduly nervous already, felt no inclination to ask what it might be. Louise smiled and said, 'See you in a little time, mademoiselle.' Then she was hurrying back down the stairs and gone.

Karen, now alone, closed the curtain and removed her top and skirt. The small room, as with the rest of the shop, was cosy and well carpeted. It reminded her, with the style of its fittings, of the beauty parlour at the house. She moved back to the curtain and opened it far enough to look outside, then, seeing nobody, she emerged and walked over to the rack of beachwear. She browsed for a few moments, looking for the item she had seen in the window, locating it and ascertaining that it was her size. She looked further, pulling other items from the rack, holding them up and whispering to herself, 'God some of these are ridiculous, I wouldn't dare be seen in them,' Nevertheless, she took a small selection back with her to the changing room.

She sat astride the bidet, the hot water bubbling about between her legs, her hand holding the soap and massaging it over her sex and under the cheeks of her behind. It felt strange, in this oddly familiar room, where anyone could enter at any moment and catch her in this intimate act. She began to think that, perhaps, she did not want to move from where she sat, but to wait, and wait in the silence, until someone came to find her.

After she had dried herself, she tried on the little blue slip with its fine gold stripes. It fitted her snugly and, in the mirror, it looked good. 'I suppose it's no less than the others wear,' she mused, admiring herself from every aspect and deciding that this was the one she would purchase. She removed the g-string and replaced it in its plastic packet. The other items still lay there, untried, and she returned to them, picking one of them up and holding it before her. It was made of soft, deep red vinyl and so minimal as to be of no value at all, she considered, except for a nightclub stripper or a model in some men's magazine. She looked at herself for a moment in the mirror then muttered, 'Oh, why not?'

In a few moments, she had carefully eased on the tiny garment and adjusted it over her sex. She observed in the mirror how the thin strip of material passed over the shaven skin just above and joined the red, elasticated vinyl band about her waist. Again, she peered through the curtain and then walked out into the room, aware of how the strip of vinyl moved with each step, stroking the focus of pleasure between the lips of her sex. She reached the big wall mirror and stood before it, running her hands about her breasts and down to her thighs, turning about and seeing from different angles how the scanty little garment fitted her. The sound of voices downstairs caused her to stop. She walked back to the curtain.

She was about to pull it shut, when a thought occurred to her. She stepped outside once more and reached out for the other end of the curtain, the end which had not yet been opened. She drew it slowly aside and looked within.

'Oh,' she breathed.

Karen was looking into the massage parlour at the house, or at least, a smaller version of it. The carpet, the walls, the lamps and the furniture, all were the same. Even the long, low bench, draped with its pink towel was there and the oddly shaped chair with its dark blue cover. She moved inside a short way and stared in silence for some minutes, transfixed with curiosity.

'Would mademoiselle care to take a closer look?' came the soft voice from close behind. Karen caught her breath sharply and spun around in alarm.

'Oh, please ... I ... I ...'

She placed her hands quickly over her naked breasts as the two faces broke into a smile.

'Please, you come now properly inside,' said Marielle as both of them pushed her further into the darkened room.

'No! Look!' she protested, 'I ... I have to go. I was just ...'

But the two sisters rained warm kisses upon her lips, neck and shoulders, one standing before her and the other behind, holding her arms.

'You like this little room, I think,' whispered Louise. 'Everybody is happy to be in here with us and you will be happy too.'

Karen could not reply for burning lips were pressed against hers. From behind her, hands reached around and held her breasts, circling and squeezing the nipples, making them hard and erect despite her initial alarm. She was being smothered by warm breath and ever more ardent kisses. She quivered as fingers slipped into the side of the vinyl strip over her sex and stroked the smooth flesh, remorselessly probing downwards until they found their way inside her.

'We have so little time, mademoiselle,' whispered Louise from behind, 'so little time.'

But they had time enough, for Karen's resistance was almost gone and the voluptuous tingle throughout her body was, she realised, about to overwhelm her. She put her arms around Marielle and closed her eyes, accepting the trap she had allowed herself into. None of them spoke further, for the room was full of their breathing and their sighs. From her moans, they knew when Karen's time was close, and they held her ever more tightly until her body shook and she cried out, entwined in their arms.

When she emerged from the shop, her eyes half closed against the dazzling sky, Annette stood waiting, leaning against the doorway with her arms folded. Karen stopped in the doorway and pushed the small plastic packet into her shoulder bag.

'Christ, where have you been? There was nobody in the shop – I wondered if you'd all fled the country!'

'Oh ... er ... er, we were just talking upstairs. I didn't realise how ...'

'Well, have you actually bought anything after all this time?'

'Yes, the swim slip we looked at ... and I'm sorry I was so long.'

'What about clothes?'

'Oh, I ... well I didn't see exactly what I wanted. I'm going back next time though.'

They strolled along the pavement, Karen fighting to appear normal but her body still trembling.

'You'll feel a lot better when you've parted with some cash, dear, I just know it,' smiled Annette. 'We still have time for you to look around a few more shops.'

By twelve-thirty they were seated at a small table with a

crisp red and white chequered table cloth. It stood beneath a tree, in a side street not far from the Allées Paul Riquet. There they enjoyed the sun and shade, with a salad each and a bottle of the local white wine.

'I can think of far worse places to be right now,' remarked Annette, pouring two glasses of Blanquette.

'Yes, me too. Sonia said I ought to see more of the towns and villages, perhaps I will.' In her mind, Karen was still in the darkened room above the shop, wondering now if it had all been a dream, for under the warm, blue sky, with people passing to and fro, it certainly seemed so.

'You get on OK with Sonia don't you?' Annette broke into her thoughts. 'That's not to say other people don't, it's just that most of us find her a bit impersonal. D'you know what I mean?'

'Yes, I do. She was like that with me at first, but working with someone all day pushes the barriers down. I like her a lot.'

Karen hoped that nothing in her relationship with Sonia had attracted notice from outside.

'You're quite close to Angie as well aren't you? I see you talking to her quite often.'

'Oh yes, Angie's sweet. She seems so vulnerable at times.'

'I think that's what men like about her,' smiled Annette, 'but don't let it fool you; Angela is as much a woman of the world as the rest of us tarts, but I know what you mean.'

'Tarts?' quizzed Karen. 'Is that how you think of yourselves?'

'No, not really,' laughed Annette. 'I leave that to others who think they know better but would give their right arms to spend a night of pervery with any of us – if they could afford it, that is. But you, what do you think of us? You obviously have a different perspective from everyone else.'

'I . . . I don't know . . . I think about it sometimes but it's not for me to say. If it had bothered me, I wouldn't have taken the job in the first place.'

'Oh well,' replied Annette, 'at least you're diplomatic. But you ought to know that we've all wondered from time to time.'

'I wonder too,' said Karen. 'Some of you must have proper, no, I mean long term relationships. Do any of you have regular boyfriends outside? I've seen you and Mike together a few times and I wondered if ...'

'Quite, yes,' cut in Annette, 'I'll have to be careful about that, won't I? But don't read too much into it, Mike is in a very unusual situation. Although it was a bit before my time, I think when he first arrived he regarded it as a dream come true. He probably expected to be in bed with a different female every night of the week, with two at weekends; but of course it's not like that.'

'Poor Mike,' mused Karen.

'Well, I wouldn't go quite so far as to say that,' breathed Annette, 'he's not exactly starving in the midst of plenty, if you understand what I mean.'

'Oh ... yes, I suppose I do. Look, d'you want a fag?' asked Karen, reaching into her shoulder bag.

'I didn't realise you smoked,' replied Annette. 'No, I won't thanks. It's one of the few vices I haven't acquired yet.'

'I think it's one of the few I have,' smiled Karen, flicking open her cigarette lighter.

'Well, it'll probably do you more harm than anything I do. You should consider giving it up and going in for something that's less of a health hazard.'

Karen regarded her with an expression of slight puzzlement for a moment then laughed quietly. 'Oh Annette you're incorrigible.'

Annette poured more wine, then, affecting a pained expression, squirmed in her chair and remarked. 'You know, it can be a bit bloody uncomfortable at times.'

'What? What can be uncomfortable?' asked Karen.

'You probably wouldn't know. Most of us shave down there, it's a sort of unwritten rule. If you leave it for a few days it gets itchy.'

'Er ... yes, I know ... I mean, I do.'

The thought of her visit to the beauty parlour on that first occasion flashed through her mind and she wondered if she should have remained silent on the subject of pubic hair. Almost as if seeing her thoughts, Annette said, 'Val has a new German method for permanent hair removal. They can do it in a single visit I'm told, but I don't think I want to risk getting rid of it for good. I might meet up with someone I really fancy one day, who likes a bit of a nest.'

Karen laughed. 'I don't think I'd mind being without it. I've never been with anyone who expressed a preference one way or another.'

'No – well, you don't meet the people we meet! If I had a choice though, I'd rather not get rid of it for good, but there's nothing at all to stop you. I think Angela's had it done, and Lorna was talking about it – you should find out when you get the chance.'

'Perhaps I will,' replied Karen, swirling the wine about inside her glass. 'Getting that sort of thing done would cost quite a lot back home I imagine.'

'Back home?' queried Annette, spearing a piece of sliced tomato on her fork and looking at Karen in mild surprise.

'Yes, in England.'

'Do you still think of it as home: I don't. This is home to me now.'

'I suppose I do. This isn't my home is it? I've got a job here, that's all. If I left, I'd have to go back there to earn a living, if there was any work to be had.'

'God, I feel depressed at the thought of it,' mused Annette. 'You should come out with us more, and with Sonia. I'm sure she wouldn't mind, though you would know more about that. Put yourself around more and you'll meet a decent bloke sooner or later – probably someone with a yacht and a private plane if they're anything to do with Sonia. I certainly intend to hook one like that eventually.'

'I'll think about it Annette – it's not that important at the moment.'

'Sorry dear; I've been a bit pushy today, haven't I?'

'Oh no,' smiled Karen. 'I appreciate your concern, and

Angela's and everyone else's, but I'm all right as I am, at least for the time being. I get well paid for doing an easy job in a nice place. It's something I wouldn't have dreamt of not so long ago.'

Annette looked at her watch.

'We ought to think of getting back with the shopping, it's after two-thirty.'

The sun was still well above the tree tops and the air was calm and warm when Karen wandered, her robe about her body and a towel in her hand, towards the swimming pool. She was now alone. Annette had gone to join Sonia and Pauline, in what would undoubtedly be a private discussion, in the main office. She saw Mike by the poolside, chatting to brown-haired Rachel and raven-haired Lorna. Both the girls, as usual, wore the most minimal of bikinis and nothing covered their breasts.

'How does he cope with it?' Karen mused to herself. They did not see her approach, so engrossed were they in laughter and conversation. Karen draped her robe over a nearby chair, some distance from them, and was at the pool edge before they noticed her.

'Hi Karen!' came three voices in succession.

She turned to face the smiles and upraised hands, and returned their greetings. She saw how Mike's gaze fell from her eyes and became fixed upon her naked breasts and on her body before she lowered herself down into the water.

She was still in the pool, swimming leisurely from end to end when she heard Mike and the two girls call their greetings to a newcomer. It was Valerie, and she was alone. She laid her bathrobe and towel next to Karen's and, after a brief exchange of conversation and laughter with the others, she too lowered herself down into the shimmering, cool embrace of the water and swam towards Karen.

'Hi!' she smiled. 'You been here long?'

'About ten minutes.'

They swam together for a time. This, thought Karen, might be a good opportunity to ask about the new hair removal treatment, but she would have to wait until they were away from the pool in case Mike and the others overheard.

'I'm going to dry off in a minute, Val. Shall I take your things with mine over to a table?'

'Yes, all right,' answered Valerie, bobbing up and down and pushing the wet hair from her eyes. 'Tell you what deary, Angela's behind the bar. Stick your robe on and poke your head around – see if she'll send us out a pot of tea in quarter of an hour. I'll be out of the water and with you by the time it comes over.'

Karen pulled herself out of the water and up the steps onto the edge of the pool. The water glistened in droplets on her breasts, her nipples stood out firm and hard. She was aware of how little of her was concealed by the small blue and gold lycra swim slip she had bought with Annette earlier that day. She liked the way it cupped her sex and left the rest of her slim body bare to the caress of the warm sun. She was aware too of how the girls and, of course, Mike, regarded her as she walked by and picked up the things from the chair.

'Are we in luck?' asked Valerie as she pulled the bathrobe about her lithe body.

'Yes, Angie should be along soon with a tray of goodies – there's nobody to keep her busy at the bar.'

Karen thought for a moment, clasping her hands under the table to hide her nervousness, wanting to, but avoiding clearing her throat, before she spoke.

'Er, Val . . . somebody was saying about this new treatment for . . . er, getting rid of hair, for good, I mean.'

'Oh, that,' smiled Valerie. 'Yes, it works very well, but it's not all that new. We've had it for a few weeks now but I think it's been around for a year or more.'

She glanced over Karen's shoulder then said casually, 'Why, are you interested in having it done?'

'Well . . . em, I thought about it but . . . I mean, I just thought I'd ask, that's all.'

Karen knew her face had flushed and reddened. She looked down and began to fidget with the belt about her robe.

'It's very effective,' continued Valerie in a matter of fact manner, 'and not at all painful – it works on ultrasound rather than electrolysis – but it is permanent, the hair will never grow again.'

'No, that's why I wondered about it ... it seems like a good idea ... sort of.'

'Well,' smiled Valerie, 'if you decide to have it done, just say the word and we'll fix a time for you.'

'That's what I was thinking, em ... that I might have it done, you know, make an appointment.'

'I'm sure we're clear after four o'clock tomorrow if that suits you,' smiled Valerie.

'Yes, that sounds OK. If there's any problem with me getting out of the office early I'll let you know beforehand.'

'Good, then we have a choice of treatment – deluxe or ordinary. You'll need to decide beforehand which you prefer. The results in the end are exactly the same; it's the method of getting there that's different. All the others know about it you see – but I assume you don't.'

'Well ... I ... I ...'

'Tea up!' came Angela's voice from behind and Karen breathed a sigh of relief.

'Here we are ladies,' smiled Angela, placing the tray down before them. 'I'll leave the tray and come back for it all later, OK?'

'Just what we needed deary,' grinned Valerie, passing a cup and saucer over to Karen. 'I was saying to Karen what wonderful treatment you get on our deluxe service. What do you think about it?'

Angela glanced, amused, from one to the other.

'Oh, absolutely, there's nothing like it,' she smiled. 'Why, were you thinking of ... ?'

'Oh no,' said Valerie, 'we were just chatting about things, that's all.'

'OK,' said Angela turning, 'I'll see you both later. Enjoy the tea!'

Karen watched her walk away back towards the house in her silver lurex, halterneck mini dress.

'She looks lovely doesn't she?' remarked Valerie, as if reading Karen's thoughts.

'Yes,' answered Karen, 'she's a lovely person through and through.'

'So, where does that leave us deary? You're down at the parlour tomorrow at four for one or the other of . . .'

'Look,' interrupted Karen, her heart thumping. 'I'll have what the others have, what Angela had. It might be as well if you don't say any more.'

Valerie began to pour the tea, a subtle smile on her face, the afternoon sun gleaming on her dark gypsy hair.

'God, I wish this door wasn't in the corridor where everyone can see you waiting,' breathed Karen as she listened for the sound of the blue door opening. She thrust her hands deep into the pockets of her pink bathrobe and looked about her. The door swung open.

'Sorry for the delay,' smiled Valerie, standing aside to let her through, 'but we were having a bit of bother with the cork in the sherry bottle.'

The inner door closed and Karen found herself standing on the familiar rich mauve carpet amidst the cosy luxury of the parlour. Three glasses gleamed in the soft light before the range of mirrors.

'I thought we'd all relax and have a little drink,' continued Valerie, 'or at least we will if Kim's got the other part of the cork out.'

'It's OK!' came a voice from the brightly lit kitchenette. Kim appeared clutching a bottle of Amontillado.

Both the girls wore white, high collar blouses with voluminous sleeves, almost Victorian in appearance. Their leggings were of sleek metallic vinyl, each with a wide belt in dark blue, of the same material, and both wore dark blue open sandals. Both had matched their hairstyles too, for Valerie's dark hair and Kim's light brown, almost as light as Karen's, were fixed with small blue clasps and hung down at their backs as pony tails.

'Come and sit down,' said Valerie, swivelling one of the

black leather and chrome chairs around from the mirrors and offering it to Karen. Valerie pulled up a stool and sat by her, whilst just behind, Kim poured out three drinks and handed one each to Karen and Valerie. Pulling up her own stool and sitting with them so that the three formed a triangle, Kim raised her glass and grinned, 'Cheers!'

Valerie and Karen did likewise and Karen sipped the drink gratefully, feeling more at ease than she imagined she could have done earlier. They made small talk for some fifteen or so minutes and, from time to time, Karen glanced between the two of them at the low bench with its pink towelling cover, for she imagined that it was there that she would eventually be asked to lie down.

'D'you want to take your shower, deary?' asked Valerie with a smile, noting that each of them had all but finished their sherries.

'Yes ... yes, I will,' Karen replied, putting down her glass. 'I'll go now.'

When she re-entered the room, warm, glowing and fresh, the bottle and glasses were gone. Kim stood at an open drawer by the sinks. Valerie, her eyes glinting in the warm light, approached Karen with a smile. Karen returned her smile and continued over the room towards the low bench, slipping off her bathrobe as she went.

'Not that one today, love,' said Valerie from behind her, 'we're over here.'

Karen turned, clutching the bathrobe against her. Valerie gestured towards Kim, who was lifting the blue cotton cover away from the strangely shaped chair at the far end of the range of mirrors and sinks. Karen walked back slowly, her eyes fixed upon the object which stood at last revealed. The chair resembled, superficially, the type usually seen in a dentist's surgery. Like so much other furniture in the house it was made of padded leather and gleaming chrome with various levers and fittings. Kim stood by, obscuring the rear part of the chair, obviously awaiting Karen. Karen, meanwhile, was aware of Valerie taking the bathrobe from her and placing it over a nearby stool. She was next aware of Valerie's arm about her waist, moving her gently towards the sinister chair. She froze.

'Oh, I thought we were . . .' Karen gestured feebly with her finger pointing at the bench.

'No, deary,' smiled Valerie, 'it's much better on here, you'll see.'

Karen let herself be guided onto the chair, which gave sufficiently to mould to her body as she settled into the seat and against the padded headrest. The earlier feeling of relaxation had left her and she glanced about over her shoulder, wondering what was to happen to her next.

Valerie looked down at her and said, 'You still have the chance to change your mind if you want you know. Once it's gone, it's gone for good.'

'Yes,' added Kim, 'it's as well to give it a quick think now because once we get started, it's the point of no return.'

'It sounds like I'm going to have my teeth out!' replied Karen, looking from one to the other with a hint of disquiet in her voice.

Valerie and Kim smiled at her and Valerie said, 'Well, it's just as permanent but much, much nicer. I promise you, it's not in the least unpleasant.'

'No, not in the least,' added Kim with a broad and mischievous grin.

The two moved around to the rear of the chair and Karen wondered why they had gone to the trouble of asking her again. She had little time to speculate, for Valerie and Kim each took hold of one of her arms and pulled it behind the narrow back of the chair.

'Really Val, you don't have to . . .'

But even as she spoke, the cool steel ratchets closed about her wrists and the handcuffs, attached to the rear of the seat, held her arms straight down behind her. She felt that her token objection was enough to absolve her from any suspicion of being totally compliant. As if to emphasise the restraint to which Karen was now subject, they took straps which hung from the edges of the backrest and secured her upper arms against it. She knew that had she not been rendered helpless on the occasion of that first visit, she would never have allowed them to take the liberties with her which had ensued. And now, equally, she could convince herself that there was no option but to let them do it again.

'Nice and comfy?' asked the smiling Kim.

Karen hesitated, wondering if some further mild objection might be in order, but Valerie cut across her thoughts.

'Of course she is; everyone is comfortable in here.'

What happened next was quite unexpected and might have prompted strong objections from Karen if she had been aware of it beforehand. A large, soft rubber plug suddenly slipped into her mouth and was pressed home. Around the plug was an equally soft, latex lined pad, like a rubber ring, which fitted firmly over her mouth and squeezed her lips. The whole thing quickly tightened and it became apparent that the leather strap which held it in place was attached to the headrest. Her head was pushed back against the upholstered leather and held completely immobile. A tube, leading from the inside of the mouth plug to a ring of perforations on the outside of the strap, meant that breathing through her mouth was not difficult, but speech was impossible.

Her eyes darted from side to side. Kim and Valerie both smiled down at her. The back of the chair tilted smoothly down a few degrees, taking Karen with it, as Valerie turned a small handle at the side. Kim moved forward and reached down. The section of the chair supporting Karen's legs and thighs folded down, lowering her feet onto the carpet. But this situation was only transitional, for Valerie and Kim reached into one of the lower cupboards in front of the chair and pulled out two chrome bars with attachments which Karen was unable to see properly from her restricted viewpoint. She was soon to understand their purpose as they were quickly slotted and locked into position in the frame of the chair. The two bars angled up and out, away from the chair. Each was topped by a horizontal, leather padded rest, equipped with straps, and Karen, seeing their purpose knew that she could do nothing to prevent their use. She knew now that she had passed Kim's 'point of no return'.

Valerie and Kim lifted each of her legs, pulling them up and wide apart, placing them on top of the padded rests and securing them in position with the straps. Karen could see herself fully exposed in the mirror opposite and wondered what was to happen next. Valerie picked up an object from beside one of the sinks. From one end of it a thin cable snaked off and coiled around to where it ended at a plug fitted into a wall socket. From its other end protruded two parallel metal prongs which ended, at right angles to them, in a metal circle some fifteen millimetres across. A faint humming noise reached Karen's ears as Valerie switched on the device and, standing to the right of Karen's outspread legs, held it poised over the base of her stomach.

Karen let out a short, stifled, 'Mmm!' as the metal ring came into contact with the shaven skin above her sex, for though it was not cold, a sensation akin to pins and needles passed through her flesh. Valerie, whilst Kim looked on, moved the device step by step over her mons venera, keeping it firmly in place at each stop for some seven or eight seconds at a time. The sensations were neither pleasant nor unpleasant, at first, but Karen felt a stirring within her as the gadget was applied ever closer to her clitoris and began to act in the manner of a stimulant.

She closed her eyes. She was well aware that Valerie knew what it must be doing to her and that if it continued she would be aroused beyond the level of self control. The device had been doing its tingling, fiendish work on the warm, tender flesh at either side of her sex for some six or seven minutes when Valerie lifted it away and switched it off. Karen opened her eyes.

'I think that's taken care of it,' remarked Valerie.

'Yes,' answered Kim and stroked her middle finger slowly

between the wet lips of Karen's sex, 'but I think the lady needs something to help her on her way.'

Karen's pelvis stiffened at her touch.

'And here's just what the doctor ordered,' smiled Valerie, bringing an object up from the cupboard which Karen was, at first, unable to see.

Valerie turned around. In her hand she held what looked like a large male penis in shining black rubber. Behind the head of the artificial organ sprouted a series of soft frills and the shaft was heavily rippled. Below it and running parallel, was a companion of plainer and smaller proportions. From the base to which both of these were moulded hung a harness of thick rubber straps and from it also ran a cable which, like the previous device, ended up at the wall socket. Karen, watching wide-eyed as Kim smeared clear jelly from a small tube about the head of the lesser of the two protruding members of the dildo, began to tremble. She was more aware than ever of how firmly the restraints held her and how tight was the rubber gag over her mouth.

The head of the larger organ was slid between the lips of her sex, lubricated by her own excitement, needing nothing more to help it spread the lips and pass slowly into her. The lower member, with its lubricant, met with little resistance either, and she felt it enter her rectum, cool and hard, just as the other penetrated and moved deeper into her sex. Valerie and Kim pulled the rubber straps under and around her, at last fastening the harness about her waist so that the two shafts were held deep inside her two most intimate places. She began to work her muscles about the two sensual intruders, for their very presence was stirring her lust and desire and making it well up to the surface.

Kim reached over to the wall socket and pressed the switch. The dildo began to writhe and pulsate within, causing Karen to jerk her pelvis in rhythm with it. She knew that they stood watching her but she could not help herself. With her eyes shut tight, she attempted to squeeze even harder than before on the larger of these two objects of voluptuous torment. As the two shafts slipped and squirmed inside her she enjoyed their ample dimensions. She pulled against the handcuffs, feeling them bite into the flesh of her wrists, for she wanted to prove even more to herself how helpless she was to prevent the rising heat of lust within. The kisses which roamed about her neck and breasts, and the sucking of her nipples, only added fuel to the black devil whose tentacles spread throughout her limbs. As her breathing became harsher and shorter, she tensed hard against the restraints, forgetting Valerie and Kim altogether, knowing only that the engine of fire which beat within her was rising to white heat. She cried repeatedly through the gag, her fingers clutching behind her at empty air as she plunged through the glittering void of orgasm.

She was relaxed and breathing more regularly when the rubber straps about her lower body were released and the dildo withdrawn from her reddened loins. The gag was undone moments later and the straps began to loosen about her legs. The handcuffs were removed last of all.

With her bathrobe about her shoulders, Karen sat between Valerie and Kim on the low bench. Each held one of her hands and each kissed her on the cheek in turn.

'You'll be as right as rain soon dear,' smiled Valerie.

'Yes,' added Kim, 'it's wonderful therapy – gets rid of all your stresses and anxieties. You should have it done regularly.'

'God, I'm not sure I could cope,' replied Karen. 'How often do you ... I mean, do many of the others ...?'

'Oh, it's like what they used to say about the Roman forum,' smiled Valerie. 'Stand here for long enough and you'll see everyone you ever knew strolling in.'

'What – everyone?' questioned Karen, glancing from Valerie to Kim.

'Er, well, not quite everyone,' replied Kim. 'You can probably guess the three or four who don't use our special services, but even they at least manage to show up for a hairdo or a manicure.'

'We're always here to help, deary,' smiled Valerie, 'we're your friends.'

'Yes,' added the soft-eyed Kim, 'we both think you're a lovely person and we're going to invite you down from time to time whether you like it or not.'

Karen smiled at them, her smile breaking into a laugh.

'I think it's coffee time,' announced Valerie, rising from the bench.

'Hey!' called Kim, as Valerie reached the entrance to the kitchenette.

'What?'

'I've just thought of a motto for the shop door.'

'Oh, God,' sighed the waiting Kim, 'go on then.'

Kim grinned broadly from Valerie to Karen.

'It's "come again soon!"'

'Jesus Christ!' groaned Valerie, disappearing through the doorway, 'you're fired!'

Karen laughed softly and squeezed her hand.

# 6

# Night Games

With late summer came the time for the annual party. Sonia had been away for much of the time in London and various other European cities. Neither of them had referred to that late evening in the office since the morning after; though Sonia continued to show Karen the affection that had led up to it and Karen showed no reluctance in accepting it. There seemed to be an unspoken agreement between them to indulge themselves no further. Inwards, however, Karen felt herself developing a dangerous curiosity.

She had occasionally wondered where Sonia's private rooms were, then one day the obvious dawned upon her. The door behind and to one side of Sonia's desk in the main office must go somewhere. It was a plain and unassuming door. Karen took it to be a storage cupboard, though she had never seen it opened. Several times of late, when Sonia was away, she had tried to open the door. It was always locked and none of her keys would fit it.

For no apparent reason, she had never thought to ask anyone. Until now, that was, the day of the party. She sat with Valerie and together, shaded by a tree, on a bench by the main pathway, they watched the comings and goings of workmen and suppliers. Karen had come to terms with the Valerie she knew as a friend, as opposed to the Valerie she knew in the beauty parlour. She had convinced herself that the second Valerie, as with Kim in that situation, was playing a role, doing her job, and that personalities and outside relationships were not important under those circumstances. Had this not been the case, Karen could never have felt so at ease in her company. She knew too, that others whose company she kept must have been restrained and driven to voluptuous abandonment in that room, though none had ever spoken of it.

The marquee and the platform for the band were going up at either end of the pool. James was to be seen hurrying to and fro in an uncharacteristic state of animation, supervising and checking on microphones, cables and lighting.

'It's odd you should ask about Sonia's living space,' said Valerie. 'It took me a while to figure it out, but she must have rooms behind the office. I'm surprised you didn't know, I really am.'

'Somebody else must know,' said Karen, 'whoever it is that does her cleaning.'

'Maybe she does her own, or more likely, young Jackie,' suggested Valerie. 'The girls who do the office at weekends never say anything about other rooms so your guess is as good as mine.'

'Odd that it should be so secret,' mused Karen, 'if it really is a secret.'

'How much of all this did you get involved in?' asked Valerie, gesturing towards the activity about the pool.

'As much as I could,' answered Karen. 'Sonia deals with the local workmen. I can't understand half of what they say, she gets along perfectly, speaks German and some Italian too. James sorts out the electrical people, they're from Lyon I think.'

'You must have some idea of who is coming,' said Valerie. 'Most of us know. After all, we do have dealings with some of these people in the er . . . course of duty.'

'Most of them are just names to me and, in some cases, not their real ones I gather,' smiled Karen. 'I sent out all the invites and details and I've entered in the money too. You wouldn't believe what some of them are paying to come here and . . .'

'Oh yes I would!' interrupted Valerie with a flashing smile.

'Well,' continued Karen, 'they don't even get accommodation as far as I can see, at least I haven't seen anything arranged and we're expecting over two hundred guests!'

'You'll see towards the end,' said Valerie. 'Most of them get whisked away by cab to Narbonne or Béziers, even Montpellier, and a select few will spend a day or so here in our special accommodation.'

'Oh, the first floor,' said Karen.

'The very place,' smiled Valerie. 'As for the media people, they'll be in camper vans near the main gate.'

'Media!' uttered Karen her face a mask of startled surprise. 'But Sonia would never allow . . .'

'No, no, not the ordinary press,' interrupted Valerie, 'it's people from the scene and fetish world throughout Europe and America.'

'But surely, Sonia wouldn't allow photographers,' insisted Karen, 'not with her clients! The last thing they want is a camera pointing at them!'

Valerie laughed, 'That's never been a problem – you'll see what I mean when it's all up and running. Doesn't Sonia tell you anything?'

'I suppose not,' answered Karen defensively, 'she probably thinks other people do, whereas all of you probably think you don't need to because Sonia does, if you know what I mean!'

'Poor little Karen, never mind, you'll see it all in full swing soon.'

Karen did not reply but purposely began to examine her finger nails.

Valerie gazed at her anxiously.

'You are coming tonight aren't you?'

'Well . . . I'm not sure. I don't have anywhere to go but . . .'

'But what, for heaven's sake?'

'Well, you're all involved with things here . . . it might be awkward for me, and anyway, what could I wear?'

'Don't you worry deary!' grinned Valerie. 'We'll go to the clothes store and fit you out with something nice but not too naughty. But understand, it is a fetish party and some of them will be a bit outrageous! Everyone will be having fun but you won't be pushed into anything you don't want – OK?'

'Oh Val, I must seem like an old frump. I'm not at all really, it's all such a different world to the one I used to live in. I guess I'm out of my depth, I'll never get used to it – all the wealth and glamour.'

'Of course you will, you'll fit in perfectly by the time I've sorted you out!'

'What about the men? What about Mike?' asked Karen.

'Don't worry about our Mike, he's in the band playing the saxophone. Sonia doesn't want him running loose, I can tell you. As for the rest of them – if you haven't been to a fetish party before, try not to look too amazed won't you? And if you feel a bit giggly, avoid some of the Germans. When you get someone as overweight as Herr Grunwald in a latex suit, dear, you're looking at a blackcurrant jelly on the move!'

Karen looked at her and laughed gently.

'You'll enjoy yourself deary, I promise, and I bet you'll be chatted up by at least six millionaires.'

When Karen stepped out into the open air the party was in full swing. The night air was pleasantly warm and the stars were out, their glory challenged by the multi-coloured lights strung about the trees, and the flickering, pulsing strobes in front of the platform where the band was in full spate.

Valerie, true to her word, had taken Karen to the clothes store and assisted her, with admirable patience, to choose an outfit for the evening. The clothes store turned out to be the next door along from the beauty parlour. They had both walked by the parlour without comment. The selection of clothes was, to Karen at least, astonishing. The styles in nylon, rubber, PVC and leather ranged from the intimidating, through to the outrageously provocative. When she had chosen and asked Valerie, 'How do I look?' Valerie had answered, 'Mega terrific sweety, you really do!'

So she stepped out into the chattering, laughing, pulsing throng in her little red halter neck dress in stretch PVC. It moulded to her slim body as she walked and, that night, it felt good. With it she had matching shoulder length gloves and silver high heeled sandals to match the silver lurex seams of her black stockings.

Flashguns were already searing the night air as she made her way through the crowd towards the bandstand and the bar. She could, at last, appreciate why nobody was concerned about the photographers. Half or more of the males, where it was possible to determine gender, and perhaps twenty-five per cent of the females, were wearing masks. Looking about her at some of the other girls, Karen was beginning to feel overdressed. Her small shoulder bag felt quite out of place.

The band was playing jazz rather than disco music. The way a few of the guests were attired, thought Karen, it would have been difficult to dance too vigorously anyway without risking some kind of accident. She was close enough to see Mike seated with the other players in a small group. Then the vocalist appeared, clasped the microphone and began to sing. It was Valerie: bathed in the swimming lights, dressed in a fishnet catsuit and gold, high heeled sandals with, about her waist, a short skirt made of thin metallic strips which shimmered in the changing light as she sang and swayed her body in time with the band.

Nearer still, Sonia stood in genial conversation with three male guests, each of whom was masked and wore a more formal style of leather suit. Somehow, Karen knew these must be men of wealth and maybe considerable influence. Perhaps they would be staying at the house tonight, in some of these secret rooms. With whom she wondered – Angie, Kim, Jackie, maybe Val or even Pauline.

As if on cue with her thoughts, Pauline appeared, walking by her with a male guest. She wore a black leather leotard with brass studded collar and black thigh boots with studded seams. About her waist was a studded belt from which swung a short, snake-like, braided leather whip. If she saw Karen as she passed close by she gave no sign of recognition.

Karen had reached the bar when suddenly an arm appeared from the side and took hers by the elbow.

'Karen, you made it!' shouted a voice over the band and the hubbub. 'Get your drink and come and join us over by the pool!'

It was Annette, and Karen could not help but look her up and down, realising as she did so that it might be bad manners, but Annette saw her expression and laughed.

'You'll get used to it soon ... you should see some of the others!'

Annette was bare breasted, her breasts held firmly in position by the support of the stiff quarter cups of her basque. The basque, in black satin with red lace trim, was laced tightly about her body and ended in red lace suspenders stretching down to lace topped black stockings with patent leather high heels. Below her broad grin was a slim black satin choker with a small red bow at the front. Her g-string panties were shimmering red satin. Karen, large Scotch in hand, followed her through the revellers, marvelling at some of the bizarre outfits as she went.

At the poolside, Annette introduced Karen to two male guests; one, a young, dark haired man in latex tank top and tight latex trousers, was not masked. He reached out, smiled and squeezed her hand. The other, an older male with a leather helmet covering his head and half of his face, was stout and thick set. He was more formally attired, his leather suit almost military in style. He reached out and took Karen's hand, lifted it and kissed it with cold, moist lips.

'Delighted to meet you, Miss Karen,' he said quietly with a gruff accent which Karen thought Scandinavian rather than German.

'I'm sure you will excuse the disguise,' he went on, 'but it is necessary outdoors you understand.'

'Quite so,' answered Karen nervously, 'of course I do.'

'Then perhaps you will join us for a drink and a little conversation.'

He gestured towards a poolside table and guided Karen, behind the others, towards it, putting his fleshy hand about her waist and letting it drop down over her behind as she turned to sit down. Karen shivered and looked coldly at Annette. Was Annette setting her up? Probably not, but she instinctively disliked the man and wanted to get away without seeming to be rude.

'You have a small drink,' the masked man said to Karen with a slight smile, 'and you, Miss Annette, you do not have any drink. I will get us some champagne and four glasses to complete our table – there are no waiters here, I think.'

He spoke a few words in a foreign tongue to the other male, both arose from the table and disappeared into the chattering, laughing and bustling crowd in the direction of the bar.

'Annette!' hissed Karen. 'What's going on? I'm not pairing up with him if that's what you think!'

'No, no sweety,' Annette nodded. 'I'm not trying to get you into anything. It's Jackie he's expecting to meet, but I can't see her anywhere. I thought you wouldn't mind sitting in until she . . .'

'Yes, OK,' Karen interrupted, 'but he's repulsive – I just couldn't – you know, anything! Who is he anyway?'

'God!' hissed Annette, looking about her. 'He's financial director of the International . . . well, never mind, we'll stay here until . . . ah!'

Annette suddenly broke off and stood up, staring past Karen and waving her arm.

'Jackie – over here! Over here!'

Jackie appeared from behind, eyes wide and smiling, her long brown hair swinging from a pony tail fixed high up at the back of her head. She wore large pendant gold earrings and a black leather collar. A sheer black nylon top with little flounced sleeves covered the upper part of her body down to just beneath her breasts, which could be seen clearly through the material. Her midriff was bare but from her waist hung a short flared skirt in the same material as her top. It did not appear to Karen as though she wore much, if anything, underneath. On her legs, as if to emphasise the flimsiness of her body attire were black latex stockings, held in place by thigh straps. On her feet she had black leather sandals with long, slim heels.

'Are they here?' asked Jackie.

'Yes,' answered a relieved looking Annette, 'they've gone for the drinks – Karen's been sitting in for you.'

'Oh thanks, Karen, you're a love. I got nailed by some bloody drunken Greek ship owner – his girlfriend, or somebody, showed up just in time!'

Karen smiled, stood up and retrieved her drink.

'I'd better leave you to it then, I'm sure the two gentlemen will excuse my absence!'

'See ya later kid!' grinned Jackie. Annette blew her a kiss.

Karen downed the remains of her drink and turned away towards the band and the lights. If only she could sit and talk to Mike, or somebody not involved in all of this.

Most of the revellers were confined to the paved areas between the house and the tennis courts, or the paths, mainly because the women, and apparently, as Karen had observed, some of the men, wore high heels. So, heading back to the bar, she found herself once more ingested by the milling throng, surrounded by laughter, movement and lights, yet feeling utterly alone and isolated as never before. On the way to the bar, she had recognised only one of the girls from the house and she, like everyone else, was by now fully occupied with one or more of the guests. In front of the stage, people were pressing in to watch another act. Valerie was absent from the stage and Sonia, who she hoped to find, was gone also.

'Make it a large one please,' said Karen as the barman lifted the Scotch from the shelf, 'no ice.' There was a wave of clapping and cheering and Karen looked up, seeing a new figure at the microphone. This girl she had never seen before but she was obviously known to most of the others. The barman stopped wiping glasses and leaned forward to take a better look.

The girl was about Karen's age but with long black hair

set in ringlets which swung about her shoulders as she smiled down at the crowd and voiced unheard words of acknowledgement. She wore a vivid pink long sleeve top, fastened by a large bow at the front. Below were sheer black seamed tights which disappeared up under the blouse and on her feet, high heeled open sandals in gold, with straps criss-crossing her ankles. She would have revealed all except for the opaque 'modesty' strip in her tights, no more than four centimetres wide, which ran vertically from her waist and down between her legs. She began to sway and sing to further applause.

'Isn't she something?' said the barman, turning to Karen.

Karen was gone.

She walked by the pool, glass in hand. There were people in the pool now, some of them wearing nothing but their masks. She passed by the small marquee and over the gentle rise in the direction of the main gate. Over the rise, the sounds of the party and the band were much diminished and the chirping of the night insects took their place. There were several groups of trees a short distance away, each with a wooden seat or two set near to it. Karen, hesitating to remove her shoes, walked over the soft grass towards one of these. She sat down, took a drink and leaned back to gaze up at the sky. The stars were so much brighter now and a full moon loomed behind the trees, long deep shadows clawing out before it. The air was calm, sweet and perfumed.

A shout, then someone laughing, cut across her thoughts. She turned. Three figures were approaching over the rise, silhouetted by the glow from the party. They whooped and laughed as they drew closer, one of them stopping to remove her shoes whilst steadying herself on the shoulder of her male companion. The third figure, also male, made for the grove of trees nearest to where Karen sat and swung himself down onto one of the seats. Karen picked up her glass and quietly moved further around the trees by her seat so as to be out of sight. She was nevertheless quite able to observe the three, who were now together talking and laughing, the first man on his feet again. The two men, one tall, one shorter, were both masked and wearing leather jackets and trousers. They were standing with their backs to Karen, facing the girl and obscuring her from view. They were talking too quietly for her to hear what they were saying, but they were speaking English with German accents. The girl sounded English.

All three laughed loudly and the men pulled off their jackets, dropping them carelessly onto the seat. One of them sat down and started to remove his boots and socks, the other did the same but remained standing. Both took off their masks. Now one of them was out of the way, Karen could see the girl. It was Angela.

Angela stood watching the men, her blonde hair held up in its clasp with whisps hanging free. She had on a strapless black mini dress with a red zig-zag pattern down the front. The soft latex reflected the moonlight in a diffused sheen. On her arms were shoulder length latex gloves which she smoothed with her fingers as she waited for the men, who were starting to remove their leather trousers.

Karen took another drink, saying to herself, 'Oh God, what am I going to do now?'

But there was only one answer – nothing! The two men were slim and well built, the shorter of the two, fair and about thirty-five, the taller and darker man a little older. One of them stood behind Angela pulling down the zipper at the back of her dress. The other peeled the dress away from her body, exposing her breasts to the moonlight before the zipper was quite freed.

'Oh!' she laughed as the dress pulled away. 'It's sticking to me!'

The men still wore their briefs but Karen saw that both were sexually aroused and eager for Angela, who stood before them in her gloves, open body tights and red nylon briefs.

The fair haired man pulled down his briefs and Karen

saw his penis swing up, rigid and well proportioned. The other placed his right arm around Angela and pressed his lips to hers as his left hand slid deftly into the front of her briefs and began to play its lustful game. She, with matching eagerness, forced his briefs down far enough so that she pulled his erection free and held him against her stomach whilst her fingers cupped his testicles. The fair haired man positioned himself behind her, reaching around to squeeze her breasts whilst forcing his shaft under her behind. Karen's heart was beating strongly. Her hand shook. She took another drink from the glass, too much this time, causing her to almost choke. It took all her efforts to suppress a cough.

Angela released her hold on the man in front and pushed down her panties. Both the men supported her as she freed her legs from them. Then she went down on her knees as if the whole act was rehearsed, turning as she went so that she now faced the fair haired man. Taking hold of his erection, she took the head in her mouth and slid her lips down the shaft as far as she could go, moving her head back and forth and gently squeezing the scrotum.

Her other accomplice moved over to the bench, took up his discarded jacket and draped it over the wooden back. He sat down and leaned back against the coat calling to the other two, 'Hey! Over here now!'

Angela withdrew the shaft from her mouth and raised herself up. The fair haired man put his arm about her waist and they walked over to the bench where the other was waiting, his erection held vertical in his hand. Angela turned her back to him, spread her legs and bent her knees so that she sank down, pushing the lips of her sex against the head of his cock. He supported her with his hands on her thighs and moved her back and forth so that the head massaged her clitoris. After a minute she bent forwards and then slid down onto him, taking the full length of his shaft into herself. In this position she was able to resume fellatio with the fair haired man whose impatient organ so eagerly awaited her open mouth.

To Karen's watching eyes, the soft, gentle Angela was the instigator of this act and at least as enthusiastic as the two males.

One of the men said, 'OK, change over time,' and Angela drew herself up from the glistening shaft, but only just, staying poised above it.

The seated man grasped her thighs and eased her forward slightly, pulling her down again until the head of his cock, lubricated by Angela's own excitement, pressed hotly and urgently against her anus, squeezing through the tight opening and forcing up inexhorably into her rear passage. She pulled away from the fair haired man and leaned back against her rearward invader so that he penetrated her all the way, then letting her head fall askew across his shoulders she spread her legs wide for the other. He leaned forward, supporting himself by his hands on the back of the bench either side of the other two. He thrust between the waiting lips of her sex and entered her fully, pumping slowly at first whilst the other male, under her weight, flexed his pelvis more rapidly, at the same time squeezing her breasts. All three closed their eyes and abandoned themselves to the inevitable.

From her hiding place, Karen saw Angela's mouth full open, heard her gasping hoarsely, then driven by lust, spread wide and impaled on the two men, she cried, 'Oh you buggers, go for it! Go for it! Now! Now!'

Her voice broke into long sobbing gasps and she squirmed on the two shafts as the enveloping tide of orgasm overtook her. The rasping breath and moans of the two men evidenced the fulfilment of their own passions within moments of hers. Karen downed the remainder of the Scotch, and now that the tableau was ending, closed her eyes and realised she was hot and sweating, not just with the effects of the drink or through the warm evening air but because of her own sexual tension and desire, a desire intermingled with guilt and anguish at having witnessed what she was never meant to see.

Then Karen heard a sound to her left and hissed, 'Oh

Christ!' as something in the dark shadows touched her ankle. She unfroze and looked down. It was Pancake, out on his nocturnal wanderings, now brushing about her legs and purring loudly. To Karen, his purring sounded like a buzz-saw in the calm night air. She looked back through the trees and saw Angela and the two men gathering up their clothes. Angela had removed her tights and gloves, and bundled them up with her dress saying, 'Straight to the pool, OK! Nobody will bother if we go in through the trees, yes? They'll think we just got undressed there.'

The two men agreed and picked up their bundles, then suddenly one of them looked at the small grove of trees where Karen stood trembling, seemingly straight at her. Angela and the other male stopped and followed his gaze, then Angela laughed and said, 'Oh, here's Pancake, come on ... come on then, back with us!'

The cat circled them for a few seconds then went on his way into the secret night, whilst they set off back the way they had come, towards the party and the lights.

Once more Karen was alone, and as if to confirm this, she again was conscious of the whirring insects and the wide spread of stars above.

After a time she returned to the pathway, put on her shoes and made her way back around to the bustle and chatter of the gathering. Again she was amongst the crowd and the lights, and Valerie was back at the microphone. Karen stopped to watch and listen as the glamorous Valerie began to sing and sway in the myriad lights. She sensed a presence at her elbow, but before she could turn, a voice said, 'Perhaps I might get Mademoiselle another drink as her glass is empty?'

She turned and found herself looking into a broad smiling face with brown eyes and thick black hair. He wore no mask but had on a soft brown suede shirt, open almost to the waist, and black leather slacks. He was slim, perhaps nearing forty. Karen smiled and held out the empty glass.

'Thank you – yes, I was about to go to the bar.'

'And what will it be?' he asked.

'Er ... nothing alcoholic, just a Coke with ice, if you don't mind.'

'But of course,' he smiled, 'and where was Mademoiselle sitting, or does she not have a table?'

'No,' replied Karen, 'I don't have one.'

Five minutes later he emerged from the crowd, a glass of beer in one hand, her Coke in the other.

'I see no spare seats,' he said, handing her the drink and looking into her eyes apologetically. 'I thought we may sit for a while and I will talk with you.'

'Never mind,' smiled Karen, 'we can talk here.'

'I am Armand,' he smiled, 'and you are?'

'I'm Karen,' she smiled in return, taking his outstretched hand. He kissed her hand lightly. 'Have you been here all evening?'

'Oh no,' he answered, 'my flight from Paris to Marseilles was coming in late you see. I have been here only one hour. I find Mademoiselle Sonia to talk about business and then I come here and I see you standing alone.'

'So what do you do in Paris?' asked Karen, wondering if she ought to have asked at all.

'Me – I am just publisher, that is why I am not so secret and have on no mask. And you, you are friend of Sonia or guest ... I have not seen you before, I think? I always am here for the party and sometimes for business.'

'I'm Sonia's secretary,' replied Karen, 'I've been here nearly three months.'

They made small talk for a while until each had finished their drink, then Armand said, 'Do you wish for another drink, or perhaps you will walk with me? The gardens, they are beautiful tonight and here there is much noise.'

'A walk would be nice,' smiled Karen.

Armand took her glass and placed it with his on a low wall at the side of the path, then turned and smiled, 'Perhaps Mademoiselle will take my arm. She can show me her favourite part of the grounds, yes, I do not know them so well.'

She took the arm he offered, smiled into his eyes and he squeezed her hand. Karen knew exactly where she wanted to go.

They were not quite clear of the crowds about the swimming pool when a voice called, 'Armand! Oh, Armand!'

A figure detached itself from a knot of people silhouetted against the lights and hurried the intervening few metres towards them.

'Josephine!' smiled Armand, who barely had time to disengage himself from Karen before the girl seized and kissed him avidly on the lips. Armand held her by the waist, self consciously glancing at Karen.

'Armand, you bad boy, you have been avoiding me all evening!'

She turned to Karen and squeezed her arm, smiling. 'You are Armand's friend, you have met him here today?'

'No, no,' answered Karen looking Josephine up and down, 'I work here, I . . .'

Armand, seeming to sense Karen's unease, put his arm about her and smiled looking from her to Josephine.

'Miss Karen and I are going for a little walk and no, Josephine, I have not been avoiding you, I have been late getting here and I found Miss Karen alone like myself.'

Karen gazed at Josephine with her round face, full lips and long raven hair. Her features were not unlike those of Sonia's but softer and she was younger, perhaps in her early twenties. Her slim figure was clad in a tight black leather cat suit, about which there were numerous short zippers and short lengths of bright chain. From a belt about her waist hung a pair of brightly polished steel handcuffs, and to complete the effect her black ankle boots each displayed a small glittering spur.

'You like this?' She grinned, turning to Karen and passing her outspread fingers down the front of her outfit.

'It's very impressive,' replied Karen, feeling more intimidated than impressed.

'The men, they all love it, don't they, my sweet?' She smiled knowingly at Armand, slipping an arm about his waist, then her other about Karen's.

'We all three go for a walk now – yes?'

Armand looked sheepishly at Karen, awaiting her response. Karen had no idea what to say and wondered if she ought not to leave them alone. They obviously had shared experiences which left her, as was so often the case here, the outsider. But Armand smiled and manoeuvred Josephine around to his left side, took each of them by the hand and began to walk along the path.

Josephine, a little shorter than Karen, her head just above Armand's shoulder, peered around him at Karen and said with a look of intense concern, 'Mon dieu! You should not walk alone with this man, I tell you Karen, he is most dangerous – no young woman should trust him! Is that not obvious from his eyes?'

'If you say so,' smiled Karen weakly.

'Oh, I am misunderstood always,' sighed Armand with a sideways smile.

A small group of revellers, some masked, headed past them and back towards the party. Karen thought she recognised Annette but the pathway was shaded from the moonlight and it was too dark for her to be sure.

'There's a place to sit if you want, over there.'

Karen gestured towards the low rise beyond which lay the groves of trees.

'We'll need to take our shoes off though.'

'Oh yes,' said Josephine, stooping at the side of the path to undo her ankle boots, 'I must not get soil in the little spurs, it is not good!'

Karen wondered who 'the little spurs' were intended for. Surely not Armand, she thought. He just didn't seem the type, but then, who could tell?

They crested the rise and started down the grassy slope. The noise of the party diminished and, once more, Karen was aware of the realm of the stars spread above them. The air was a little cooler than before but none the less pleasant.

They were still some way from the trees, still on the

gentle slope, when Josephine said, 'It is nice here I think, the grass is very soft.'

They stopped and Karen looked from one to the other. Armand glanced at his watch.

'Almost midnight, the magic hour and so beautiful here.'

He stroked Karen's hair then placed his hands on her cheeks.

'But I think this night is just a reflection of your own beauty, Mademoiselle.'

He pulled her face close up to his own until their lips met. Karen placed her hands on his arms as if to resist him but wavered in uncertainty, feeling the presence of Josephine next to her, wondering if, perhaps, she would now go away and leave them alone. Maybe if she responded to Armand, Josephine would take the hint and go. She felt very uneasy but made her decision and, putting her arms about Armand's body, she returned his kisses with enthusiasm.

Then she felt Josephine's arms slip about her own waist and Josephine's warm breath on her neck. Before she could protest or move, another pair of lips closed upon her, just below the ear. Karen shivered and a sensation like a mild electric current passed through her. Josephine and Armand held and squeezed her, their lips in turn finding hers then roaming about her neck and shoulders as far as the tops of her long gloves. They paid little attention to each other, concentrating only on Karen, sensing that their attentions were beginning to have the desired effect.

Armand whispered in her ear, 'Would Mademoiselle prefer that I send Josephine away?'

Josephine's hands moved slowly down below Karen's waist until her fingers were splayed out and pressing on the base of her stomach and the soft lips brushed against her ear.

'Oh, I . . . I . . . please Armand . . . I don't know.'

Josephine's hands moved away from her stomach and glided up over her shoulders, and Armand's lips closed upon hers.

She felt the halter neck of her dress loosen as the nylon zip moved slowly down and Josephine whispered, 'We play a little game now, I think.'

Karen told herself there was no point in struggling as Armand was holding her too tightly by the upper arms, nor did she take her arms from around his body as the dress loosened all the way down to her behind. Armand released his hold on her and Josephine pulled the dress down over her arms. Karen half turned, her breasts exposed, and reached down to stop Josephine from pulling the dress away further.

'Look, both of you ... I don't think we should be doing this ... really ... I don't ...'

But Armand placed his fingers and thumbs about her breasts and his lips found her nipples, sucking and twirling his tongue about them until they were hard and erect.

Josephine had the dress around her ankles and pulled away each of her feet in turn so as to remove it from under her. Armand pressed his attentions onto Karen with greater fervour but now Josephine moved away and began to undo the leather belt about her own waist. Karen was aware of the rasp of the buckle and the metallic rattle of the handcuffs and assumed that Josephine too was getting undressed.

If any signal passed between Armand and Josephine, Karen was not aware of it, but suddenly he took her wrists and forced her arms around behind her back whilst pressing his lips hard against hers. Karen felt the cool steel of the cuffs fitted quickly about her but they had snapped shut and secure before Armand released his hold.

'Oh, wait – no!' Karen cried, twisting her head from side to side to look at her manacled wrists.

Armand smiled, 'Just a little game, Mademoiselle.'

Josephine lifted Karen's manacled wrists up, pulling them by the attached belt which she passed around the girl's neck. Armand took the belt and assisted Josephine to fasten the buckle just behind Karen's neck. They adjusted it and pulled Karen's wrists higher until her arms were trussed up between her shoulder blades before securing the buckle and taking their hands from her. Karen twisted and turned, backing away from them, her mouth opened in silent protest.

'You can go now!' laughed Josephine. 'You can run away from us if you wish. Go on – go!'

Karen's eyes darted from Josephine to Armand, 'Look! ... Please ... what are you doing with me?'

Armand stepped forward and held her trembling body in his arms.

'Miss Karen, you are a very beautiful lady, we want you very much!'

Josephine stepped up close behind her and again the scorching breath and devouring lips engulfed her neck and throat. Armand's fingers slipped suddenly under the elastic of her flimsy little briefs and invaded between the lips of her sex. Karen gasped and cried out once, then again, as another hand slid down between the cleavage of her behind and met the fingers which already danced upon the stage of her sex. She closed her eyes and her breath shortened as the fingers began to electrify her entire body. Josephine used her free hand to tug down the briefs as did Armand with his, then they eased her legs apart. Armand sucked hard on her nipples then slowly sank to his knees, biting and licking down her chest and stomach until he reached the hard, smooth flesh just above her sex.

'Oh,' he cried, 'she is shaved and smooth, this is beautiful!'

His tongue darted into her, teasing and burning her clitoris as Josephine's fingers spread her sex from the rear. Karen began to moan into the dark sky when they pulled her down onto the grass, choking and gasping, seated upright on the gentle slope.

Josephine sat down behind her and slightly to one side with her knees each side of Karen. She slipped her arms around her, pulling her backwards so that Karen's body lay partly across her, giving Josephine's hands access to her breasts and nipples and her mouth within easy reach of her face and neck. Karen's blonde hair shone in the moonlight against Josephine's black leather suit, whilst Josephine's long hair cascaded over Karen's naked and bound body.

With Josephine so occupied and Karen, with eyes shut tight, returning her kisses, Armand struggled with urgent haste out of the leather trousers and thrust down the white nylon briefs which at once released his flushed and erect organ. Karen part opened her eyes and saw Armand drop down to his knees in front of her. Josephine reached forward and slipped a hand under each of Karen's knees, pulling hard so that her thighs were spread apart and back against her chest. Her mouth again pressed on Karen's nipping and plucking at her cheeks and lips, her breath a perfumed furnace.

Armand's tongue did its fiendish work about her sex and anus, burning and inflaming until her breath quickened and she murmured hoarsely, 'Please ... please ... please ...!'

She closed her eyes again but saw in her mind the reddened, swaggering shaft poised above her as Armand raised himself as though to pierce her through to the heart. Karen let out a cry as if in despair as he entered her ravenously and began stroke after devilish stroke. Josephine pulled her knees harder and wider apart still and continued to suck and bite about her neck. Karen moaned loudly. Having earlier concerned herself that others might come by and see what they were doing, she now wanted them all to see her, bound and spread in the blazing, pulsing lights, penetrated and unable to stop herself from crying out, for cry out she did, again and again as he convulsed within her.

'Oh, sweetheart,' whispered Josephine, 'it is wonderful, you enjoy it so very much.'

When they had released her and helped her to dress, Armand took Karen's hand and kissed it, giving a little bow and smiling, 'Oh, Mademoiselle, you must visit us in Paris, we must spend much more time together and make this music again!'

# 7

# Ritual of Chastisement

Two days had passed by and everyone had recovered from the effects of the party. Gone was the marquee, the bandstand and gone were most of those privileged few who had stayed on through the following day. Karen sat at a table near the bar, chatting to Angela. This was the old Angela again, the one she had come to know, not the Angela of two nights ago. What she had seen in the gardens on that night was of a different world and another time.

It was seven o'clock and people were thinking of eating. Angela said, 'I don't know about you, but I wouldn't mind the village bistro for a change, rather than here. I always feel a bit unsettled after a do. I like to get out and about more.'

'Fine by me,' agreed Karen. 'I've heard it's quite nice from some of the others.'

'Oh, I thought you'd been a couple of times already with Mike – it's only a small place where the local people go but it's . . .'

She was interrupted by a shriek of laughter from a table nearby. It was Jackie, who had been deep in conversation with Kim, now giving vent to her mirth over whatever it was they were discussing. Kim's face was a mask of surprise and she could be heard saying over and over again, 'No – he didn't, you're kidding!' Jackie, unable to reply, just kept nodding, then Kim burst into laughter too.

It was at that point that Pauline entered the room, dressed in her long, slim fitting black gown with gold braided high collar.

Everyone noticed her silent but purposeful glide across the room, except Jackie, whose face changed abruptly as

Pauline came to a halt by the table. She leaned over and spoke a few words into Jackie's ear, then turning, left as quickly as she had come, neither looking nor speaking to any of the eight or so people who were scattered about the room. Jackie pulled a face after her, put her thumb up to her nose and wiggled her fingers.

No one spoke for a few seconds, then Valerie, sitting with an orange juice at the bar, said, 'Oh dear, now what have you been up to?'

'Nothing I can think of,' answered Jackie nonchalantly, pushing back the hair from the sides of her face, 'unless I forgot to water that stupid little plant on her bloody desk again!'

'It must be more than that,' said Valerie, 'she was smiling! Didn't you notice? It's always a bad sign when she smiles!'

'No I didn't!' replied Jackie. 'But it can't be that bad, she just said to wait in my room tomorrow morning, that's all. I wasn't going anywhere particular anyway, so the old cow isn't going to spoil anything!'

'I wouldn't bank on that,' said Angela quietly, looking from Jackie to Karen.

Shortly after nine o'clock the following morning, two figures emerged quietly from a room at the end of the first floor corridor. One of the two, Cheryl, a slim woman in her early thirties, had short, blonde, loosely permed hair which framed a face of undoubted beauty. She had full lips, an upturned nose and sultry blue eyes; but it was a face which conveyed a look of authority and a manner which implied that she was used to being in charge of a situation, as in this case she undoubtedly was.

The outfit she wore suggested that she fulfilled the role of a hospital nurse, which indeed was her original training and career. Her uniform was mid-blue with white edged, short sleeves and white edged collar open at the neck. The pockets, one over each of her full breasts, were white edged too and the casual observer would not have been surprised had she worn a small cap as well.

This outfit, however, would not have been approved by any health service. Not only was it not made of the traditional materials but of soft vinyl instead, it was also considerably shorter than regulation length and revealed black, seamed stockings and black patent high heeled shoes.

The outfit, and Cheryl's services in this role, were much appreciated by a number of Sonia's wealthy and influential clients in London, where she provided services and treatment of a more esoteric nature for those in need, and made 'house calls' of a kind not specified by the National Health Service.

Two-thirds of her time saw her at her 'consultation' rooms in Knightsbridge but Cheryl had returned for the party and would remain until the end of the following week.

The figure in front of Cheryl presented a different appearance altogether. Jackie wore a white cotton surgical gown, held in place by tapes spaced at intervals down the back fastening just below her knees to reveal her stockings, black and seamed like Cheryl's. On her small feet were fastened black patent leather sandals, held about her ankles by thin patent straps, and poised on stiletto heels of some fifteen centimetres. Walking in these shoes was made all the more precarious as she also had to contend with steel ankle cuffs, joined by a short chain so as to restrict the length of her step.

Cheryl walked at her side saying, 'Stand up straight and get a move on!'

Jackie almost stumbled and had to be steadied, turning her face to Cheryl and protesting, 'If I try to go any quicker I'll . . .'

'Shut up!' came the response. 'Just keep moving!'

Jackie obeyed and kept up the pace as best she could, the arms of the gown swinging loose and empty at either side of her.

They reached the door of Pauline's office, Jackie with a mixture of relief and apprehension. Cheryl knocked twice sharply, then opened the door and ushered her in.

The layout of Pauline's suite was similar to that of Sonia's, but the office area was not as extensive and the remainder of the room more domestic in appearance. There were a small number of rooms leading off it, one of which was not lit by natural light but was surrounded by black drapes and furnished with a number of items in chrome and black leather which Jackie knew only too well were not office furniture. The door was, ominously, standing half open.

'How nice to see you again, my dear,' smiled Pauline, as Jackie was brought to a halt in front of the oak desk behind which she was seated. Pauline appeared to be dressed in the same manner as Cheryl.

Cheryl undid the tapes down the back of the surgical gown and pulled it away from Jackie's shoulders.

'Oh, very good,' said Pauline smiling again. 'Did she behave herself – no problems?'

'She wasn't too much trouble,' replied Cheryl. 'She didn't want the restraint on at first, but she saw reason in the end.'

Tightly fastened about Jackie's waist was a heavy black leather belt, some fifteen centimetres deep, buckled at the rear and having a steel cuff at each side which held her wrists close to her body. Above the waist she was naked, her breasts firm, her nipples prominent and pinkish brown. Below the restraint she was dressed only in a black elasticated garter belt which served to hold up her stockings.

She had been in Pauline's office many times of course, normally as part of her duties and on several occasions to be punished, but this was different. She had never been collected like this from her room before, in restraint, and it had always been just her and Pauline. The punishments and humiliations meted out to her in the past were just a game. She sometimes provoked Pauline into chastising her, they both knew that, and Pauline knew how far to go with Jackie. Perhaps Cheryl wanted to join in the charades too. She had no doubt that much, if not all, of what was happening now was being recorded.

Jackie looked about the room. Pauline was usually tidy, and she should know as she did much of the tidying for her. It seemed odd that there were items of what appeared to be black rubber clothing piled on the deep orange cushions on one of the chairs by the window. Pauline never left clothes laying about.

Pauline saw where Jackie was looking and said to Cheryl, 'Perhaps we could slip her into something more stylish, don't you agree?'

'Of course I do,' replied Cheryl and, walking over to the chair, picked up the largest of the garments laying there and walked back behind Jackie, saying, 'Now you do not move or turn around, do you understand?'

Jackie asked, in a high pitched, nervous manner, 'What are you doing?' But nevertheless obeyed the order.

Neither of them replied to her question but Pauline got up from her seat behind the desk and walked around to a position directly in front of her. Pauline held a small key with which she proceeded to unlock the cuffs on Jackie's wrists. Cheryl released the belt about her waist at the same time so that Pauline lifted the dangling restraint away and lowered it carefully onto the desk top. Cheryl passed the garment she held around in front of her, so that Pauline took one end of it, indicating the sleeve running across the inside, and ordered, 'In here, left arm first!'

The unmistakeable odour of latex asserted itself as Jackie complied with the order.

'That's it, right in, now the other!'

She crossed her arms over inside the cool, smooth material of the sleeve whilst Pauline and Cheryl pulled the heavy black rubber about her upper body. She knew exactly what it was they were putting on her, it was certainly not her first acquaintance with the straitjacket. Pauline held her tightly by the upper arms and Jackie felt the collar tighten about her neck. There was not the sound of straps and buckles being done up, the sound she expected to hear, but a faint swishing and intermittent tugging as Cheryl's hands worked down the back.

'This is the tedious part,' muttered Cheryl. 'Always takes such a long time.'

'So much neater when it's finished though, I always think,' replied Pauline.

Jackie began now to realize what it was that kept Cheryl so occupied. They were fastening up her restraint with laces which criss-crossed down the back through metal eyelets. So far, the straitjacket was not especially tight but then, as Cheryl reached the waistband, Pauline moved around behind and Jackie felt the heavy rubber begin to constrict. She swayed on the stiletto heels as two pairs of hands tugged and adjusted the laces from the collar down, so that the two halves of the jacket met down the middle of her back.

'A perfect fit,' muttered Cheryl, 'it could have been made especially for her.'

'It was made especially for her,' responded Pauline.

This restraint was tighter than the ones Jackie had known before. As she twisted and flexed inside it, the latex conformed and moulded to her body, squeezing down on her breasts and almost squeezing her fingers into immobility. Her upper body was enveloped in a sleek rubber skin, fitting like a glove from neck to waist.

'There now,' announced Pauline with a smile of satisfaction, 'nice and secure! Are we nice and comfortable?'

Jackie did not reply but looked from one to the other.

'I think that style suits her rather well,' remarked Cheryl.

Pauline moved back behind her desk, opened a top drawer and pulled out a small white packet. She looked Jackie in the eyes and said, 'I really hope you are comfortable my dear, you're going to be wearing that for a long time, a long time indeed!'

'All right!' Jackie finally spoke up. 'What's going on – what have I done wrong now?'

Pauline did not reply but reached down into the drawer again and withdrew two short, black braided whips; the kind she had worn in her belt at the party. One of these she handed over the desk to Cheryl. Jackie looked at her in alarm then twisted about to look at Cheryl.

'Look! You mustn't . . . you . . .!'

'Just to make quite sure you do as you're told!' said Cheryl.

'I will! Just don't go on at me – I can't do anything can I?'

Pauline returned to where they stood, putting the whip down within easy reach and picking up the white paper packet.

'Close your eyes and your mouth – tightly!'

Jackie was about to protest but thought better of it and obeyed. She heard the packet being ripped open by Pauline just in front of her, then she felt Cheryl's hands grip the sides of her head from behind.

'Tightly!' Pauline repeated, then something cool and moist was pressed hard over her mouth and held firmly there for a few seconds.

'That will do the trick!' announced Pauline. 'Now you may open your eyes.'

Jackie opened her eyes but her mouth was held securely shut. Sealing her lips was a strip of white adhesive plastic tape, some ten centimetres long. It no longer felt cool, but had an odd synthetic smell about it.

Cheryl moved around to her side and remarked, 'Hm, nicely packaged.'

Pauline reached into a red plastic filing tray at the corner of her desk, turned back to Jackie and said, 'This will explain why you're here.'

She held a colour photograph up in front of Jackie's face. Jackie stared at it for only a moment before her eyes widened and she let out a muffled, 'Mmmm!'

'Sonia's own photographer took it,' continued Pauline. 'You were too preoccupied to notice. James processed the films yesterday. The silly little bitch kneeling in front of that man, we know who that is don't we?' She pushed the photograph closer and repeated loudly, 'Don't we?!'

Jackie felt her knees weakening and the blood rush to her face. Suddenly, Pauline lifted her arm and struck with the palm of her hand hard across the taped mouth. Jackie staggered back and might have fallen, because of the ankle cuffs, if Cheryl had not held her.

'Yes,' continued Pauline with subdued anger, 'and the man you gave the blow job to was very happy at the time, even though you were both so close to the house that the bloody photographer saw you!'

Jackie looked away but Pauline seized her chin and forced her head back so that their eyes met.

'Now I appreciate that you were both probably pissed, but do you understand what would happen if the wrong people got hold of a photograph like this? The old fool with his pants down and his mask off is a government minister, and one of Sonia's most important clients!'

Pauline released Jackie's chin and put her hands on her hips.

'The first thing Sonia said when she saw this was, "Her father will have to know – she'll have to leave here." Then her busy body secretary, little miss prim and bloody proper poked her nose in and said it would be safer if you stayed – so here you are!'

Pauline reached for the whip curled like a black rattlesnake on the table, and thrust it into Jackie's face. Jackie trembled and felt her bowels churning.

'Do you know what your father would do to you if you were chucked out of here? We all know why he pays what he does to keep you with us, don't we? It's because it would cause him no end of bloody embarrassment with a randy little bitch like you on the loose! With your sexual appetite, you'd end up in every tabloid paper with your knickers down and his political career would be finished! Well you're going to learn a bit of discipline starting now, and from today you'll do nothing without telling me and go nowhere without my permission!'

Pauline looked at Cheryl and said, 'Let's take her in there first.'

Jackie was looking straight ahead and so did not see what Pauline meant by 'in there'. However, they turned her around and began to propel her towards a doorway on the right at the far end of the room. Jackie knew it was the bathroom – for want of a better term, for it was more than just that. She wanted to object, to make some excuse for her behaviour at the party, to put the blame on him, to absolve herself, but the tape kept her as silent as the straitjacket made her helpless.

It took a little time to cross the room because of the short chain connecting her ankles and at one point she faltered. Cheryl drew back slightly and brought the whip down across her bare behind with a crack. Jackie jerked her head back, the shock displayed in her startled eyes, a sharp high pitched moan coming from behind the taped mouth.

'Walk properly and stand up straight!' ordered Cheryl.

Jackie endeavoured to do as she was told, the hot sting across her buttocks almost bringing tears to her eyes.

The room they took Jackie into was not unlike the shower room of the beauty parlour to which she made frequent visits, except that in here, the lights were not rose pink, but white and rather harsh on the blue tiled walls. They guided her to a low level, blue porcelain bowl, set out from the wall. It was similar to the combined bidet and toilet bowl in the parlour, with a rubber padded support rising up at the rear and sloping backwards. This one, as well, had been fitted at various places with leather straps, and hanging from the wall behind it were more straps and fittings.

'Especially for you, my dear,' smiled Pauline, as they brought her to a halt before the sinister looking bowl.

Pauline stooped in front of her and, with a small key, released the ankle cuffs and placed them with a metallic clatter onto an adjacent shelf stand. Cheryl took her by the shoulders and both of them pulled Jackie back against the edge of the bowl, then lowered her down onto it so that she was seated on the cool ceramic with her legs apart and positioned over each side. Straps were next secured about her neck and waist so that she was held against the padded back at an angle of forty-five degrees, her thighs and the rear of her behind supported by the bowl, but with nothing directly beneath her.

Cheryl disappeared through a pair of louvre doors set into an arched opening in an adjacent wall, whilst Pauline reached for something inside a wall cupboard.

It was whilst they were so occupied that Jackie realised that she could see herself reflected in a full-length mirror which, about three metres away, filled the area between the shower cubicle and the next wall. The mirror was a new addition; she knew it had not been there on her previous visit to the room.

When Cheryl reappeared, she was carrying a pink rubber hot water bottle and a coiled length of clear plastic tubing, whilst on her hands were flesh coloured latex surgical gloves. She joined Pauline at the sink and Pauline said, 'Here's the soap.'

Jackie knew perfectly well what the bottle and the tube were intended for and tensed her body against the straps and the straitjacket, pulling up her feet against the edge of the porcelain bowl in front of her. It was a futile effort. Her shoes squeaked against the rim and Pauline came over, laid the whip about her thighs with short, sharp strokes, saying sharply, 'Little bitch! Little bitch!' with each stroke.

Jackie's face reddened and she gave out a muffled cry which rose in pitch as tears welled up in her eyes. Cheryl moved over to face Pauline with Jackie in between. Each took one of her thighs and lifted it up, at the same time pulling out the hanging straps on the wall which were suspended some way from her head at either side. Each strap ended in a collar which they buckled firmly about her, above each knee, holding her thighs up and apart. Their fingers quickly moved to the buckles half way up each connecting strap and these they pulled tighter until Jackie was held spread and exposed with her high heeled shoes swinging level with her head and with the dubious advantage of being able to view her predicament fully in the mirror opposite.

Cheryl reached into the sink and lifted out the hot water

bottle, removing the cap and adding warm water from the mixer tap. She next added a measure of liquid soap from a small plastic bottle, followed by more warm water.

'By the way,' remarked Cheryl, inserting the end of the plastic tube through a hole in the cap, 'I don't think she shaved this morning. I'll deal with that first I think. That thing is usually kept charged isn't it?'

'Yes, it is, but we shouldn't have to do it,' remarked Pauline, 'I think I'll have her depilated permanently by Valerie after this. It will give her something to remember us by if she ever leaves this place.'

Cheryl handed Pauline the bottle and walked around to the other side of the helpless Jackie, removing the cap from the shaver head and switching it on. She knelt down beside Jackie to gain access from beneath rather than above the thighs, and as the electric razor began its work on the slight stubble about her vulva, Pauline suspended the rubber bottle from a bracket on the wall some two metres above the floor.

'D'you know what!' said Cheryl, after working with the shaver for a minute, 'She's oozing! I think she's going to come; it can't be just the vibration from this.'

'No!' barked Pauline. 'Don't let her, the little slut mustn't!'

'Don't worry, I've finished. Have you put soap on that nozzle?'

'Yes,' replied Pauline, 'and I've let the air out of the tube – it's all ready.'

Cheryl took the pink rubber nozzle, some ten centimetres long and flaring out to a disc at the base. Behind the disc was a small valve, from which the clear plastic pipe, now visibly filled with soapy water, coiled up to the suspended rubber bottle. The nozzle snaked down in Cheryl's rubber skinned hand, down under Jackie's thighs until she saw it in the mirror, poised, then she felt the hard, cool tip between her legs. She tightened her anal muscle to prevent its entry, but so smooth and well lubricated was it that she could not do so. She felt it slide up into her, cool and insistent, all the way up to the flared base.

'Time for potty training now, my sweet,' smiled Cheryl as she twisted the small valve.

Jackie felt the warm water surge up into her rectum as the rubber bottle above deflated. Her body felt hot and she was sweating inside the straitjacket. She saw Pauline, reflected in the mirror, reach above her head and rotate a large, chrome, wall-mounted tap and water began gushing down from the inside rim of the bowl. Cheryl withdrew the probe from her anus and swished it about in the water before putting it aside in the sink. Then they released the straps about Jackie's legs and lowered them down until her feet once more touched the floor, only to refasten her, this time by the ankles, with straps at either side of the bowl.

'Can't take chances with naughty girls!' remarked Cheryl.

Jackie could feel the hot water playing between her buttocks. She could also feel the increasing sensation of urgency pulsing through her lower innards. She closed her eyes and at first resisted the shamefully sensuous movement growing within her bowels which became more insistent by the moment. She breathed hard through flaring nostrils as her body took over in uncontrolled release of its contents, whilst her captors witnessed her shame and humiliation, a shame all the worse because it held within it dark seeds of ecstasy.

'I think that's it,' said Cheryl, and reached over to the sink for a tablet of soap.

Pauline reduced the water to a moderate flow and Cheryl again brought down her hand between Jackie's legs. The soap lathered about her groin and the cleft of her behind, a rubber skinned finger slipping several times into her anus so that she stiffened and moaned.

'Be careful!' warned Pauline. 'You're going to make her come.'

'No, I won't let her, I've done. Turn up the water will you, I'll rinse away the soap.'

'I've never known such a randy little bitch!' said Pauline.

'No,' agreed Cheryl, 'it doesn't seem to take much, does it?'

Released from the bowl and dried, Jackie now found herself back in the office standing in the centre of the room with the ankle cuffs back on, whilst Pauline stood beside her and Cheryl, still in the bathroom, put away the rubber gloves, washed, dried and powdered.

As Cheryl entered the room, Pauline smiled into Jackie's eyes and said, 'Now we know you won't be needing the toilet for a while, I think we'll carry on with our little lesson in discipline and obedience!'

'Yes, we're going walkies now,' said Cheryl, moving towards the main door. 'Come on, over here!'

Jackie glanced from Cheryl to Pauline in alarm but did not move. The braided whip in Pauline's hand stung sharply across her behind. She let out a strangled cry and her whole body jerked, but she started walking, as quickly as the ankle chain would allow, towards Cheryl, who pulled open the door.

Jackie, with Pauline directly behind, found herself on the threshold of the corridor but again stopped, an incoherent, muffled protest coming from her taped mouth. This time Cheryl applied the whip, as Pauline stood to one side, her steadying hand on the cocooned shoulder of the unfortunate Jackie whose muffled shriek did nothing to solicit pity.

Out in the corridor, with the door shut behind them, Pauline looked into Jackie's tearful eyes and said, 'Now you're going to walk right up and down this corridor from end to end ten times between the two of us. People are going to walk past and see you like this, but you will not on any account look at them or make a sound. Do you understand?'

Jackie gave no response and as if by pre-arrangement, Cheryl took her by the shoulders and Pauline applied the whip to her reddened behind repeatedly between each word and syllable as she shouted out at her, 'Do-you-un-der-stand?'

The muffled squeals gave way to a flood of tears as she writhed against Cheryl's grip then nodded her head up and down with a plaintive, 'Mmmm!'

'I think she understands,' said Cheryl, releasing Jackie's shoulders.

'Good!' replied Pauline, observing with a smile of satisfaction, the inflammed stripes across the girl's behind.

'Now!' she continued, 'you will walk in a regular and upright manner and look straight ahead! You won't turn around until you have gone all the way each time! If you disobey, you'll be thrashed hard!'

Cheryl walked away and took up her position at one end of the corridor whilst Pauline moved to the other, then turned and called, 'All right! This way first!'

From the outset, she knew it was not going to be easy. With the height of the heels and the restriction of the ankle cuffs, Jackie needed to progress with short careful steps, not too slow to provoke the whip, not too quickly to cause her to stumble, which she did not doubt must have the same result.

The corridor was some twenty metres long but to Jackie, after her first few passages each way, it began to seem interminable. She was becoming so wet with perspiration inside the confining latex that she could slide her hands about a little and, by flexing her shoulders, make the thick rubber slip over her skin. A thin trickle of sweat ran down her spine from under the straitjacket, only to be stopped when it reached her suspender belt. To her relief, not many others passed along the corridor. Amongst those who did were Valerie and two of the girls on maid duty who glanced at her several times as they passed by.

When her punishment parade began, Jackie had counted each way and had reckoned as far as five when her thoughts began to wander. The stinging on her behind was almost gone, replaced by sensual warmth which seemed to reach deeply into her sex. She could do with a man now, she thought, Mike maybe. She wondered what he would do if he found her like this, helpless and unable to speak. He could do anything he liked, she thought. Take her any way he wanted, perhaps with a friend. They could ...

She had almost reached Cheryl when she stumbled and

propped herself against the wall to regain her balance. Cheryl stepped over and pushed her around to face the wall. The whip fell one, two, three times across her already tender buttocks, bringing up fresh wheals on her flesh, with renewed moans and spreading tears, though the strokes were not as hard as she might have expected.

'Think yourself lucky,' hissed Cheryl, 'that it didn't happen at the other end!'

She pulled the weeping Jackie away from the wall and started her back on her way again saying, 'Try to be careful, she'll hurt you a lot more than me!'

So Jackie continued back and forth, her behind a furnace of heat, rivulets of perspiration trickling down her stomach and back until, reaching one end of the corridor, Cheryl said to her, 'Last lap.'

She turned to see Pauline waiting for her by the door, hands on hips, whip in hand, prepared for her to falter again.

Once back inside the apartment, they took her into the room with the black drapes all about the walls, a room familiar to Jackie, sinister, frightening and erotic; it could be any and all of these things to her. In the centre stood a black leather upholstered bench, no more than a metre and a half long, a half metre from the floor and under a metre wide. On either side of it but a little distance away, was a chrome post rising from floor to ceiling, with leather straps hanging from metal rings on each of them. Pauline touched a switch and the bench stood out in bright illumination from the lights above.

They pushed Jackie down onto the bench and then laid her on her back with her head only a hand's width from the end. From deep pockets within the upholstery, they pulled out straps and buckles with which they secured her upper body at the neck and waist. Pauline fished about momentarily in one of her uniform pockets and produced the small key with which to remove the ankle cuffs.

On her back, Jackie looked up and again saw an image of herself, for on the ceiling above the bench there was mounted a long mirror surrounded by spotlights. She knew how they were going to fasten her, Pauline had done it before. But this, she felt, was going to be different.

Pauline and Cheryl, on either side of the bench, took her ankles and pulled her legs up, apart and backwards. Jackie felt the firm coolness of leather enclose each of her ankles and heard the rattle of the buckles as they were tightened and fixed in place. Her legs, now fastened to the metal posts at each side, were pulled straight as the connecting straps were shortened. As in the bathroom, earlier that morning, she could watch herself spread, exposed and helpless but now more comfortable, at least for a minute or two.

'It's her natural position in life,' commented Pauline. 'Just look at the little bitch, it wouldn't take much to bring her off right now would it?'

'Her arse must be burning,' remarked Cheryl, 'look at those marks!'

'Yes, well we'll give her something else to think about now,' smiled Pauline, pulling a small white tube from her tunic pocket.

Jackie watched her unscrew the cap, wondering what the tube contained.

'This will be a new experience for you my dear,' smiled Pauline, squeezing a length of pale amber coloured cream out onto her middle finger. Jackie stiffened as Pauline bent forward and spread the cream over her sex, running it between the moist lips and over her clitoris, then down to her anus and back again.

At first, it merely felt cool, and she wondered why Pauline had done it. Pauline replaced the cap on the tube and turned to Cheryl. 'I think it's coffee time, how about you?'

'Yes, I agree. I don't think she'll be going anywhere while we're out!'

They closed the door behind them, leaving Jackie helpless and splayed out as she was, with a well illuminated view of herself and her predicament.

She was still hot inside the rubber cocoon but not

sweating as much now that she was immobile. Her behind pulsed and throbbed from the effect of the whippings and it was only gradually that she became aware of another, more intimate sensation. The area where Pauline had applied the cream was beginning to irritate. The irritation was no more than just that, for the first few minutes, but she was aware of it growing in intensity as time passed. Soon it was beginning to burn. Jackie tried to twist and turn in the restraints, this way and that; then she tried clenching the muscles around her groin, all to no avail.

After a few more minutes, the burning had become a torment.

She heaved against the straitjacket and began to sweat again, tugged first one leg and then the other against the straps but the torment just increased. She wanted to cry out but the tape over her mouth prevented it, so she began to cry out inside, her head twisting from side to side as the real trial began.

Only twenty or so minutes had gone by since the door had closed upon her, but when Pauline and Cheryl returned, Jackie was a picture of misery. Her hair was bedraggled and the black leather at either side of her head was wet with her streaming tears. Long moans, punctuated by muffled sobs, exuded from her.

'We're not enjoying ourselves so much now are we?' taunted Pauline. 'Perhaps we'll release you in another half an hour or so – perhaps we won't!'

The moans became louder and Jackie once more began to writhe helplessly against the restraints.

'You'll be able to see yourself on video soon my sweet,' continued Pauline with an ironic smile, bending over and looking into Jackie's wet and pleading eyes. 'Perhaps I'll have them show it in the bar, and you shall have a souvenir copy of your very own.'

Fresh tears welled up and Jackie squeezed her eyes shut.

'I think she's had enough,' said Cheryl, 'look how inflamed she is!'

'Oh no,' answered Pauline, 'she has a while to go yet, I

think. That stuff's harmless anyway, even though I used a bit extra.'

Cheryl looked Pauline hard in the eye. 'I say she's had enough! She's becoming distressed, even you can see that! We're not keeping her like this any longer!'

Pauline returned her gaze for a few moments, clutching hard at her whip but saying nothing. Then she averted her eyes from Cheryl's intimidating stare and said, 'All right then, you do as you bloody well please with her. I'm getting changed and going out for a bit.'

She turned and walked towards the door. 'Just one thing though! The straitjacket stays on and she stays put in here 'til I get back – I want to talk to her, all right? And I don't want her walking around either!'

'If that's what you want!' answered Cheryl coldly as Pauline disappeared.

Cheryl listened to Pauline's bedroom door close, then pulled apart one of the black drapes at the side of the room and exposed an alcove set into the wall. From a shelf she took down a bottle of methylated spirits and a roll of cotton wool. She uncapped the bottle and pulled a wad of cotton from the roll which she soaked with the methylated spirit. She bent down over Jackie and, with her fingernail, pulled at a corner of the white plastic tape which still so effectively sealed her mouth, then squeezed the soaked cotton wool about it so that the adhesive began to dissolve.

'Hold still!' she ordered as the tape started to ease away.

With the tape gone, Jackie gasped, then pleaded, 'Cheryl! Please! It's fucking murder!' Fresh tears welled up in her eyes. 'Cheryl! Cheryl! Please – I can't stand it – it's driving me fucking insane!' Cheryl, her back to Jackie was occupied at a nearby wall cupboard.

'Cheryl – Pleeeease!' Came the desperate appeal from behind her.

Cheryl turned, and as she sat down on the soft leather in front of Jackie's wide spread legs, the bound girl saw through tearful eyes what she was holding.

It was realistic and pink, but more ample in its

dimensions than the average male erection. Beneath it sprouted its lesser companion and behind the two a handgrip about which Cheryl's finger tightened.

'You stupid girl, you don't deserve this!' she said and brought the plump rubber head into contact with the red and swollen lips of Jackie's sex. It was obvious that no lubricant was needed. Jackie, with the effect of the intense irritation, was providing enough of her own.

She massaged the clitoris for a few moments but Jackie squeezed her eyes shut and cried out, 'Christ, Cheryl, don't torment me! Please, don't!'

Cheryl slid the rubber cock part into her until the companion butted and probed her anus. With a little extra push, both shafts entered her eager body fully and she gave a long quivering moan, so that Cheryl herself could almost feel the relief. She started to work the dildo quickly back and forth.

'Aah!' Jackie cried. 'Do it harder, harder, harder!'

Cheryl worked more vigorously, faster and harder. It seemed as though the writhing and gasping Jackie wanted to swallow the dildo inside her so urgent was her need. At last she tightened and heaved against the straps and enclosing rubber, her mouth agape, her teeth bared. She let out a sudden cry that was almost a scream, so that Cheryl thought she was going into convulsions.

Then she was calmed and opened her eyes. 'Christ, that was bloody wonderful. Just let it go on a bit more Cheryl, please ... just a bit more!'

'God, you're insatiable,' breathed Cheryl, beginning with the dildo again, slowly at first, then building up the rhythm and thrust.

Her second orgasm took a little longer to arrive, and when it did, culminated in a series of high pitched moans before she finally relaxed with a long sigh. Cheryl withdrew the dildo slowly, seeing her body quiver as if regretting its departure.

'I hope you feel better now,' grinned Cheryl, placing the instrument of Jackie's lustful relief into the nearby handbasin.

She reached up and undid the ankle straps, letting down first one leg and then the other. Jackie moved her knees up and down awkwardly.

'God my bloody legs ache,' she groaned. 'Cheryl, are you going to let me go?'

'No,' replied Cheryl, 'you're to stay in the straitjacket and on there. You're still in detention until Auntie Pauline gets back. She'll let you go.'

'I thought you'd seen the old cow off,' sighed Jackie. 'I tell you, I'm sweating like buggery in here!'

'Well I don't suppose she'll leave you in restraint after twelve o'clock; she's got a meeting with Sonia. Anyway, you do ask for it. We all know how you provoke her and what you did was really stupid! You could have gone further away from the party quite easily and it wouldn't have mattered.'

Cheryl leaned over her and undid the straps about her neck and waist. Jackie struggled over onto her side and watched Cheryl reach into the alcove again. On the spot where she had lain, the leather showed a line of wetness where her perspiration had seeped through the eyelets and the join at the back of the straitjacket.

Cheryl turned to her, holding something black in her hands which she quickly slipped into one of her pockets. She pulled Jackie around and upright until she was seated on the edge of the bench.

'What are you doing?' she asked, as Cheryl reached back into her pocket.

'Just a little re-packaging. It's for your own good really.'

To Jackie the object in Cheryl's hands first looked like a soft black wallet, or at least, something folded several times over, until she unfolded it.

'Now hold still whilst we slip this on.'

Cheryl stretched out the neck of the rubber helmet and pulled it over her head. Jackie instinctively closed her eyes as it slid tightly and reluctantly over her face and ears, covering her head completely, moulding and fitting like a thick black skin. A small circle of holes at the nose and mouth allowed her to breathe easily but her world was rendered pitch dark. Cheryl pulled the black latex away at each side of her head in case her ears were trapped awkwardly, then released it back again. Jackie could hear her moving around then felt Cheryl pass something behind her knees.

'Just a little strap,' said Cheryl, 'and another around your ankles then you can lay down and rest.'

'Why?' came the muffled voice. 'Why are you leaving me like this?'

'I told you,' came the reply out of the darkness, 'it's for your own good. She won't gag you again with that on and she won't fasten your legs up, probably. Tell you what though, if you upset her again today, I can assure you that you'll be standing up for dinner this evening, let alone lunch!'

'Oh! Please, no!' came the muffled appeal. 'Please, she'll hurt me anyway!'

'Well my love,' came the slowly receding voice, 'it's not the first time, and knowing the way you carry on, it certainly won't be the last!'

# 8

# Beyond Bounds

It was early afternoon and Angela, her fair hair fallen loose and streaked wet about her shoulders, pulled herself out of the sparkling water. A short distance away along the poolside, reclining in her little red naturist brief, the raven haired, slim form of Lorna basked in the sun. Angela pushed back her dripping hair and walked along the poolside. Lorna stirred and opened her eyes.

'Hi, Angie!'

'Hi, are you coming in for a swim or are you just going to fry?'

'I'll come in for a bit,' answered Lorna, 'but weren't we supposed to be playing doubles this afternoon?' She raised herself up from the sunbed. 'Mike and Rachel went off looking for Jackie. I don't suppose you saw her wandering around before you came down did you?'

'No, sweety, I didn't. Maybe she's in her room.'

'No,' replied Lorna, stretching up her arms and feeling the warmth of the sun caress her naked breasts and her body like a lover. 'I tried up there after lunch but there's no reply. We arranged the match yesterday and she seemed keen enough then.'

'Well,' mused Angela, 'our Jackie isn't the most reliable of people but I know she was summoned to Pauline's office this morning. What it was all about I have no idea. I don't suppose you've tried there have you?'

Lorna noted the wry smile on Angela's face and said, 'Rather you than me – I want to get through the day in one piece!'

'Oh well,' continued Angela, 'I dare say she'll make an appearance soon.'

'Don't bet on it!' came a voice from the chair beneath a nearby sunshade. Valerie lifted up her sunglasses and peered around the side of the reclining chair.

'Sorry, Val,' smiled Angela, 'I didn't see you around there.'

'No, nor me,' added Lorna.

'I was having a bit of a snooze,' answered Valerie, 'but I heard you mention Jackie. I don't know what's happened but Pauline and Cheryl were giving her a hard time this morning over something.'

'Cheryl?' said Angela with surprise. 'I thought she'd gone back to London.'

'No, she's here for a day or so yet,' replied Valerie. 'I did her hair yesterday evening, after Karen's.'

'She doesn't mix much does she?' remarked Angela.

'No, not much,' replied Valerie. 'She's a very cool girl is Cheryl – knows just what she's about, but she's not as hard as a lot of people think, not underneath it all anyway.'

'Not like Pauline,' remarked Lorna.

'Oh God no! I could trust Cheryl as a friend, she's a good sort when you get to know her, not like the other one I'm afraid – she's plain bloody vindictive.'

'Yes,' sighed Angela, 'tell me about it. I've been on the wrong end of her often enough so I can't imagine what Jackie goes through.'

'Oh, come on Angie,' said Valerie, 'the randy little sod nearly has a climax every time Pauline, or Mike for that matter, looks at her! I reckon she fantasises daily about being trussed up and pushed into a rugby players' changing room!'

'Ooh! I can think of a lot worse,' grinned Lorna.

'Anyway,' continued Valerie, 'I don't expect she'll be around this afternoon. Mike's gone into the village – I wouldn't be surprised if she's gone along with him just to get away for a bit.'

Indeed, Jackie did not appear that afternoon, nor had she left the house. She had heard Lorna tap on her room door earlier but had remained laying on her bed, her behind an angry, pulsating furnace.

'Bloody old cow,' she muttered repeatedly into her tear stained pillow.

When Cheryl had left her earlier that day, she had lain helpless and unable to see for a while, not more than ten minutes she judged, before she heard the door opening. The person entering the room had not spoken, so that when a hand was laid upon her rubber cocooned shoulder, Jackie had asked, 'Who's there? Cheryl, is that you?'

'Yes, it's me,' had come the reply.

'Oh good,' Jackie had said, 'I thought it might have been that old shitbag!'

Then, close to her ear, the voice had whispered into her darkened world, 'What a pity for you, my little bitch, that Cheryl didn't leave that mouth of yours taped shut, because now it's got you into trouble again, hasn't it? Just the way it always does!'

Jackie had begun to tremble, realising that any effort at an apology would be a waste of breath. She had then expected the worst. She had got it.

Pauline had pulled her over, face downwards, then fastened on the waist strap which had helped to keep her in position on the leather bench earlier. When the thrashing had begun, it had been all the worse because Pauline now laid the short whip across that part of Jackie's anatomy already tender from its previous application. She had not counted the number of strokes, but in the end, with her face soaking from the tears trapped inside the rubber hood, she had begun to scream. Perhaps that was why Pauline had stopped.

It was past seven o'clock that evening before the pangs of hunger overcame humiliation and acute soreness. Jackie lifted herself slowly up from the bed and walked over to the full length mirror.

'Oh God, what a bloody sight,' she muttered, pushing bedraggled hair away from her face.

She walked tentatively into the bathroom, opened the wall cabinet door and took down a bottle of paracetamol. Two of the tablets she threw into her mouth and followed them with a glass of cold water. She replaced the bottle and closed the cabinet door. Swollen and reddened eyes confronted her in the cabinet mirror. She was glad nobody had seen her when she returned to her room for vanity is not so easily extinguished. She began to brush her blonde hair and the words, 'You've only yourself to blame,' passed through her mind. How many times had she heard those words? From how many different people? But the burning was not just in her behind, it was in and about her sex. She was inflamed there too. What Cheryl had done for her would have been enough for most of the others, but for Jackie it wasn't.

She had done the best she could to make herself look presentable, and when Jackie walked into the bar, wearing the softest and most comfortable dress she could find, two or three of the others looked up at her, though none of them spoke. It was as if they knew she wished to be left alone. At the bar, she ordered a Bacardi and Coke then scrutinised the menu. Kim, who was on bar duty that evening, leaned over to her and asked, 'Where've you been love? What's up?'

'Oh nothing . . . nothing. Just make the Bacardi an extra large one will you?'

Despite the burning soreness she sat at the bar to eat a chicken curry, with her back to whoever else might be in the room. When she left, it was without speaking to, or acknowledging anyone. She walked out into the garden, into the soft and pleasant evening air. The lights were on around the pool so she decided to go and watch whoever might be out there taking an evening swim. Nobody would notice her swollen eyes in the darkness. She never reached the pool, for Mike appeared on the pathway heading straight towards her, his face breaking into a wide smile.

'Hi lovely! Where are you off to?'

She stopped and moved to one side.

'Oh, er . . . nowhere in particular. How about you?'

Mike seemed a little taken aback by the question but replied, 'Ah, yes, well – just a quick drink, that's all, then back to watch today's cricket match on the telly.'

Jackie linked her arm into his and squeezed, lowering her head.

'What's up?' he asked. 'Where were you this afternoon?'

'Oh, er nowhere,' she smiled weakly.

'You're upset sweetheart, what's the matter?'

'Nothing, Mike, really. I just want a bit of company.'

On any other evening, he would have welcomed such a statement, for knowing Jackie as he did, the implications were mouth watering. They had spent enough time together in the past for him to appreciate her sexual appetite, but tonight of all nights, the answer had to be no.

Before he could detach himself, she had slipped an arm around his waist and leaned her head on his shoulder. He sensed that she was crying. A feeling of indecision beset him and he stood holding her for long seconds, not knowing quite how to deal with this unaccustomed situation. Then a nearby voice called, 'Hi, you two!'

It was Valerie, fresh from the pool, her black hair hanging in ringlets over her white bathrobe.

'Oh, I'm sorry,' she smiled, 'didn't mean to interrupt.'

'No, no, that's OK,' responded Mike. 'Poor kid's upset about something – I don't know what.'

'Really,' insisted Jackie, 'really, it's nothing!'

'It's bloody Pauline isn't it?' said Valerie with a hint of anger.

Mike looked at Valerie, almost pleading. Valerie seemed to understand.

'I'll talk to her Mike, OK?'

'Sure Val, thanks,' he responded, trying to disguise any hint of relief in his voice.

'Come on deary,' said Valerie, 'let's go in and make you a nice cup of coffee. I'll do your hair and we'll get you nice and relaxed with a little rub down.'

Jackie smiled at Valerie, turned and kissed Mike who then watched as they walked arm in arm back towards the lighted portico of the house.

He followed them a short way until they disappeared through the main doors, then checking to see if anyone else was in sight, he hurried off along the front of the house to the far right-hand end, turned the corner and vanished into the darkness.

'You're late,' whispered Annette sharply as he slipped through the half open rear door.

'Only a couple of minutes. I got waylaid by Jackie.'

'It seems like an age when you're waiting here and hoping nobody is going to see you.'

She slid the bolts back into place and turned the key, kissed him and said, 'OK, let's get going.'

He followed her, looking about anxiously. This was his second visit to the house by this means, his second transgression when he was willing to risk so much. They hurried up the rear stairs, neither of them speaking until they reached the end of the first floor corridor.

'Same place?' hissed Mike from behind her.

'Yes, same place,' she answered, pulling out the small key.

The corridor lights were dimmed, which gave him a false sense of security, but there was nobody to be seen. Annette fumbled with the lock for interminable seconds, then the door swung inwards. Moments later, they were safe inside the room, bathed in the warm, intimate pink half light and sensing the rich aroma of the black leather seating.

'God,' he breathed, leaning back against the door, 'it doesn't do my nerves any good knowing her door is only over the corridor.'

'Never mind,' smiled Annette, looking mischievously into his eyes, 'I've got you into my lair again big boy.'

They kissed for a few moments then Annette turned and walked over to the group of leather seats, the scene of their earlier sensual encounter, when she had him under her control, on her own terms, serving her the way she thought men should. She considered Mike a very fortunate man. Her, or Sonia's, clients paid a good deal of money for the privilege of her services. On the other hand, they were by no means all as attractive as Mike. She sat down on the soft leather of the two seater and turned, expecting to see him coming over to join her. She looked up to see that he was still by the door, leaning against the wall, arms folded and watching her in the warm, subdued light.

'And what do you think you're doing?' he asked in a low voice.

'Me – doing, what do you mean?'

'Remember our agreement?' he continued.

'Er ... well ... yes, but why?'

'Well, it's my turn this evening – my turn to call the shots.'

'Yes, OK,' she smiled. 'Look, if you'd said, I could easily have come around to your place like before. It would have been less of a risk.'

'Oh no, we have what I need in here, not at my place.'

'What do you mean?' she asked, rising slowly from the chair.

'I mean it's my little game this evening,' he answered walking over to her, 'and I have plans for you.'

Annette put her arms around him, looked wide eyed and said softly, 'Yes, I know I agreed but I didn't think you meant ... I mean ... I didn't think you would be wanting to ...'

'Didn't you now?' he responded with mock seriousness, pushing away her arms.

She smiled into his eyes. 'But you enjoyed it so much didn't you, and I am rather good at it aren't I? It's the way I am.'

'It's the way I am too,' he smiled in turn, 'and an agreement is an agreement.'

'Mike, sweetheart,' she went on, bringing her face closer to his, 'let's sit down and relax a little with a nice drink.'

She brushed his ear with pouting lips and he felt his resolve beginning to disintegrate.

'Now be a good girl,' he whispered, 'go and take a nice hot shower and Michael will have a special little treat for you after.'

'Pig,' she whispered back.

Annette basked in the private world of the shower, relaxed in its enveloping intimacy. She was going to take her time. Perhaps if she took long enough he would come in to find out what she was doing. It shouldn't be too difficult after that, she considered, to get him inside the cubicle with her then she could exploit every voluptuous resource of their bodies and have their sins washed away as quickly as they were enacted, in the water's hot caress.

A sound outside the cubicle broke her thoughts. She fancied she saw a fleeting movement in the room, wiped the condensation away from the door with her fingers and peered out. He was not there, and neither were the clothes she had left on the seat outside. Though something else was.

Mike was seated and waiting, a gin and tonic in his hand, when the hairdrier stopped. The bottles and a spare glass stood waiting on the coffee table. He was mentally congratulating himself on his planning and resourcefulness when she appeared at the doorway, silhouetted against the pink glow of the shower room. She had put on the soft cream bathrobe he remembered her wearing on their first visit here. Without looking at her feet, he could see from the way she walked towards him that she had put on the delicate, silver, open toe sandals with their thin, criss-cross ankle straps and long stiletto heels. She moved with poise and measured steps, and her auburn hair cascaded over her shoulders. He stood up to meet her but even before they were close enough to kiss, he could smell her warmth and perfume.

'You took your time,' he whispered.

'Did I?'

'Well, no matter, it gave me a bit of time too. Want a drink?'

'Mmm, yes please – time for what?'

'Oh,' he grinned, 'time to rummage about in the cupboards and have a good look in there.'

He gestured over to the curtained archway and his grin broadened.

'Oh,' she remarked as he poured her drink and she sat down on the two seater next to him.

'Cheers!' he smiled, 'here's to a lovely lady.'

'Cheers,' she replied, 'and here's to a nice considerate man – I hope!'

After the drinks were finished, he stood up, looked down at her and slowly unbuttoned his shirt, pulling it off and casting it over onto one of the chairs.

'OK,' he said, holding out a hand to help her up from the seat. She arose and put her arms about his neck, and kissed him ardently. Even through the jeans he was wearing she could feel his enthusiasm for her as she moved her pelvis slowly against his. He moved his arms to the front and pulled the belt of her gown so that it slipped undone. He felt her hands on the buckle of his belt but he took hold of her wrists and whispered, 'Not yet.'

Their hips met again and his hands moved up to her shoulders, pulling away the bathrobe so that it slid down from her soft body.

'Don't move,' he whispered, stepping around her and reaching down beside one of the chairs. Then he was at her back and she felt his hands upon her wrists, pulling them behind her and saying, 'put your palms together.'

She did so, resisting the temptation to look over her shoulder, even when a rustling sound reached her ears and something cool, with the unmistakable feel of leather, brushed against her. She felt the leather pouch pulled over her hands and a tightening about her wrists. She knew what it was he was putting on her but still said nothing. After all, as he had recently taken the trouble to remind her, it was only a game. She heard the zipper begin its ascent and felt the cool, soft leather closing about her, pulling her elbows back as it tightened upwards, encasing both of her arms together in the bondage glove as far as her shoulder blades. He passed the straps from the back of the glove under her armpits, crossed them over her chest and took them back over her shoulders where he fed them through the buckles attached to the top of the glove, just below her neck. He tightened the straps so that Annette's arms were now encased rigidly behind her back, and the tension of the leather sleeve caused her full and firm breasts to stand out with greater prominence.

He spun her around saying, 'There! Gotcha!'

'Mike, you swine,' she retorted, 'you put that on me like an expert. I thought this sort of thing was new to you.'

'Yep,' he grinned, 'but I've seen pictures of them being used and you gave me plenty of time while you were in there to figure it all out.'

He kissed her and she pressed her swollen nipples against his chest. He stepped back from her and said, 'Annette, turn around slowly.'

She smiled, knowing the effect she had upon him, even with her arms enclosed behind her in the leather sheath, or perhaps more so because of it.

'God, you're a dream,' he breathed as she moved around and his eyes feasted upon her body. Above the silver sandals, her legs were clad in fine sheened, gossamer black stockings held up by a black and red lace trimmed suspender belt. The matching g-string she wore was merely an elasticated lace ruffle passing down between her legs and held in place by a waist band of similar material, fastened with a small hook at each side. She stopped turning and faced him, the soft, warm light glowing in her eyes, her full lips slightly parted. He moved around behind her and kissed her neck, cupping her breasts in his hands and rolling the nipples with his fingers. After a minute he turned aside and quickly reached down behind one of the leather cushions. She felt his hand against the back of her head and opened her mouth to speak when his other hand came around in front of her face. It took only a few moments to press the red rubber ball into her mouth and to pass the thin strap around, buckling it firmly at the back of her neck.

'Nnnnnng!' was all Annette could manage by way of protest. He kissed her ear and whispered, 'Now who's in control?'

She looked at him wide-eyed but made no effort to resist as he led her over to the other side of the room where a square, leather covered stool stood. He sat upon this and manoeuvred her onto his knee, not sideways, but facing him with her legs either side of his. In this position, the sight of the lace ruffle stretched over her shaven sex, barely hiding what it was meant to conceal, was even more appealing than if she had been totally naked. He supported her by one arm about her waist, whilst with his free hand he reached under the ruffle where it passed between the cheeks of her behind, stretching it back and forth to make it stroke between her parted legs. With her arms held behind her in the bondage glove, her breasts were thrust out close to his face and he could suck and tongue about her nipples, keeping them hard and making them glow a deep pink. Annette closed her eyes and sighed through the ball gag.

After a few minutes he stopped and whispered, 'God, I could eat you.'

He eased her off his lap so that she was standing before him then slid down from the seat onto his knees in front of her as he had knelt once before. But this time he was free to do as he pleased and she was not. He placed his hands about her thighs, kissed and brushed his lips about the elasticated ruffle, pushing it aside with his tongue, not quite reaching but sensing the warmth and perfume of her sex. He ran his hands down her stockinged legs, down to the silver sandals and up again, feeling her tense in anticipation and sensing her murmur each time his tongue came close to the object of his desire.

He rose to his feet and turned her around, taking her by the shoulders and pushing her along the room towards the black curtain hanging behind the arch. He felt her resist, her head turned and she let our a sharp, 'Mmm – mmm!'

He ignored her muffled protest and propelled her more firmly onwards until they reached the ominous curtain. He pushed it aside and guided her through. The rose pink lights were already on.

He turned her left and they continued across the soft carpet until it became obvious to Annette which of the chrome and leather pieces was to be their destination. She stopped and twisted against his grip, working her elbows from side to side within the tight leather sheath and letting out a series of stifled protests, one of which, 'Ooo hig!' was just about comprehensible.

He brought the palm of his hand sharply across her behind with a resounding slap, then half pushed, half lifted her around and onto the firm black leather. The chair was waiting for her, with its gleaming chrome fittings, levers, bars and hanging straps. He held her with one hand so that her restrained arms were pushed back into the upholstered leather support, whilst with the other he buckled the first of the straps about her slim waist. This left him with both hands free, for she could no longer rise from the chair. The rest was much easier, as he found when he placed the padded strap about her neck and immobilised her against the headrest. He had used his time usefully during her long stay in the shower and felt quite confident about adjusting the chair to his will, and Annette with it. The lever which enabled him to tilt the chair back and lock it into position had readily been identified and he quickly eased it over so that her body was inclined as far back as he wanted it to be.

A chrome extension bar protruded upwards and outwards from either side of the chair and each of these was hung with two leather straps. No further protests ensued as he pulled each leg out in turn, securing first the ankle straps and then a tight strap around each of her soft thighs. He next reached down and released the small hooks at her waist, pulling away from under her the lace ruffle which he threw over onto a nearby table. It was on that table too, during his earlier exploration, that something else had caught his eye and registered in his mind.

Annette was now spread helpless and on display in front of him with her spiked heels pointing up and outwards at head level. She watched with a wide gaze as he loosened his belt and lowered his jeans to reveal blue cotton shorts which did little to obscure his excitement. She waited for him to slip those off too but he smiled and walked around the chair, stooping to kiss her on the forehead before turning to the table where, next to the tiny garment he had removed from her moments earlier, lay a short length of black strap, one end of which was split into three tails. He picked this up and moved around the back of the chair only to reappear at her right.

'Now then,' he smiled, 'let's warm you up a bit.'

She saw, with obvious alarm, the strap in his right hand and let out a muffled protest, which he ignored. He leaned over and brought the strap down sharply against her exposed behind, seeing her lurch against the restraints as she let out another sharp, 'Mmm!'

Stroke followed stroke in rapid succession on both sides of her behind and around her upper thighs, each accompanied by a stifled protest and a twitching of her bound body. When he ceased wielding the strap, that part of her which had fallen under its sting was suffused with irregular pink blemishes. When he put the strap aside he saw her eyes blazing at him in helpless anger. He knew this was no time to lose his resolve so he leaned over and kissed her cheek, saying, 'Rough with the smooth, sweetheart, OK? Now just you relax and see what my mouth and tongue can do with every bit of your lovely body.'

He was true to his word. True that is if you take the body to begin at the breasts and to end between the legs. He aroused her teats to a reddened hardness before pressing his kisses on a remorseless course downwards over her warm stomach. He gave full rein to his tongue once he reached her sex, teasing and penetrating her in that manner more skilfully than anyone before had done. Despite the indignity she had suffered and despite the growing discomfort in her arms, pinned so rigidly behind, she was beginning to feel the currents of pleasure trickle through her. The electric dance of his tongue about her most intimate parts began to draw her into a golden whirlpool of pleasure and she could not prevent herself from drifting towards the well of sensual light around which it spun. It took him but a moment to slip his shorts, rise up and enter her with the hard and burning strength her body craved. She moaned louder with each stroke until both of them spun and plunged together, out of control and into the glittering vortex.

Annette emerged from the bathroom still aching and burning. Mike was dressed already and sprawled in one of the chairs, his hands clasped behind his head.

'Did I say I'd give you a good time or did I?' he grinned.

Annette pulled on her T-shirt and looked at him coldly.

'Yes, Michael, you did. I haven't come like that in months. I thought I was going to have a bloody apoplexy!'

He sensed that all was far from well and waited.

'The trouble is,' she continued, 'I feel like I've had a serious case of lockjaw! My arms and shoulders, not to mention my legs, ache like buggery and my arse feels as if I've been sat on a bloody barbecue! Apart from that, everything's wonderful!'

'Christ!' he breathed, standing up. 'Don't talk so loud – someone might hear outside.'

'Mike, I don't care who hears! Orgasms come and go but I could be feeling like this for days. And those bloody strap marks! I just hope they're gone by tomorrow afternoon because I've got work to do – if you know what I mean!'

He approached closer, holding his hands up defensively.

'Look, Annette, I'm sorry, honestly ... I just thought that ... well, look, it's only a game and I thought that ...'

'Thought Mike? You didn't think to ask did you?'

'OK, OK, I didn't mean to hurt you but you're the one who got me into ... into this after all so I ...'

'Mike!' she cut in. 'I'm not a submissive. Not all women are – as you ought to be fully aware. If you want someone like that then try Angela, Kim or Lorna, or better still, Jackie, you can do anything you like with her and she'll love it! You probably know that anyway!'

Annette turned towards the door, leaving him lost for words. Before opening it, she swung around and said, 'By the way, there's a bit of cleaning up to do, not to mention the glasses and bottles! For once in your life you'd better leave the place just as you found it and not with stuff draped all over the bloody place! If anyone starts asking questions, I might just have the answers Mike, remember that!'

She pulled open the door and without bothering to check the corridor, or to look at him again, slammed it hard. Once on the stairs she smiled to herself, picturing the look of alarm on his face, and in her mind she saw him hurrying about, glancing at the door, tidying the room up, making sure everything was exactly as it should be to avoid leaving any clue in case he got found out. Well, she thought, it serves him right. And next time, yes, give him long enough and there would most certainly be a next time, he was going to pay the penalty.

# 9

# Forbidden Images

It was Karen who saw them first, from the office window. At around three o'clock under a bright, cloudless sky, a red car flickered by the trees along the road beyond the driveway. She called into the main office where Sonia was occupied at the word processor.

'I think our visitors are here!'

'Thanks!' came the reply. 'They're a bit early but no matter.'

Karen kept an eye on the drive where it curved around beyond the pool and the tennis court. She had heard Sonia describe them as two of her 'star performers' and she had to admit to herself that she was more than a little curious to see them.

The Alfa Romeo coupé pulled up with a soft murmur at the front of the house, its polished vermilion lines accented by the glare of the sun on its spotless chrome. The car was out of sight now in front of the portico but after a short time, Karen heard voices and laughter in the corridor outside the office and saw Sonia going towards the door.

'Hi, Sonny!' came a girl's voice, loud and exuberant.

'My pleasure to meet you once again, madam,' followed the deeper, more subdued voice of her companion.

'Carlene, Roddy, lovely to see you, come inside. How are you both?'

'Great, Sonny! Just great!' responded Carlene. 'And you're looking better than ever, isn't she, Roddy?'

'Ah yes, but then the signorina, she always looks divine.'

'Karen!' called Sonia. 'Don't hide away in there, come and meet our guests!' It was an invitation she seldom had, or wanted, but on this occasion she arose with enthusiasm and went out to join the small group.

Sonia's guests were a striking couple. Carlene was apparently the product of a Caucasian and African union and certainly displayed the best features of both races in looks and physique. Her face was soft and round, her skin the colour of pale coffee and her full lips pouting and sensual. Under the fringe of her dark, bobbed hair, her eyes flashed with mischief and humour. Karen guessed her age as early to mid-twenties. She wore an open biker jacket of soft brown leather with sharp, padded shoulders and an ample complement of studs and zippers. Under this was a cobalt blue, stretch nylon top and below, skin tight gold lamé trousers and lace-up white ankle boots.

Rodolfo was tall and slim with black swept back hair, blue eyes and broad, clean shaven jaw. The black hair on his sun-tanned chest and a large, gold medallion could be seen through the half opened front of his black needle cord shirt. The maroon slacks he wore beneath this flattered his slender hips. Both wore gold earrings, Carlene's glittering and prominent, Rodolfo's more discrete, and both wore Cartier wristwatches.

Carlene did not wait to be introduced but turned about with a flashing smile and outstretched arms.

'Hi, Karen baby!' she exclaimed. 'Sonny's told me all about you. I'm so glad we could meet at last!' She took Karen by the shoulders and planted a warm and generous kiss upon her cheek.

'This sultry looking guy here,' she said, turning and gesturing with her thumb towards her companion, 'is Roddy.'

Rodolfo broke into a wide smile and stepped forward, reaching out and seizing Karen's hand, then pressing his lips against it whilst effecting an elegant bow.

'Nice to meet you both,' said Karen, a little taken aback.

'Signorina,' he replied, in a low voice, looking with intense concern into her eyes. 'I am most honoured to meet so beautiful a lady.'

Sonia appeared to have difficulty in keeping a straight face, whilst Carlene pulled Karen's hand from Rodolfo's grasp and exclaimed, 'Jesus Christ, Roddy! This kid runs the accounts here – remember.'

She turned to Karen with a look of mock despair.

'His brains are down the front of his pants kid, just ignore him!'

Rodolfo responded with a half smile and a shrug.

Sonia said, 'Come on all of you – sit down and I'll put the coffee on.'

'Sonia, no, leave it to me,' pressed Karen. 'You sit down with Carlene and, er, Roddy and I'll . . .'

'Oh how awful!' cut in Carlene with an expression of startled concern, her large brown eyes flashing from Karen to Sonia. 'You mean somebody broke in and stole the drinks cabinet?'

Sonia smiled and turned to Karen.

'OK, forget the coffee, bring out the glasses.'

Karen sat with them for a while, sipping a Martini, and although the exuberant Carlene kept her involved in the conversation, she felt that her presence might be blocking discussion between the three of them on other matters. When she arose and said, 'If you'll all excuse me, I have a few things which need sorting out yet,' Sonia answered, 'No my dear, forget about it until tomorrow. Go and enjoy yourself in the gardens; I'll talk to you later.'

When Karen joined Angela at a small table by the bar, it was after eight o'clock on a warm, calm evening. The ceiling fans turned lazily above the chattering heads and the sounds of Oscar Peterson blended with the congenial atmosphere of the room. This evening, nobody wore jeans or appeared too casual, because Carlene was back. Carlene always had that effect.

Angela wore a short, halter neck dress with leopard skin print and Karen, also subject to the sudden outbreak of style consciousness, had put on a sleeveless white crochet dress with braided shoulder straps, as short as Angela's but not quite as tight.

'Did she look glamorous?' asked Angela.

'Oh yes, quite put me to shame I have to say.'

'Well she spends a fortune on clothes,' continued Angela. 'It's all part of her image. And that car you saw, she owns that too.'

'I see, I thought it might belong to her boyfriend.'

'Oh, hot Roddy – no, he's a hanger on. He's been here with her the last few times but nobody is permanent with Carlene. The last one was Canadian, I think, and before him a Swede. I think Roddy comes from a wealthy family – he's just a playboy.'

'God,' breathed Karen, 'she must own a fortune, how on earth does she . . . I mean . . .?'

Angela smiled one of her sweet understanding smiles. 'Karen dear, if you really don't know, ask James if you can see the video when they've gone.'

Karen did know, of course. She had opened her mouth without thinking. Before she could speak again, the louvre doors sprang open and in walked Carlene, followed closely by the suave and smiling Rodolfo.

'Hi Babes!' her voice rang out with flashing smile and upraised hands.

'Hi Carlene! Hi Roddy!' They all responded.

Rodolfo gave a small bow and passed his arm across his waist, his eyes attempting to encompass the whole roomful of girls in one sweep.

'Just take a look at him,' grinned Angela. 'He thinks we're some kind of sexual smorgasbord, I think he's so funny.'

They had both changed outfits. Carlene had on an electric blue satin catsuit with wide, flared collar and metallic grey ankle boots. Rodolfo now wore a blue denim shirt, open to the waist and dark leather trousers, almost skin tight, with broad, hand tooled leather belt and silver embellished cowboy boots. About his neck hung a silver Egyptian ankh. Carlene began to circulate, amidst increased chatter, infecting them all with her zest and exuberance, going from table to table with more than enough good humour for everyone.

'She's a walking sound and light show,' mused Karen.

'Yes,' responded Angela, 'everyone likes her – except you-know-who of course.'

'Oh, but why?'

'Because Carlene takes the piss out of her in front of everyone – at least that's the way Pauline sees it. That's why you'll never see them in the same place at the same time.'

'They were earlier,' responded Karen. 'Her, Carlene and Romeo were in with Sonia.'

'That's different. They have to get together to discuss business whether she . . .'

'Hi, Angie baby and Hi again, Karen!' cut in the bubbling voice and wide smile.

'Oh, it's great to see you again, Carlene!' grinned Angela, rising from her seat to hug and kiss their visitor.

'And you baby,' laughed Carlene. She turned to Karen and squeezed her arm, saying, 'Sonia's told me what a great help you are, sweety. She really does appreciate all you do; take it from me!'

Karen felt a surge of embarrassment but couldn't help other than to smile back into her eyes.

'It's a shame you couldn't make the party,' said Angela. 'It was one of the biggest and best we've had.'

'Oh, I heard,' replied Carlene, 'and it's the first one I ever missed, but do you know where we were? Well, we were in Hamburg for the international banking conference. We had all these wealthy old guys to entertain! Not Roddy, of course, he was back in Italy visiting his poor old mother, or so he made out.'

Her eyes flashed and she burst out laughing.

'Some of those old guys in Hamburg needed oxygen just to get into their limousines you know. Now Francesca, do you remember her? I darn't think what she got up to, but one of the guys she called in on had a coronary in the hotel room! Like I was saying to Val, she hot footed it out of there as fast as you like and rang the concierge from a phone box. It was just as well for Sonia they'd all paid up front because not only did the medics show up, but the security people were in on it too!'

'I hope he didn't die,' put in Karen.

'Oh, you wouldn't believe!' laughed Carlene, 'some of those guys are dead before they even show up. But it's not a bad way to go is it? Or so I'm told.'

Carlene glanced around as a squeal of laughter came from the direction of the bar, then continued. 'We're off to England in a few weeks time for the Tory party conference. Cheryl and Annette are coming as well, so maybe we'll see off a couple of the old boys there too!'

Carlene turned again as more laughter emanated from the bar and Rodolfo could be heard exclaiming, 'Ah, bello, signorina, bello!'

'Guess I'd better sort Roddy out quick,' announced Carlene with a startled grin, 'looks like he's about to split his pants!'

Karen and Angela turned to see what had attracted Carlene's attention.

Rodolfo was leaning back against the bar, his arm around Jackie's waist. She stood pressed up against him, her lips slightly parted, one arm hanging limply by her side, the other raised, with her fingers tracing through the hair and around the pendant on his chest. She had on a low-cut, sleeveless white top which ended well above her waist and hung loosely over her breasts, and below this a red mini skirt, very mini, in stretch PVC. This, together with her fine, black lace tights and red, high heeled sandals must have impressed Rodolfo deeply. His eyes were concentrated with intensity upon hers and his fingers stroked up and down her body, down her spine from under the white top and down over behind.

'Hey, Rodolfo!' sang out Carlene, with a brief wink at Angela and Karen. 'Put that child aside or you'll be hitch hiking back to Milano!'

'Oh, Carlene!' he responded with a look of injured dignity. 'The signorina comes to me for a little advice – you are jealous I think!'

'Jealous my arse!' she responded, to everyone's amusement. 'It's your jewels I gotta keep an eye on – remember who's got a busy day tomorrow!'

'Poor Jackie,' smiled Angela, 'she just can't get enough. I don't know how Mike stays out of her clutches.'

'How do you know he does?' asked Karen.

'I suppose I don't really. Her room is on the first floor so that Pauline can keep an eye on her but I don't think she locks her in at night. Knowing men, I wouldn't expect Mike to be too far away if she was out and about at night, and the gardens are pretty extensive.'

Karen felt the blood rush to her face as she recalled what she had seen Angela and the two men doing, and what had happened to her in those same gardens on that same moonlit night. Then who was she to pass judgement on anyone, she thought. She had not complained at Sonia's intimacy with her on that evening when they had both been drinking together. What if it started again, if she perceived herself about to be taken advantage of? Would she resist next time? Would she even want to? Sometimes she felt as though a shadow was stalking her, but a shadow of what? Was it a manifestation of her own guilt or was it that which she tried so often not to admit to herself? The episode in the beauty parlour earlier – the thought of that made her physically tingle. She would never herself request another such course of treatment but when she went to the parlour and sat having her hair or nails done, she trembled in anticipation in case Val should again invite her to submit herself. She dared not even glance at the towel covered bench with its hidden straps, but if only Val would say something, even a hint. She knew she would not refuse.

'Penny for your thoughts!' broke in Angela's voice.

'Oh,' blinked Karen, 'sorry, I was ... em ... I was just thinking about ... well, nothing really.'

'Want to share it with me, sweety?' smiled Angela softly.

Karen ran her finger about the pinewood table top in a decreasing circle.

'I don't know Angie, it's something I ... well ... no, I'm

just being silly, it's nothing at all. Let's have another drink.'

After two days, Carlene and Rodolfo were gone though Karen had seen little of them during their stay except at the bar again for a short time on the second evening. She would never forget that infectious laugh and those flashing eyes.

'I wish I'd had a chance to say goodbye,' remarked Karen over morning coffee.

'She didn't say goodbye to anyone,' answered Sonia. 'They had to leave very early to get to Marseille airport. But she'll be back eventually, she always keeps in touch wherever she is. I'll get a fax or a phonecall soon enough, you'll see.'

Later that day it started to rain, though Karen was sufficiently occupied for the weather not to cause her any concern. The cat appeared from time to time, being more inclined to remain indoors rather than to get wet, and so made himself known to everyone he could gain access to during the day. Sonia spent a great deal of time on the telephone and Karen was glad each time Pancake appeared at her door. At four o'clock, Sonia called her and said, 'Don't forget, I'm off myself this evening dear. I've a meeting with some people in Geneva tomorrow lunch time. I'll be back on Friday, late afternoon with a bit of luck.'

At five o'clock Sonia was packing some documents into a briefcase and Karen was preparing to leave the office. As was usual now, Sonia kissed her before she left. This time the kiss lasted a little longer, this time it was a burning kiss, like the kiss she remembered from that evening which neither of them ever spoke about. It was as though Sonia was reminding her secretly about it, and it made her tremble and catch her breath. Even after she had reached her room to change for the evening, she felt a strange, dark excitement within her.

At three-thirty on Friday, the day Sonia was to return, the telephone rang. It was Sonia herself. Some twenty minutes later there was a knock on the main office door and Karen, looking out from her own office called, 'Come in!'

The door swung open and the tall figure of James, complete with large spectacles, stepped inside.

'Hello,' he smiled, 'I think Sonia's due back soon, yes?'

'She was,' replied Karen, 'but there are problems at Zurich airport so I'm not sure if she'll be back until tomorrow now.'

'Oh well,' he said gently, 'I'll leave this with you if I may, Sonia knows what it is.'

He handed her a clear plastic bag in which was a video cassette tape. She took it from his slender, waxy fingers and smiled into his gaunt face saying, 'I'll put it on her desk where she'll see it as soon as she gets back.'

James cast his gaze further into the office and said, 'So this is where he's been hanging out today.'

Karen turned and they both regarded the recumbent ginger form sound asleep in front of Sonia's empty desk.

'Oh, poor Pancake,' smiled Karen, 'Sonia usually shoos him off but he's been keeping me company today even if he has slept through most of it. I'll be chucking him out soon, too, when I lock up the office.'

James departed, hesitating at the doorway and saying, 'Well I hope you have a pleasant weekend. I'll talk to Sonia on Monday. Bye-bye now!'

The door closed and Karen looked with curiosity at the videotape as she walked slowly across the room to Sonia's desk. She put the tape down next to the player, behind which stood the large monitor screen. On the tape she saw a white label upon which two dates were written. She thought for a moment. Were those not the two days when Carlene and Rodolfo were here? This must be the video to which Angela had referred. She contemplated the videotape for a minute then examined the controls on the player. It was perfectly straightforward, like the one in her room. She looked at her watch. She had a tennis game arranged with Annette after work, then she would get changed and be off with Mike and Valerie to the village restaurant. Perhaps later ... perhaps if Sonia had not come back ...

'Wakey wakey, Pancake!' she grinned, scratching the yawning cat under the chin. 'We're closing shop.'

As she was turning the key in the lock, a voice from behind said, 'Have you heard from Sonia? I'm supposed to see her this evening.'

'Oh, Pauline, no ... I mean yes, I've heard from her, but no, I don't think she's going to be back.'

Pauline, wearing a heavy white satin blouse, fawn jodhpurs and riding boots, regarded her coolly.

'I believe James has left a tape here – you'd better let me have that before you go, please.'

Karen hesitated, then slipped the office keys into her shoulder bag.

'Sorry, it's been left in my charge – I have to leave it where it is.'

Pauline looked at her, unblinking, for a few uneasy moments. 'I'm supposed to see that recording,' she insisted, placing her hands upon her hips. 'I'm asking you again to open that door, please, and hand that tape over to me now!'

'Well, I'm not going to,' responded Karen firmly. 'If Sonia's given you a set of keys then there's nothing to prevent you from going in and getting it for yourself!'

Pauline's eyes narrowed.

'You're a snooty little cow aren't you? You think you own the place just because you work in there. Well you don't!'

Karen felt an unaccustomed anger well up within her and she resolutely held Pauline's gaze.

'Pauline, I don't own anything and as far as I am concerned neither do you. You're an arrogant bitch and you can take it out on some of the others but you don't have any control over me – none at all!'

A scornful smile crossed Pauline's face and before turning abruptly away, she said in a low voice, 'Well, you'd better watch yourself, miss bloody prim, because one day, I just might.'

* * *

Karen had intended to read for an hour before going to bed. At least that is what she felt she ought to do. She had undressed, opened the drawer below the vanity unit and taken out the shining pink object which she caressed in her fingers. She switched off the main light, then the bedside lamp, and lay gently down upon the bed, her head sinking into the apricot pillow, her eyes closed and her legs spread apart. The sound of the electric vibrator broke the silence of the room as she ran the smooth head slowly back and forth between the flushed lips of her sex. Her free hand she brought up above her head and pushed deep under the pillow. After a time, her breathing became more audible and she started to moan, her moans becoming louder as the seconds passed by. She began to move the vibrator faster and deeper, her breath coming now in hoarse short gasps, until, almost sobbing aloud, she arched her back and spread her legs wider, feeling the electric sensation overwhelm her body and mind in a golden stardust of orgasm.

Afterwards, she took a hot shower, tying her hair up first so as not to get it wet. In the warm, private embrace of the cubicle, she closed her eyes and her thoughts returned to the black cassette, lying on the desk, waiting alone in the silent office.

After drying herself, she pulled on a sheer blue nylon bikini brief and her deep pink bathrobe. She glanced at the unopened paperback book on the bedside table and then at her clock radio. It was eleven o'clock, almost, and there had been no word from Sonia. She pulled on her gold sandals and, rummaging about in her shoulder bag, took out the office keys and slipped them into the pocket of her robe.

There was nobody in the corridor and the back stairs were likewise deserted. It was on the ground floor she had to be careful. If anyone had seen and spoken to her, she had intended to say she couldn't sleep and was going to see if she could find anyone in the bar. No comment would have been made about her attire as, late on in the evening the others often went down for a night-cap dressed so.

Passing the beauty parlour, she heard voices ahead, but they were ascending the main stairs and she reached the office door unseen.

She thought it most odd that she should feel so guilty about entering a place where she spent most of her weekdays and yet was more than a little relieved when the door clicked shut behind her and she was in darkness. She dared not switch on the lights in case they should show outside through the door and window blinds. Eventually, though, her eyes began to adjust to the gloom and she could make out the vague, still shapes about her. She knew well enough the direction of Sonia's desk and it was only some eight or nine metres away. The air was warm, still and ominously silent as she negotiated the green leather chairs.

'God,' she breathed, 'why don't I just switch all the lights on and sit down as large as life to watch the damn thing? What's it got to do with anyone else? I work in here, not them.'

But she knew the answer as she felt her way around the desk. Only Sonia, sometimes with Pauline, viewed the tapes and she had seen the cassettes behind Sonia's desk in a cabinet which was usually kept locked. She was guilty by implication though she told herself that Sonia would have no cause to admonish her for what she was doing. With that in mind, Karen sat down at the desk and took the cassette from its plastic bag, plugging it into the player and seeing the 'ready to play' lamp come on. Her fingers glided along the fascia below the screen and found the monitor switch. Soon, she was bathed in the ghostly light of its blank glow and her shadow loomed eerily over her on the wall behind. She took up the remote control which had become visible at the side of the player. She pressed the play button, sat back in Sonia's chair and waited. The seconds passed. She had no idea as to how long the tape would last but was quite prepared to fast forward it if necessary. The colour test sequence appeared, so she realised, this was not a final copy. A rainbow of lights danced across her face and reflected a kaleidoscope of colours in her eyes as she sat in her small island of illumination. Then the title 'Maid to be Punished' appeared and the music began. She had given no thought in advance to the sound but now quickly located the volume control and reduced it to near inaudibility.

The scene opened in what appeared to be a hotel bedroom and there, in the picture, were Carlene and Rodolfo. Karen had no doubt that this was one of the rooms in the house. The two in the sequence were dressed as if for a formal dinner but were evidently in no hurry to leave the room as they alternated between conversation and kissing. Karen speeded the tape up but it was obvious even with the figures jerking about the screen in comic fashion, that the kissing was becoming more frequent and passionate. Eventually Rodolfo's hand found the zipper at the rear of Carlene's black satin dress and began to pull it down. Karen released the button and the tape returned to normal speed.

Carlene, at first appearing to resist his advances, was becoming more receptive and released his arm so that the zipper could continue its descent as far as the base of her spine. Rodolfo, without taking his lips from hers pulled, the dress from her shoulders and the camera zoomed in to show her exposed breasts with their prominent brown nipples which quickly began to occupy his attention. Suddenly the camera angle changed and the bedroom door was seen to swing open. A figure entered and Carlene with a look of outrage, immediately drew back the top of the dress in an attempt to cover herself, whilst Rodolfo moved quickly away from her and made so as to adjust his tie in the mirror. The 'maid', it was obviously Jackie, now filled the screen, going about her duties but glancing frequently at Rodolfo. Karen sped the tape on, but it was clear that Jackie, in her low-cut and short skirted maid's uniform was playing up to Rodolfo and that Carlene had noticed as well. She leaned towards him, giving him ample opportunity to observe her breasts and then, working with her feather duster, bent over sufficiently to make it obvious that beneath the short skirt she had on only the most minimal of garments.

When the 'maid' completed her tasks and left the room with a last, seductive, glance at Rodolfo, he and Carlene appeared to argue for a time before getting deeper into whispered conversation. Rodolfo smiled, kissed her and the screen went dark for a moment as they faded from view.

In the next sequence, Rodolfo, now dressed in jeans and T-shirt sat by the bedroom window reading a newspaper. As the maid, again Jackie, entered the room, Karen let the tape slow down to normal and relaxed in the chair to await developments.

At first, Rodolfo ignored Jackie as she went about her duties but, as Carlene was not in evidence, she behaved even more provocatively than before. It was when she stood next to his chair, reaching upwards with her feather duster, that he placed his hand on her thigh and ran his fingers up to the bare flesh at the top of her stocking. Jackie recoiled in mock alarm with fingers across her open mouth. Rodolfo arose from his chair and took her in his arms. She put up token resistance, looking apprehensively about the room. But this soon gave way to compliance and after a few moments, their lips met. Rodolfo found the zip at the back of her dress and with one smooth action, had it down to her waist and was soon pulling it past her knees. The dress was cast down onto a nearby chair and Jackie stood before him in black lace suspender belt, sheer black seamed stockings, a minimal blue lace g-string and black patent leather high heels. Rodolfo took her in his arms and after some kissing and no little attention to her breasts, they moved across the room towards the bed.

It was at this point that Carlene entered from the bathroom, dressed in a high neck maroon cat suit with black leather belt and tight black knee boots. She leaned against the door for a few moments, one hand on her waist, the other swinging a leather, three-tailed strap. Jackie, effecting a look of horror, dashed across the room to grab her dress from the chair by the window. She had just retrieved it when Carlene strode quickly over and wrenched it from her, throwing it over the room and smacking her hard across the mouth. Jackie recoiled and took refuge behind Rodolfo only realising that she had been set up when Rodolfo turned and pulled her around to face the full wrath of Carlene, holding her arms rigidly against her sides whilst Carlene again slapped her face. Jackie protested so vigorously that Karen had no desire to turn up the sound. Rodolfo continued to hold her whilst Carlene strode over to a suitcase which had lain unnoticed by the bed. Having opened this with some haste, she pulled out a garment, the appearance of which was not altogether unfamiliar to Karen. She proceeded back to the hapless Jackie and both she and Rodolfo struggled, then succeeded, in forcing the girl's arms into the straitjacket. Jackie, her face a mask of fearfulness, glanced wildly from Carlene to Rodolfo as the heavy black latex closed around her upper body. Rodolfo held her at the elbows whilst Carlene fastened and tightened the straps down the back. Jackie struggled, but the straitjacket, with its dull sheen, encased her form neck to waist and held her fast.

Carlene again struck her across the mouth then dragging her around, pushed her onto the bed. She struggled against the restraining rubber for a few seconds, rolling back and forth and kicking her feet as Carlene and Rodolfo looked on. Carlene retrieved the strap which she had placed upon the bedside table after entering the room and proceeded to lay about Jackie's behind and thighs with it, whilst Rodolfo unfastened his trousers and slowly removed them. This must be a very noisy affair thought Karen as the camera came in close to show how vigorously the strap was being applied and how Jackie's mouth opened and closed in animated and vigorous protest. When the camera zoomed back, Rodolfo was quite naked and Carlene pulled Jackie around on the bed to see his very obvious erection. They pulled her from the bed and down onto her knees so that she faced what Carlene had been heard to describe as

Rodolfo's only real asset. Carlene knelt down behind her and held her head as the swaggering and more than ample pink shaft moved closer, guided by his hand. Jackie watched it as if mesmerised until the glistening head touched her lips, then opened her mouth wide to take it in as far as it would penetrate. With one hand on the side of Jackie's face, Carlene reached forward with the other and slipped her fingers under Rodolfo's testicles, whilst he began a rhythmic back and forth movement of his pelvis. This went on for some time in close up and Karen wondered what was on the sound-track. Then Rodolfo's thrusting began to quicken. Carlene moved her hand down to Jackie's shoulder and pulled her back from him just as he ejaculated, his pelvis jerking wildly.

Slowly, the camera backed away, showing Jackie kneeling with her eyes closed, semen streaked about her mouth and chin, and meandering slowly down the front of the black latex. Then the scene faded out. Karen did not know whether she considered what she had seen to be shameful or whether she ought to feel ashamed of herself for watching. Was the fact that she had come here at all to sit and view the tape a reflection of her own hypocrisy and dishonesty? If she was not fascinated by it, if she did not have her own guilt and deep yearnings to contend with, what was she doing seated in front of the screen at all?

She was about to reach for the rewind button when another title appeared. This one read 'Girls on Top'. The episode began outdoors at an open air café. Two girls sat at a table sipping drinks. One of these she recognised as Carlene but the other face was in silhouette against the blue sky and impossible to identify. In the background a small harbour with fishing boats was just visible. It might or might not be very far from the house but Karen did not recognise anything familiar about the scene for she had not made many excursions to the villages on the coast. The two girls had moved their heads close together and were discussing something which they obviously did not wish to have overheard and occasionally, the camera would zoom in on the waiter, who proved to be Rodolfo. The viewing angle altered eventually so that the face of the other girl could be clearly seen. It was Valerie.

There were glimpses now of a picturesque village above the harbour, then the viewer was returned to the table, where the girls had been joined by Rodolfo who, whilst picking up their empty plates and glasses, was treated to the sight of their short skirts calculated to reveal legs which crossed and uncrossed in a markedly provocative manner. The waiter had obviously taken the hint as it appeared that some kind of arrangement was being made. Karen sped the tape on, catching glimpses of the girls, Rodolfo getting changed and setting off in his car, the girls talking and laughing in their room. Karen wondered what the time was and realised that she did not have her watch. She looked around the desk for a clock but there was none, nor, she knew was there a clock in her own office. She turned back to the screen and released the button on the remote control, letting the tape slow again. The scene now was another hotel room and the centrepiece a bed. Upon this lay Rodolfo, spread-eagled and immobile, held fast by a leather cuff and strap attaching each of his limbs tightly to a corner of the bedstead. He was naked and his erection stood like a small mast between Carlene and Valerie who sat either side of him. Karen wondered how, having missed the sequence, they had contrived to get Rodolfo into that situation, though, for the purposes of this drama, it was probably not of paramount importance.

Carlene, wearing a red satin corset and black lace stockings ran her fingers up and down the flushed and rigid penis. She was smiling and talking to Valerie, who wore a tight black PVC mini dress and long, shining black gloves. Carlene appeared to invite Valerie to make use of the helpless Rodolfo, who she began to slowly masturbate. Valerie evidently agreed and getting up from the bed, commenced undoing the zip at the rear of her dress. Carlene stopped her sensual play with Rodolfo, slid from the bed and joined Valerie, who she helped to remove the dress. Valerie stood only in her long gloves, black suspender belt and seamed stockings. Carlene kissed her eagerly and Valerie returned her kisses with equal enthusiasm. Soon, they were occupied with each other, mouths and fingers doing their voluptuous work whilst, for the time being, the bound Rodolfo lay all but ignored though still no less aroused.

It seemed from the way that Valerie and Carlene became distracted, that Rodolfo had uttered something to gain their attention, for they released their hold on each other and turned their activities to him. Valerie took the inflamed shaft and started to work it with her hand whilst enveloping the head with her red lips. Carlene moved up the bed, positioned her thighs on either side of Rodolfo's head and lowered herself slowly down so that her sex was directly over his face. She moved down further and now the camera closed in to show his tongue darting and coursing between the reddened lips of her most intimate place. Valerie stopped the play of her hand and mouth and she too climbed astride Rodolfo, over his pelvis. She moved herself back and forth, letting the head of his organ furrow between the lips of her sex for perhaps a minute before lowering herself down so that it entered her up to the root. The two girls took advantage of the position they were in, to lean forward and to kiss and caress each other, Carlene adjusting herself a little to give Rodolfo's tongue full play, Valerie moving up and down on the glistening shaft to a rhythm which gave her greatest pleasure. Their arms closed about each other, their lips sealed together and both began to sway in unison, their eyes closed, their bodies becoming more agitated.

Whether Valerie and Carlene actually came at the same time, Karen could not say, though they both appeared to do so with their heads falling back and their mouths open in a silent cry which was almost audible inside her own mind. As for Rodolfo, it could be taken for granted that his satisfaction was never in doubt, and Karen wondered if he actually got paid for doing it. The camera closed in upon the faces of Carlene and Valerie, showing them with their eyes closed and their lips brushing together as their heads moved gently from side to side. Again, the scene ended and the screen became a uniform grey. Karen did not wait to see if there was a third episode but pushed the rewind button and heard the muffled hum of the player spinning the tape back.

Sitting in the small oasis of light, she had lost all sense of time and place. With the dimming of the monitor screen, the surrounding darkness closed in and drew her attention to her own situation. She reached out to switch off the monitor but, realising that she would not be able to see anything, first switched on Sonia's green shaded, brass desk lamp. A few moments later the tape machine clicked to a stop and she ejected the rewound tape. Placing it back into the plastic bag she was aware of the still silence of the room and that she, seated at her employer's desk and centered in that pool of light, had no business to be there. She arose and switched off the lamp, hesitating sometime for her eyes to readjust to the gloom.

'Really, my dear, you do surprise me!' came the voice from the darkness. Karen froze, her mouth agape. The small lamp on the coffee table snapped on.

'Oh Sonia! I didn't know ... I mean, I didn't realise ...'

'No, I don't suppose you did! You were much too engrossed to notice anything at all!'

Sonia arose from the green leather chair, silhouetted against the light from the small table lamp, and walked towards Karen. She reached down and switched back on her own desk lamp, as though to illuminate the guilt which already flooded throughout Karen's body and soul. Her heart beat rapidly as Sonia stood and fixed her with dark penetrating eyes. Karen thrust her hands deep into the comforting pockets of her bathrobe.

'Look ... er ... James left it with me ... I didn't think you'd mind if I ...'

'Nobody is supposed to view those tapes without my permission!' cut in Sonia sharply. 'That's one of the reasons why no one else has keys to this office – not even Pauline.'

Karen felt herself in turmoil, her mind seethed in an agony of confusion.

'Well, nobody ever said ... and ... it, it was left with me ... I mean I ...'

'So why do I find you down here at this time of the night with the lights off? And what else have you been prying into behind my back?'

'Look, I haven't been prying into anythng!' Karen protested. 'I was just curious about ... well ... Carlene and Rodolfo and ...'

'I thought I could trust you!' cut in Sonia. 'All you had to do was ask!'

'Yes ... all right! I know I could have bloody well asked, but ... but I felt a bit embarrassed. You're making me feel like a criminal, Sonia! I know what these people are here for – it isn't a secret is it?'

'No, it isn't. But what I need to know is how often you have been down here like this and what else have you seen Karen? What else?'

Sonia moved forward, her face weirdly illuminated by the green lamp. Karen looked at her for a moment, trembling and feeling unsteady, feeling tears well up in her eyes.

'Look, I've never seen a blue movie before and I've seen nothing else; nothing at all, that's all there is to it. I've done nothing wrong. If you think I have, then I'll go ... I'll pack my things and leave tomorrow!'

Sonia regarded her tearful eyes for long moments then said, 'Please come here.'

It was not quite a request, not quite an order. Karen walked around the desk and stood before her, her moist eyes fixed on the carpet. Sonia reached down, took Karen's hands from her pockets and clasped them.

'Karen, my dear, what are we going to do with you?' she said quietly.

Karen felt more miserable than she could account for, but looked up at Sonia and said, 'Perhaps I should leave here you know – I don't belong – I don't have anything in common with the others.'

Sonia squeezed her hands and kissed her on the cheek before releasing them.

'Look my dear, I was a bit annoyed at first but not now. I didn't want to upset you. Come and sit down and I'll pour us both a drink. I've had a trying day and I could certainly do with one.'

Karen said nothing, but moved over to the green leather chairs grouped around the low table and sat down. Sonia, a glass in each hand, returned and sat opposite to her.

'Well,' she smiled softly, 'now you have seen one of our little productions, what do you think?'

Karen looked down at the glass of neat scotch, recalling the last time she had spent alone drinking with Sonia in the warmth and intimacy of the soft lights.

'Well ... I ... I don't know. Like I said, it's the first proper blue movie I ever saw. I know you might find that difficult to believe but it's true.'

'Do you disapprove of what you saw?'

'I don't know I ... no ... not really, it's not that. I suppose I've led a bit of a sheltered life. Sex was never mentioned at home, let alone seeing books or magazines. I was at a private school up in Scotland for most of my teens, as you already know, so the big wide world passed me by I'm afraid. I didn't know blue movies even existed until after I left. In a place like that, you get a very different perspective of the world, I can tell you.' She took a drink from her glass. 'After such a closed upbringing, life can be a bit difficult.'

'I can well imagine,' smiled Sonia. 'You might be surprised in turn to know that I was raised in a convent school.'

'Yes ... well, then perhaps you can understand, the things you have to hang on to are your old school friends. At least they were there to fall back on when things got tough. And I always feel guilty about things Sonia, that's my trouble. I've always felt guilty about physical relationships, always except with ... well ... someone I grew up with. I felt guilty about going for a massage – some of the others go often, I wouldn't dare to ask. Did you know about that?'

'No, my dear, I didn't. Why should I? It's a private matter and I assure you, the girls are entirely discrete – you should know them well enough by now.'

'Yes, I suppose I do. I know it's my problem. The last time we were together down here .. afterwards I mean ... I lay awake wondering who the hell I was, you know. Sometimes I feel there's someone inside me trying to get out and live another existence. It's not easy to explain at all.'

'Perhaps you are in the process of finding that other existence,' answered Sonia in a low voice. 'Perhaps it is an existence of which you are afraid to admit.'

Karen looked at her and held her gaze for a few seconds, then finished her drink.

'Perhaps you're right. I suppose I spend too much time feeling sorry for myself. I know I'm really lucky to be working somewhere as nice as this; some people would jump at the chance to come and work here. Everyone – well nearly everyone, is so friendly and helpful to me. I'd really miss them all if anything happened.'

'And what could possibly happen, my dear? If you're worried about Pauline, don't. I need her here to keep the house running smoothly and to keep some of the girls in check but, as you are quite aware, she has no more jurisdiction over you than she has over Cheryl or myself.'

Karen remained silent for a moment, then finished her drink, smiled, and rising from her chair, said, 'Look, you've had a long day and I shouldn't be here, I'll leave you in peace.'

She stood and again thrust her hands deep into her bathrobe pockets, not noticing that the belt had loosened and slipped away. Sonia stood up and faced her across the table.

'I'm sorry for creeping down here at night and being a bit nosey,' she smiled sheepishly. 'I know it must have seemed underhanded. I'll wait and ask next time, honest.'

The gown fell open to reveal her body, naked apart from the almost transparent briefs stretched tightly over her sex.

'Oh ... oh, bother,' she stammered, hurriedly pulling the towelling and the belt back around herself.

Sonia, a wry smile on her face, moved around the table to face her.

'My dear,' she breathed, putting her hands on Karen's hair and smoothing it away from her face, 'if you have no arrangements for Saturday evening, come back down and have a drink or two with me.'

Her dark eyes looked deep into Karen's.

'We can share a bottle of wine and talk some more. I assure you, I do appreciate your company.'

'Y'yes ... all right, I will,' she answered softly. The touch of Sonia's hands on her face passed through her whole body in a wave of electric sensations. Sonia's eyes engulfed her and their faces moved closer until their lips met. Karen trembled and drew in her breath sharply. If the gown had loosened again, if she had felt those slender fingers glide down the flesh of her stomach and seek out the focus of her sensuality, she did not know if she would want to resist. But Sonia released her.

'So, about eight o'clock, yes?'

'About ... about eight, yes.'

'And don't be formal about it, you can just come as you are now if you like – nice and comfortable, nice and relaxed.'

'Perhaps ... I don't know ... thanks for the invite, I'll see you then,' answered Karen as the door opened and she slipped out, still trembling a little, into the deserted corridor.

'Goodnight, my dear,' followed the voice as she approached the stairs, but when Karen turned to reply, the door was shut.

# 10

# Treat and Trick

She sat at a small table just inside the conservatory, partly hidden by a climbing vine but with a good view into the bar. She was part way through a chicken salad when she saw him enter through the louvre doors, look about the room briefly, then stroll over to where Lorna stood drying glasses and chatting with two of the other girls across the counter. Annette couldn't hear what was being said but Lorna, handing him a drink, smiled and gestured towards the conservatory. Annette smiled to herself.

There were several people in the conservatory as the day was cool and wet. Indeed, Pauline and a male visitor had not long since left and even Sonia had spent some time in conversation at the bar earlier. She watched with barely concealed amusement as Mike turned away from the bar and, with a glass in one hand and the other thrust into the pocket of his denims, strolled casually, and with a look of innocence, in her direction.

'Annette!' he said with an expression of innocent surprise. 'Can I er ... do you mind if I ...?'

'Mike, for Christ's sake sit down, you're making the place look untidy.'

He sat down but held onto his glass and looked about the conservatory with enforced nonchalance. Annette continued eating.

'A bit like being back in England isn't it?' he smiled.

'What is?'

'Out there,' he gestured. 'I mean ... er, the rain. I should be working on the gardens but it's too wet.'

'What do you want?' she asked, putting down her knife and fork.

He rested his glass on the table.

'Look, I know you've been avoiding me, but this is silly. I'm sorry about ... well, you know, I said at the time didn't I – I never meant to hurt you. I thought we were having a bit of fun as we always have. Why the cold shoulder?'

As if in response, she stabbed her fork into a slice of chicken, put it slowly into her mouth and looked up at him with an expression of indifference.

'Look,' he continued with deeply furrowed brow, 'I'm only trying to be ...'

'Mike!' she interrupted. Two or three heads turned nearby. He gazed, embarrassed, down at the table. 'My glass is empty. Orange and diet tonic please – no ice!'

He was stirring out of the chair before she finished speaking and hurried over to the bar without further comment. Jackie, sitting nearby, looked at her and grinned.

Annette arose quickly and stepped over to Jackie's table. A few words passed between them. Jackie nodded with grinning eagerness and Annette passed some small object to her which she pushed out of sight under the rim of her plate. She had returned to the table and winked at Jackie when she saw Mike approaching from the direction of the bar again with the glass of orange and tonic in his hand. He returned to the seat, placed the glass before her and waited. She picked it up slowly and drank whilst gazing past him, but said nothing.

He began to shuffle uneasily, rubbing his chin with the palm of his hand and glancing about the room. Still, Annette said nothing. He finished the remainder of his drink quickly, then said under his breath, 'All right, if that's what you want, I'll shove off.'

He had begun to push back the chair when she said, 'Mike, before you go I have to tell you, you could be in big trouble.'

'What?' he responded, lowering himself back into the chair.

'It concerns the little lady on my left,' she smiled knowingly, her eyes glancing momentarily in that direction. 'You-know-who has been asking questions about you and her. She wants a word with me about it since nobody else seems to be spilling the beans.'

He glanced at Jackie and back at Annette with an expression of muted dismay, leaning forward on his elbows.

'What's she been saying? Who's been talking to Pauline?'

'Oh don't fret Michael,' winked Annette. 'I might not tell her what I know as long as you're a good boy.'

'As long as . . . what? What do you mean?'

'Well, you have overstepped the mark a bit haven't you – one way and another?'

'All right,' he said in a half whisper, 'but I'm only human. What do you expect? I'd have to be like bloody James not to . . . I mean, be fair, you've done more than anyone to encourage me and you know it.'

'Quite so,' she smiled, 'but then I'm the whore, Michael. You're only the handyman.'

He watched her silently for a few moments, unable to compose a meaningful response. She began to eat again.

'Annette, be fair,' he said in a low voice of exasperation.

'I thought we had something going before. I know I went a bit over the top but I don't deserve all this. All I wanted to do was make it up with you again. What the hell's wrong with that?'

'Nothing really,' she replied in an offhanded manner, 'as long as you do as you're told.'

'What do you mean?'

'Just that lover boy. If you want to get off the hook and see me again, you do as you're told. Simple.' She put down her knife and fork and leaned back in her chair, waiting for his answer.

'And Pauline' he asked, leaning further in her direction, 'what do you intend to say to her?'

'Oh,' she shrugged, hesitating and looking intently across the room before picking up her knife and fork once more, 'that rather depends on you.'

He glanced about to see what had distracted her, then

abruptly back as a high pitched little cry of 'Ooops!' came from her lips and he returned his attention to the table.

'Oh dear,' she said, glancing aside then looking him in the eye. 'I've just flicked an olive off my plate. It's gone under the table, Mike, under there, see?'

She indicated towards the table where Jackie and Kim sat in uncharacteristically serious conversation. On the floor between the two pairs of feet rested a green olive.

Of the two pairs of legs he also observed, one, Kim's, was clad in mid-blue cotton slacks, whilst the other pair, Jackie's, was covered with sheer black nylon up to the hem of her metallic plastic mini-skirt. Annette watched his eyes move from the olive to the more obvious attraction then quickly back to her.

'Go and pick it up,' she said quietly, the fork swinging like a pendulum in her left hand.

'What?' he said, glancing back at the marooned olive.

'I said, Mike, go-and-pick-it-up!' She leaned forwards, holding his gaze. 'Now! And don't you dare peer up her legs. I'll be watching you.'

He did not reply but slowly got up and stepped over to where Jackie and Kim were seated, watched by Annette who again winked at Jackie. Mike excused his intrusion and went down on his knees in order to reach underneath the table, shuffling forewards until his head almost disappeared from view. Jackie at once began to cross and uncross her legs, one of her black high heeled shoes nudging the olive further from his grasp.

'Oh, Mike,' she cooed, 'you need a bit more room – I'll move back.'

Jackie slid her chair a short distance, at the same time opening her legs to give him the best possible view up her skirt which, with the shuffling about, had ridden higher up her thighs. By now he had grasped the elusive olive and was halfway under the table. Jackie stretched her right leg forward and he felt her nylon-skinned flesh brush smoothly against his face. The temptation to glance at the forbidden zone was too much for him and he had every reason to believe, from the position he was in, that Annette would not observe the transgression.

By the time he extracted himself and returned, red faced, to his seat, Annette had turned her chair away from her table and sat back, watching him.

'There, are you happy now?' he asked in a low disgruntled voice.

Annette leaned forward, eyes narrowed.

'You looked, you bastard,' she breathed.

'God!' he mouthed, 'how could I avoid it? She was ... she was ...'

'Shut up, Mike, I don't need to hear any feeble excuses! Now listen. Despite the way you've been behaving, the way you treated me and, just now over there, I might be able to forgive you. We could be friends again and you would be in the clear with our camp commandant.'

He looked at her, a smile of relief broadening, though with some hesitation, on his face.

'Well, I suppose I've earned it,' he said, finally letting the half squashed olive drop onto her empty plate.

'No you haven't,' she responded, 'not yet.'

'Will it help some if I get you another drink?' he smiled.

'No, it won't.'

'Well, go on, what do I have to do?'

'You're coming back to the house tomorrow afternoon. We're going to play a little game.'

'The afternoon's too risky,' he whispered.

She brushed the hair from the side of her face and looked at him gravely.

'It's your last chance lover boy. All you need to do, is go out of the bar or straight through the main entrance and down the corridor. By the time you get to the kitchens you're almost at the back stairs.'

'Look, what if I'm seen by someone? Sonia, or, or ...'

'Sonia's out tomorrow afternoon. If the worst happened, just say you're trying to find Lorna. She'll be on duty in the kitchen so it'll be all right.'

'Annette, please,' he leaned forward, head resting on the

palms of his hands. 'I'm not supposed to go down there at all and you know it – I wouldn't get away with that excuse or any other.'

She leaned forward and stared intently into his eyes, running her index finger down the side of his face.

'Well unless you're at the first floor landing by three o'clock, you've had it anyway.'

She arose from the chair with a forced smile, keeping her eyes on his. He sat unspeaking, mouth slightly parted and a look of mild bewilderment on his face. He watched her slim form, in its T-shirt and denim skirt, pass down the bar and out through the far doors.

'Have we made it up now?' came a voice from the table nearby.

He turned and saw Kim beaming at him. Jackie was looking directly at her, hand over mouth as if she would explode into laughter at any moment.

'Mm, I suppose so,' he replied dourly, raising himself up.

He strode around their table and over to the French windows. The rain had stopped and he headed off towards the main pathway. Once he had left the room, Jackie had indeed dissolved into helpless laughter, whilst Kim, managing a degree of self control said, 'Poor Mike, she's really giving him a hard time of it!'

The following day saw a return to warm sunshine and almost cloudless skies. By one o'clock, Mike had finished a morning's work on the gardens and was entering the bar room. Angela was on duty and smiled as he requested a beer and sandwich from her.

He sat up at the bar, eating and watching her as she moved about in her little black fitted dress with its modesty panel of black lace which clung to the tops of her breasts. About her neck was a black velvet choker with a ruby red stone set into a silver cameo. As they chatted, about nothing in particular, he considered the beauty of her face and watched every nuance of her body whilst she moved about. It seemed to him that whichever of these girls he found himself in conversation with appeared more beautiful and desirable than the rest. Angela did so now.

He had finished lunch when Valerie, Rachel and a fair haired girl of around twenty appeared at the bar. Valerie usually made herself the focus of conversation, so, finding himself unable to command as much of Angela's attention as he would have wished, Mike said, 'See you later, Angie!' and left the bar room via the conservatory. He half expected to see Annette there again but found himself subject to the gaze of Pauline, who sat eating with Kim. Kim turned and grinned, whilst Pauline smiled too, but with the expression of an executioner, pleased at the prospect of being about to despatch a long sought after victim.

'Busy day?' she remarked as he passed by.

'Er, oh, lots to do . . . yes, all sorts of things!'

The smile remained frozen on her face.

He reached the French doors and struggled for a moment, trying to rotate the iron knob around in the wrong direction, imagining her eyes on the back of his neck. Eventually, the door opened and he turned to give a nervous little wave as he went through. Neither of them were looking.

'God, I'm not going through with this,' he muttered, ambling along the pathway and hoping for a glimpse of Annette, hoping that those green eyes might soften with understanding if he once more tried to explain his anxiety.

There were signs of life by the swimming pool. Two of the chairs were draped with towels, a sunshade was up over one of the tables and someone was in the water. He headed in that direction. The figure in the pool was that of Jackie, propelling herself gently along on her back, her nipples standing dark and prominent as the clear water washed over her breasts, her sex concealed beneath a minimal gold lamé g-string slip.

'Hi Mike!' she smiled from the shimmering blue water. 'Coming in?'

'Oh . . . er, no, I'm just taking a break!'

The prospect of spending the afternoon at the pool held

considerably more appeal than the risk he was expected to take, in ... he looked at his watch. It was almost ten past two. Then, moving around the pool towards the tables he saw her, sitting in a mauve and white beach dress. She was talking to Cheryl. Neither of them appeared to notice him, so he determined to wait around and hope that one of them would go into the pool, preferably Cheryl, and leave the other alone for five minutes. On a nearby table he spotted a magazine, its cover lifting slightly in the warm breeze. He sat down facing away from the pool with the two girls to one side, but able to see if one of them got up. Annette had her back almost to him, but Cheryl he could see easily.

Cheryl was a closed book to Mike. He knew her less well than any of the other girls, except for the occasional new arrival. She was the least accessible of all, appearing only for a few days, then being absent for sometimes weeks at a time from the house. Her cool, almost arctic beauty fascinated him. He had wanted to make her acquaintance ever since seeing her with Sonia in the restaurant one evening but the chance had never presented itself. He picked up the magazine and stared at it with disappointment. It was a tourist guide to London. 'That's all I need,' he breathed and replaced it on the table. He let the chair back into its half reclining position and stretched out his feet, intending to appear relaxed in the sun but ready to move when the time came. Birds twittered and called idly in the nearby pine trees. The warmth of the sun and the caress of the breeze with its perfume of flowers all began to conspire. Soon, his eyes closed and his breathing became soft and regular.

Someone called his name. He was startled at first by the open air and the searing light all around.

'Wh ... what?'

Jackie stood on the opposite side of the table, covered now in a white bathrobe. He shook his head and sat upright, then peered over to his left. The table under the sunshade was empty.

'Sorry to disturb you,' smiled Jackie, her hands deep inside her pockets. 'Annette said to check your watch. Don't know what she meant, do you?'

'Oh, er ... I'm supposed to be shifting some furniture, nothing too important.'

He glanced down at his watch. It read five to three. He stood up and looked towards the house. There was no sign of Annette between there and the pool.

'Are you going now?' asked Jackie.

Mike bit his lip and forced a broad smile at her.

'Yes, I suppose I ought to make a move.'

With some trepidation he approached the house, avoiding the conservatory and walking straight up to the main entrance, watched with interest by Pancake, who sat in a shaded area on the upper step.

Inside, there was no one to confront him though he glimpsed Valerie and Angela still in conversation together at the bar. He did not even glance at the main office even though Sonia was said to be absent. The thought of her reaction to his being there, and its consequences, was something he did not wish to linger over. Now past the closed door of the beauty parlour and the part open door of the kitchen, he reached the end of the corridor and, without a backward glance, disappeared up the back stairs.

She was waiting for him as he reached the first floor, leaning against the wall just inside the corridor, wearing a cream bathrobe and purple furry house slippers.

'Good boy, you made it,' she commented as he stood before her, eyes darting up and down the corridor.

She turned and walked along, not hurrying as much as he felt she ought but the thick oatmeal carpet deadened their tread so that at least they moved in complete silence. She withdrew the keys from her pocket but, to his surprise, continued by the door through which they had passed on the occasion of their two earlier meetings. It was at the next door, some way further along, that they finally stopped and she inserted the key into the lock. They at once entered into a small chamber, already lighted, but this was only an ante room, furnished with two easy chairs and a small table. With the soft click of the door, he felt he could breath normally again, and speak too.

'This is a different room,' he hissed.

'Brilliant deduction,' she responded, shrugging her eyebrows and tutting in mock despair at his inane observation. In front of them stood an arched doorway with a maroon curtain hanging across it and concealing that which lay beyond. Annette walked the two metres across the room and pushed the curtain aside; he trailed close behind her. Beyond the curtain was total darkness until she reached around and switched on the lights, holding the curtain aside for him to follow her in.

Mike saw at once that this room was quite different from the one next door. It was equally luxurious, however, with thick maroon carpet and the familiar chrome and leather seating. The same soft pink intimate lighting pervaded everything but what took his attention was the most prominent feature, a heavy black curtain, suspended from the ceiling on a circular track of some two and a half to three metres diameter.

'What's inside there?' he asked.

'Never you mind,' she answered with a fleeting smile, 'the bathroom is the right hand door over that way.'

She indicated towards a pair of doors across the room in the wall to their left, the right hand one of which stood ajar. He regarded her properly for the first time that evening. Her auburn hair was held up in a clasp at the back of her long neck. He looked her up and down, noting the familiar bathrobe, seeing her smile at him the way she always used to before their disagreement. He reached up and put his arms around her shoulders, pulling her close, feeling her sensual warmth and kissing her.

'I know what you're thinking,' she whispered in his ear.

'Go on,' he answered, brushing his lips about her cheek and neck.

'You're wondering what I've got on under here aren't you?'

'Well, you don't need to be Sherlock Holmes to figure that one out, but yes, you're right, I am.'

'That's what I like,' she smiled, kissing and squeezing him, 'enthusiasm.'

'So we're friends again?'

'As long as you do as you're told this afternoon.'

'All right,' he answered, releasing her, 'the alternative has go to be far worse. I agree.'

He emerged a little later, showered and dried, naked except for the brief nylon posing pouch she had given him to wear. Annette, relaxed in one of the plush leather chairs, regarded him as he approached silently over the thick carpet.

'Good boy,' she smiled as he stopped before her, 'everything under control as it should be!'

He stood, hands on hips, waiting for her to make a move, wondering what were her plans, looking about to see if some kind of restraint had been made ready. He wouldn't mind if she did it to him again, as she had on his first visit. It had been good fun, different, even more sexy with her in control in an odd way, even when she teased him about leaving him in the straitjacket.

'Time to get started,' she grinned mischievously and pulled a white plastic bag from behind the chair on which she was seated. She placed it in front of him upon the coffee table. From the shape and size of it, it obviously did not contain what he had anticipated. Annette got up, and still smiling, took the bag and spilled its contents out onto the table in full view. He recognised most of the items immediately and stood wide-eyed, his mouth half open. He looked at Annette then back to the table.

'You aren't going to get me to . . .?'

'Oh, but I am,' she smiled, 'come on now!'

'You're joking, this is blackmail!'

'It most certainly is!' she answered, holding up the black and red lace trimmed waspie with its four elastic suspenders dancing and swinging about beneath it. 'We can put this on now, or I can pop over the corridor and have a word with the vampire. Sonia will probably want to replace you with one of the retired locals I should think, they'd be far less trouble than you as well.'

'Annette ... you ... you ... oh, all right, anything you say!'

She walked up to him, smiling broadly.

'I'll give you a hand with this first, we don't want the laces taken out so you'll need to step into it and pull it up.'

The waspie was about twenty centimetres deep with black laces strung between rows of metal eyelets, their ends hanging loose at the bottom. She moved around behind him and helped to ease the garment up his legs and over his thighs, tugging each side alternately until it rested about his waist. He felt it tighten suddenly as she pulled hard on the laces and he leaned forward to compensate as she tugged harder still, until the two halves met in the middle of his lower back and she could secure the laces with a knot.

'Perfect fit,' she announced.

'It's tight,' he responded.

'It's supposed to be, that's why it's called a waspie.'

She moved to the table and picked up a small plastic packet inside which was an inner sleeve printed with a colour picture of a pair of stockinged legs.

'I'll help you with these too,' she smiled, removing the seal and pulling the packet open. 'You'll probably ladder them if we're not careful and we can't have that, can we?'

Neither of them spoke for the next minute or so as she attended to pulling up the sheer black stockings and straightening the seams before fixing on and adjusting the suspenders.

'Now these,' she said, handing him a pair of black, open sandals with high stiletto heels and cross-over ankle straps. 'I'm sure you can manage on your own if you sit down first. In fact,' she grinned, 'you've taken to these quite naturally so far. I wonder why.'

'What do you mean?' he asked, his face showing the hue of one openly embarrassed.

'Oh come on Mike, you got to know Sonia originally through one of her girls, long before you became her broker. Need I say more?'

His face turned a deeper crimson still, but Annette avoided looking directly at him.

'It's nothing new to me,' she continued, 'it's part of what I do for some of our clients, remember. And, just think about it, it isn't costing you a bean!'

He had by now fastened the ankle straps on the high heels and risen to his feet. She stood back from him, arms folded, a broad smile of satisfaction across her face.

'Oh, fantastic, perfect fit – everything. You have small feet for a man; that's just as well I suppose.'

She walked over and placed her arms around his neck. He saw that she too had put on her own high heels so that the difference in their height was unchanged. She kissed him and ran her hands down his back and over his behind. She felt the pouch stir and harden as she slipped her fingers under the suspenders and tugged gently on the elastic cord running under his buttocks.

'Doesn't it feel nice wearing these?' she whispered, 'Oh, so sensual. You look great, Mike – we should dress you up like this often.'

'Are we going to do it like this?' he asked under his breath, his hands seeking the form of her body through the soft towelling.

'Oh, no dear – I said we were going to play a little game. We haven't actually started yet!'

She turned and took his arm, leading him towards the ring of black curtain. She pulled a section of curtain aside and led him through. He stared about in astonishment, up and around in the dim light.

'God, it looks evil,' he breathed.

Inside the curtain the carpet gave way to a polished wooden floor. Above this, dully gleaming, hung an array of chains and straps, and around this, on a circular track concentric with the curtains, were mounted a number of spotlights, presently switched off. The lighting track was broken, towards the rear of the area, by a square section wooden column which sprang from the floor and terminated at the ceiling, nearly three metres above.

'It's waiting just for you sweety,' she whispered, pulling him forward.

He resisted.

'Look, just a minute, you never said anything about . . . well . . .'

She turned and kissed him.

'Mike, I never said anything about anything. You've been a very naughty boy and you have to do as you're told – or else!'

He sighed but said nothing more as their heels tapped over the hard surface and they stopped in the centre of the circle. She turned him around and positioned him back against a chain which ended at the level of his neck with a wide, padded leather collar. This she pulled around his neck and fastened at the side with two small buckles. Some thirty centimetres above his head, swinging to and fro and glinting in the subdued light, was a horizontal steel bar of around thirty centimetres length. This was padlocked by a ring at its centre to the hanging chain and bore at each end a black leather cuff with buckle.

'Up here we go,' she smiled, and took his right arm, lifting it directly upwards and quickly securing it to one end of the bar. When she took hold of his free left arm and lifted that too, he tensed and resisted.

'Look, I don't see the point in doing this. I won't be able to do anything . . . I mean, how can we . . .?'

'Ah!' she responded sharply. 'Don't argue!'

He relaxed again and in that few moments felt the leather cuff enclose his left wrist and tighten as the free end of the strap passed through the buckle. In those final moments he still had the chance to reach over, free himself and thwart her intentions. But those vital moments had passed and now it was too late. His hands were spaced too far apart for one to be able to reach over and undo the other. He couldn't escape.

She immediately dropped to her knees and seized his right ankle, pulling it outwards.

'Come on, foot on the block!'

'Hey!' he protested. 'I can't stand like that with these shoes on – I'll twist my ankles!'

'No you won't, not on here. Try it, come on!'

She tugged hard until she had his foot, in its stiletto heeled shoe, positioned on the wooden block so that the shoe rested at the correct angle to support his foot. This ankle was promptly secured by another cuff, connected by a short length of chain to a floor bolt next to the block. The remaining limb offered no resistance and was rendered immobile in turn.

She arose and stepped back with her arms folded, looked up and down his stretched out form and smiled.

'Well, considering I figured this out in advance, I reckon I guessed your height and reach perfectly didn't I?'

'Years of practice dare I suggest,' he muttered.

'Oh, yes, that reminds me,' she responded. 'Just one more little thing.'

Annette pulled a small plastic container from her pocket, withdrawing a moisturised tissue from it as she moved back up to him.

'What . . .?' he began as she wiped the area around his mouth.

'Good job you shaved before you came out.'

'Yes, I always do – look, I've let you get me into this; what are you up to now?'

She next produced a flat, translucent packet and proceeded to rip off one end.

'Close your mouth,' she ordered, removing the contents of the packet.

'Hey, no! What d'you want to do that for?' he protested, seeing the oblong strip of white adhesive plastic tape.

'Never mind. If you don't do it now, I'll find a much less comfortable means of keeping you quiet. Remember the ball gag last time we were together? I might tape your eyes shut as well!' He closed his mouth and waited.

'I can promise you,' she continued, applying the tape tightly across his mouth, 'that this will be much more comfortable than the alternative. And don't think it will pull off if you try hard. It won't!'

She pressed her thumbs outwards all around the tape until she was sure that the adhesive had sealed completely to his skin. Then she took her hands from his face and gazed into his eyes with a whimsical smile. She ran her fingers delicately up and down his body, reaching around and stroking the area about the base of his spine, pressing her pelvis against his, feeling his organ stir and harden inside the nylon pouch.

'I bet you're wondering what I'm going to do with you, aren't you sweety?'

'Mmmm.'

'Well shall we see what I have on under here?'

She stepped back and released the belt of her bathrobe, seeing how intently his eyes were fixed on her, letting the garment fall slowly from her shoulders then draping it over one of the leather chairs.

'Do you like this Mike? Do say if you don't won't you and I'll change into something else.'

She placed her hands on her hips and turned slowly, provocatively. The basque was of glistening red PVC, edged with black lace where it supported her exposed breasts with small wired cups. From her slim waist hung a short, flared skirt of black lace. Her sheer black tights were accented with raised gold seams and her stiletto heeled open sandals were of red patent leather. She moved closer to him, smiling, pressing her body against his, feeling the penis, as captive as its owner, straining to be free. She kissed him on the lips then felt his body jerk as her fingers slid coolly over the flimsy nylon pouch. Her grin widened into one of mischievous triumph as she turned away from him and pushed the black drapes all the way back to the wooden pillar so that the area where he stood fastened was open to the rest of the room. He attempted to twist about in order to watch her but found this impossible and so did not see her reach behind the pillar. He did hear the click, however and blinked as the six spotlights above him burst into illumination. He registered a stifled protest as she circled him again, still smiling. Blowing him a kiss, she walked back to the group of chairs, swung about and called down the room, 'Readieeee!'

There was a sound from the end of the room. He twisted his head, his eyes expressing consternation, staring to the right as far as the obstruction of his upstretched arm would allow.

The figure who emerged from the door next to the bathroom carried a tray upon which rested an opened bottle of white wine, already glistening with cold condensation, two glasses, and an anonymous black object he at first could not identify. The short, permed fair hair, the full, firm red lips set against a cool, almost marble beauty, he recognised immediately.

'Well now,' announced Cheryl, putting the tray down on the low table, 'that's splendid! Did he give you any bother? I heard you raise your voice a couple of times.'

'Bother? Oh, no – he was more than willing – especially with the dressing up bit. Shall I pour?'

'Yes, please do,' she answered, picking the black object up from the tray, letting it unravel and swing to and fro in her hand. 'I'll go and take a proper look at him, then we'll sit down for a bit and have a natter.'

He was only too aware how vulnerable he was, stretched up on the chains with legs held apart and mounted like an exhibit in an island of light for all to see. Even so, he feasted his eyes on her slim form. Her short, halter neck dress fitted her like a skin, its metallic grey latex throwing back the light in scintillating gleams as she moved towards him, her legs sheathed in gossamer black, her silver high heels tap, tapping on the wooden floor as she walked around and studied every detail of his attire. Moulded over her hands and arms were shoulder length latex gloves in the same colour as her dress. It was what she held in her hand that caused him to twist hopelessly against the restraints and utter a muffled protest, a protest which simply brought a detached smile to her face. She stood directly before him, alternately winding the strap about her fingers then snapping it straight. It appeared to be the same strap he had previously used on Annette.

'You know,' she declared, looking from Annette to the strung-up Mike, 'someone said once that in little games like this, it's the victim who is really in charge because he's determined the situation in advance. Do you think that is true? Is he really in charge?'

'Absolutely not!' replied Annette.

'Absolutely not,' repeated Cheryl, moving around behind him.

A sharp crack rang out and he jerked hard against the restraints. The strap descended on his behind repeatedly between each syllable as she pronounced once more, 'Ab-so-lute-ly-not!'

His muffled groans through the tape became more urgent.

'Well that will get him warmed up a bit won't it?' she mused as she reappeared in front of him and went to rejoin Annette.

They sat either side of the table but turned partly towards him sipping their wine.

'I like the little corset,' commented Cheryl.

'Yes,' responded Annette, 'it pulls him in nicely – shapes his figure.'

'And did you choose those glossy stockings? They definitely suit him – he has the right legs.'

'No, they're all his. He loves dressing up – he's got quite a wardrobe.'

'I wouldn't have guessed,' responded Cheryl. 'Mind you, you never would with some of the people I deal with in London – real sanctimonious bloody tyrants 'til you get them under your wing.'

'Yes, then they're like dough.'

'Does he have dresses and such?' asked Cheryl.

'Oh yes, dresses, skirts, lingerie, wigs – you name it.

Mind you, I choose most of his underwear. I bet if he went down into the bar dressed up, the others would never guess until he opened his mouth, which is something he won't be doing for a while.'

'It suits him though, I think. He has the right kind of features, soft rather than scrawny.'

'That's through living the easy life of a city gent,' replied Annette. 'They never do any real work.'

Mike, twisting in the straps and chains, heard his own words loudly enough in his head. 'No! It isn't true! Don't believe her!' But, of course, no intelligible protest could pass his taped and sealed lips.

He could not help but watch them both as they sat talking and drinking, and seeing how they crossed and uncrossed their legs in a deliberate and provocative manner. The sight of them both and his own predicament, the fact that he could not conceal himself or turn away made his excitement all the more obvious and unavoidable.

'Just look at him,' remarked Annette, 'wouldn't you think he could control himself?'

'Disgusting!' responded Cheryl. 'It's obviously a problem he suffers from. I think a little treatment might reduce the swelling, don't you?'

'Yes, but a little something else first,' she answered, then arose and pulled open a cupboard to one side of the main door. 'That will do,' she remarked and both returned to Mike, leaving the table with its now empty bottle and glasses.

'Perfect,' commented Cheryl as Annette stepped back from him. The long, silver-blonde hair of the wig fell down over his shoulders. Annette stretched out her fingers and coaxed the fringe across his forehead.

'Hmm, I like that,' she commented, stepping slowly back. 'He could wear it for maid's duties with one of those little black dresses, with hand and leg cuffs of course. I'm sure Pauline would love it.'

'And Sonia could make him keep to it regularly,' added Cheryl, 'as a condition for letting him stay on.'

'I think so too, I'll have a word with her later, but meanwhile . . .'

Annette stepped over to one of the leather chairs and retrieved the strap.

'Let's see what we can do about his little problem.'

She moved around behind him whilst Cheryl, hands on hips, regarded the skimpy nylon pouch, bulging and gaping around the sides with his constrained erection. With eyes closed tightly, he shook with each stroke as Annette applied the strap to first one side of his behind and then the other until he was sure that his flesh was aflame.

'Is it working?' she enquired, letting the strap hang limply.

Cheryl ran her hand down over the straining pouch, cupping and squeezing, feeling the heat and the strengthening hardness through her latex glove.

'No, it's just as bad,' she answered with a look of serious concern, at the same time running two of her fingers under the top of the pouch and down each side of the base of his penis. 'If anything, it's getting a lot worse.'

'Then,' announced Annette, raising the strap again and bringing it down with a sharp whack between each syllable, 'we'll-have-to-try-some-thing-else!'

Each stroke, descending with a burning sting, made him jerk against the restraints. With each jerk, Cheryl's fingers slipped a little further down over his aching shaft. Annette threw down the strap and Cheryl moved aside to let her take up position in front of him. She passed her arms around his torso and he felt her warm, perfumed sensuality as her body pressed against his. Cheryl moved behind and he tensed as her smooth latex fingers slipped around and under his suspenders. He felt her tug at the two small knots, was aware of the cord about his waist suddenly giving way and felt his penis spring free and upwards.

'Ooh, bad boy!' sang Annette with the eager head pushing under her lace skirt and between her thighs. 'A few little poses now I think,' she smiled, stepping back, then slipping her fingers about the swollen and reddened shaft and working it slowly back and forth.

His eyes darted with some alarm up and around the room. The bright lights, all the pre-planning, her last remark – surely they were not ...! When the cool latex fingers caressed gently about his testicles, he ceased to care. Annette released his penis and moved aside whilst Cheryl, her gloved hand still under him, fell to her knees and slid her lips over the head and down the shaft. Mike groaned and moved his pelvis back and forth to culminate this act of fellatio in the way he so urgently desired. But it did not last long enough, for Cheryl knew only too well how far to go before the point of no return was reached. With a few short seconds to spare, she released him and Annette took her place. This time it was not her mouth she would use in this voluptuous game but another part of her beautiful anatomy. She took her breasts in her hands and squeezed them together over the moist shaft, moving them up and down so that the glistening head appeared and disappeared between her cleavage. He was not aware of Cheryl's brief absence from the spot but was aware of her voice upon her return when she said, 'Careful ... not much more or we won't need this.'

By now his loins were like a dam waiting to burst. He felt a moment of despair as Annette ceased the play with her breasts, so close to the edge was he, and willed her mentally to go on.

They heard him take in a sharp breath and felt his body tense as Cheryl's hand returned and closed about the shaft, working it quickly and firmly. Annette cupped his testicles in one hand, whilst with the other, held one of the empty wine glasses, which Cheryl had a moment ago handed to her, directly over the head.

'Best wank he's ever had, I'll bet,' she commented. Then he groaned, his body jerking rigidly against the restraints, his pelvis shaking as he spurted repeatedly into the glass, his organ pulsating against the firm latex fingers.

'Oooooooh! There's a good boy!' grinned Annette, whilst Cheryl's hand continued its sensual task until they were sure he was done. In a short time his body relaxed, his eyes opened, and he waited, sagging visibly against the restraints.

Annette replaced the wine glass with its warm contents, next to its empty companion on the table, then returned holding a paper tissue.

'Better clean him up for the next shift,' she said, wiping the head of his still, red and erect penis.

'Does he know he's a star?' asked Cheryl, looking him up and down as she began to peel off the long rubber gloves.

'Well, if he didn't before,' she answered, looking into the eyes of their helpless prisoner, 'he probably does now.'

'I'm going to powder these and get my bathrobe,' said Cheryl, moving towards the bathroom.

Annette returned to the table and pulled on her own bathrobe, ignoring the stifled, 'Mmmmm-mmm-mmm!' from the floodlit figure behind her.

Cheryl emerged from the bathroom, tying the belt of her robe. 'See you downstairs for coffee?'

'Yes, give me fifteen minutes to get sorted out.'

The muffled protests became louder and more urgent as they approached the door.

'Is he trying to say something?' asked Cheryl, turning to regard him with a look of amused perplexity.

'I don't know; he's been making a lot of noise the last few minutes.'

Mike wasn't struggling. He had realised long since how futile that was.

'Don't worry!' came Annette's voice from over the room. 'The maids will be coming to clear up in ten minutes.'

'Kim and Lorna are on duty today,' added Cheryl, 'they'll just love to see you dressed up like that!'

'And,' added Annette, 'they have strict instructions to make sure you fill that other wine glass before they undo you!'

The door closed and he was alone, a captive mounted on display and waiting with no hope of escape on the illuminated stage. The room was silent except for the creaking of the chains as he adjusted his body. In his mind he counted the seconds and the minutes, minutes which drifted by with ponderous slowness. In this contemplative silence he became more aware of the things he was wearing and their feel against his skin. He could deny their sensuality to others, laugh it off even, but he could not deny to himself the secret and daring fascination he felt in wearing them. Even the unyielding straps and chains which held him and the firm tape which sealed his mouth closed were oddly reassuring now. He couldn't move, couldn't protest, so why feel any guilt about his bizarre situation?

He was still in deep thought about these novel sensations when he heard a key turning in the outer door, and the sound of voices approaching. The sound of laughter reached his ears as the inner door began to open.

# 11

# Lure of the Web

It was pleasantly lonely here, away from the house, the friendly chatter and company of the others. Except for Karen, few people came to the seat under the tree, to feel the breeze or watch the sun on the distant water. She had seen nothing of Karen even though it was a Saturday and a mellow, warm autumn day. She took up her magazine and began to read but soon, something caught her eye. Two figures strolled along the rise between herself and the house, two figures with whom she had not the slightest desire to spend any time in conversation. It was with a feeling of some relief that she observed Pauline and James were moving away and not towards her.

'Angie,' came a voice from her other side. She turned abruptly.

'Oh, Karen!' she smiled with welcoming gesture.

'Sorry to creep up the other way but I wanted to avoid...'

'Don't worry, I saw them over there. Where have you been? I've looked out for you all day – you weren't around for lunch.'

'No,' she answered sitting down by Angela, 'I didn't feel hungry – I went for a walk as far as the main road.'

'God, that's half way to the village. When did you get back?'

'Er, about half an hour ago. I did start over here once but I saw you reading. I thought perhaps you might not want...'

'Karen, sweety, what's the matter?'

'Nothing, maybe I'm homesick.'

'Come on, we both know it's not that. Something's bothering you and has been for a while, I can tell. Is it her?'

'What, Pauline?'

'Yes, Pauline!'

'Oh, no, nothing like that.'

There were decisions Karen had to make, and one in particular, one that followed her like a shadow others could not see and a shadow of which she could not talk. She saw the look of concern on Angela's lovely face and smiled into her soft, blue-grey eyes with an attempt at reassurance.

Angela took her hand and said, 'You can talk to me if you have a problem – it will never go beyond the two of us.'

'Yes, Angie I know. I'm almost tempted but ... well I don't see how I can.'

'Look,' smiled Angela, picking up a white paper bag at her side. 'I scrounged a couple of chocolate cakes from the kitchen before I came out – one for you and one for me. I know it's utterly decadent but they're full of fresh cream!' She opened up the bag and held it out.

'Oh, thanks Angie, I will then. I really appreciate you trying to cheer me up and I'm glad you're here.'

Angela watched her take the cake and Karen smiled as if to say that this simple act had lifted her spirits a little.

'Angie, how do you fit in to all of this?'

'Fit in – how do you mean?'

'Well, you're such a sweet and gentle person. How do you cope with ... with ...?' Karen sighed and looked out towards the sea. 'I'm trying to understand you see – to make sense of everything.'

'You mean the sex, the videos, all that?'

'Yes, that's what I mean. You're a real person with things you love and hate, things that make you laugh and cry, things you find in the world that are special to you and yet ... yet, every thing here seems to me so far from the normal world. I'm no longer sure who is out of step, me or the rest of you.'

'It's strange,' replied Angela, 'strange hearing you put it like that. We – I, if you like, don't really see things in that way at all. We all have our bodies, our needs, our urges – we just express them differently here from how we would elsewhere. All right, it's contrived most of the time but so is almost everything else we do in life. D'you know where my first experience of sex was? I'll tell you. It was in the back of an old Ford Escort in a pub car park! We were both pissed when I had my first intercourse and I was in tears afterwards. I thought for weeks, if that's what it's all about then you can bloody well keep it. Here, the blokes, and the girls have got class – no one is going to hurt me, I can enjoy a good screw with people I find attractive and I get paid well for doing it! When I look back at the alternatives, I really don't feel I have any problems and nobody forces me to stay.'

'Yes, OK,' answered Karen, 'but you are made to do things; you're compromised. Look, that day in the hotel, at my interview, you had to come in wearing those things, how do you . . .?'

'Karen dear!' interrupted Angela, with a broad smile. 'You join a club so you expect to comply with the rules. If you don't like the rules, you go elsewhere; simple. But what you saw as some kind of degradation, and I remember your face, I really do, that was no more than a charade. You looked so worried and embarrassed, it wasn't easy for me not to laugh. I think Sonia had a job keeping a straight face too.'

'Oh, Angie, you're much more of a realist than I am and I used to think I was the one who had everything in perspective.'

'Look, love,' smiled Angela, 'there are all sorts of perspectives on all sorts of things and what is right or wrong is often a matter of fashion, let alone somebody's opinion. Whatever is worrying you might not be a problem at all to someone else, if you see what I mean. But then, I don't know what it is, or, perhaps you don't think I do.'

'Do you know?' sighed Karen.

'I think you're getting involved in something that scares you, with someone we both know.'

'Yes, Angie I am, and I really am scared.'

'Well, I'm not going to pry but I'd say that nothing you or any of us does in this place is final. It's not like marrying some beer swilling yob back in England, then living in poverty with three or four kids on some damned estate. You can go as far as you want but if you don't like what you find, you can always turn around and close the door behind you. Am I making sense?'

'Yes, I understand perfectly – but it's not that simple – there's feeling, involvement and ...'

'Karen!' cut in Angela. 'Life isn't a set of rules to be followed blindly. None of us was born with everything planned out in advance either. I've had relationships at different times and with different people; some of them seemed permanent and deadly serious at the time but none of them were in the end.'

She placed her hands on Karen's and Karen smiled, watching the warm breeze move the fringe of silver-blonde hair across her forehead.

'I know you have pent up feelings, sweety. I realise how lonely you sometimes feel, but the difference between you and the rest of us is quite superficial you know. If you find you've made a mistake, it's not the end of the world is it? It's not as though you've signed away your life! It's funny isn't it – in a place like this where you can find yourself subject to so much control, I actually feel freer than I ever did before. To me, you're neither one thing nor the other. You're a prisoner of indecision, or even worse, a prisoner of your own guilt.'

'Angie, you really surprise me. I've never heard you speak like this before. You're like a rock that weathers the tides and storms whereas I seem to be drifting out of control with no real direction at all.'

'Karen, I really think there's more to you than that. Forget your past hang-ups and forget the self righteous people you were brought up with. What the hell do most of them get out of life anyway? We're all only here once, at least that's my feeling, so why bother about what you do as long as you don't hurt someone else by doing it?'

'You make lots of sense Angie and I can't argue with what you say, but if I still have doubts and anxieties it's because I'm me and not you, and I can't help it.

'Oh come on! You have your own strength, I can see that. Maybe I'm preaching to someone who's really figured some of it out a lot better than I have.'

'No, no, you've been a great help, you really have. I feel a lot better and it doesn't seem like preaching to me, honest.'

'Well there you are, just let youself go for once – get it all out of your system. Tell you what, why don't you go and see Val at the beauty parlour and have one of their special massages? Some of the things they . . .'

'I have,' cut in Karen, 'and I didn't know what it was about the first time around, until it was too late. Actually, even I have to admit that it's good fun.'

Angela laughed. 'Karen you're so sweet.'

Karen felt her face redden, remembering who else had used those words to her not so long ago. They talked and laughed in the sun, forgetting the time, feeling the breeze and hearing the birds.

'Well, I don't know about you,' said Angela eventually, 'but cakes or no, I'm still hungry. Fancy a bite to eat?'

Karen eyed her watch; it was a quarter past six. It was unusually early for either of them to eat but . . .

The sun was getting low on the horizon now and the air was beginning to cool. A leaf fell lazily, spiralling down onto the empty seat where, until a few moments ago, they had sat, two warm friends together.

Karen sat before the mirror, brushing her golden hair, still naked, her skin tingling and warm from the soothing effects of the shower. She laid down the brush and contemplated herself, running her hands over her firm, full breasts and feeling the nipples harden. In a half open drawer beside her lay the instrument of her secret pleasures, pink and smooth, always ready to serve her in the quiet seclusion of her apartment, to feed her wild and secret fantasies,

fantasies that even now, she never dared to admit fully, even to herself. She reached down to touch it but stopped with her hand resting on the edge of the drawer. The small clock above said twenty to eight. Not long to go.

'God I could do with a drink now, not later,' she breathed closing the drawer and rising from the seat.

It did not, at the time, occur to her as odd that she should knock at the door of the rooms to which she always had full access, but knock she did before entering, well aware of the sounds of chatter and music coming from the bar and restaurant around the corner to her rear. The world outside was shut out as the door closed behind her and she found herself in semi-darkness. A voice from the island of light at the other side of the room reached her.

'Go and sit down, dear, whilst I tidy these few bits of paper away!'

She walked silently over to the green leather chairs, observing that all the blinds were closed on the inside as well as the outside windows, giving the room that air of secret intimacy she had experienced when she had come down to watch the tape during the previous evening. She smoothed the bathrobe under her and sank into the perfumed, sighing leather.

'Am I . . . am I a bit early?' she asked nervously, locking her fingers about her knees and concentrating, from the corner of her eye, on the brass desk lamp with its green shade.

'A little, but it doesn't matter in the least,' came the reply and the lamp clicked off.

Sonia appeared and stood before her, a dark figure, almost sinister in her black, ribbed sleeveless top with its high collar, her wide, maroon leather belt, black satin tights and black, lace-up ankle boots with long heels. They were the boots, thought Karen, that Sonia had worn when they first met in England. Sonia looked slim, lithe and cat-like.

'I take it you've eaten, my dear – if not, I can . . .'

'Yes, thanks, I have.'

'I put some champagne in the fridge earlier – would you like champagne?'

'Oh, I've not had champagne for ages, I . . . yes, please I would.'

From the lighted kitchenette, next to her own office, Karen heard the pop of the cork and the click of glasses. She allowed herself to relax, settling back into the chair and resting her hands across her lap. But as Sonia poured the champagne and, smiling, passed the glass with its effervescent contents over to her, she realised she would not be able to hide her apprehension easily. She leaned forward to take up the glass, self consciously pulling the bathrobe tighter about her knees, wishing, now it was too late, that she had put on proper clothes, feeling that she might appear to be offering herself and . . .'

'Cheers!' cut in Sonia's voice through her thoughts.

'Cheers,' replied Karen, lifting the glass to her lips with a trembling hand. Sonia looked at her eyes as she replaced the glass on the table a little harder than she had intended, a little emptier than it should have been.

'Well, at least you came down and I'm very glad. I half expected you not to turn up at all. Instead, here you are, fresh and lovely despite your ordeals.'

'Ordeals? Oh, nothing has been an ordeal Sonia, really – I wouldn't be here if I thought that.'

'Good, because I like to have your company my dear. As much as I think of all the others, you are rather special.'

Karen felt herself blush and was glad that the nature of the lighting did not reveal this to Sonia.

'I like your company too,' she answered, raising her glass once more. 'You're very understanding, like Angie, Val and Kim, but different.'

She hesitated whilst Sonia refilled their glasses.

'I ought to try a bit more . . . to fit in, you know. The idea you had about modelling some of the things . . . I'd like to have a go . . . I don't mind what.'

She felt a current running through her body and almost

209

caught her breath. What was she saying? What was she letting herself be drawn into? But, deeper down, she knew, and her deeper self wanted to go on, and on.

'Let's keep all that a secret between ourselves shall we?' smiled Sonia. 'All those nice things – just between you and I, and when you feel like it – well ...'

'Yes ... yes, if you think so ... just between ourselves.'

'Everything I mean; our having a drink together – everything.'

'Sonia, you know I wouldn't ... I haven't ... I just don't discuss – look, I'd hardly be sitting here talking to you now if ...'

'Please sweetheart,' interrupted Sonia, 'I know I can trust you. If I couldn't trust you, I probably couldn't trust anyone. I know I was quite wrong to say what I did the other evening.'

She leaned over and took Karen's hand.

'You weren't trying to deceive me – you were only curious and I don't mind that; really I don't.'

Karen did not move her hand away, nor did she avert her eyes from the dark gaze which searched into her. Rather, she found herself drawn towards those eyes and carried along as a flower by a secret stream in a deep cavern.

'I'll put on some music. What would you like this evening – Gershwin, Porter, or something more modern?'

'Something soothing, I think, something for a warm evening even though it's cool outside.'

'All right then,' she said, rising from her chair, 'let's see what I can find. You drink up and I'll refill your glass, yes?'

'God, I shouldn't drink any ... oh, yes all right, why not?'

Karen felt a dark sensation running through her being. It was more than the effects of the champagne, more than just the result of few drinks. She was aware too of a burning in the pit of her stomach and in her loins. She wondered if Sonia understood, if Sonia felt it too.

Their conversation carried on deeper into the evening.

Sonia opened more champagne and Karen lost track of the number of glasses as well as of the passing time. Now, she felt relaxed and easy, and the outside world mattered no more than did the far side of the distant moon.

At length she said, 'Sonia, what's behind the door near your desk; it intrigues me. You said yourself I'm curious and . . .'

'And now seems a good time to ask,' cut in Sonia with a low voice.

'Well, I just wondered, that's all. Somebody asked me the other day if I knew and I said that I didn't.'

'I think most people know my room is down here simply by a process of elimination.'

Sonia arose from the chair and stood by Karen, arms folded.

'Perhaps I'll let you come and have a look.'

Karen downed the remains of her wine and stood up a little unsteadily to find herself facing Sonia. Again their eyes met and Karen opened her mouth slightly as she felt Sonia's hands brush her cheeks and hold the sides of her face. Then Sonia's hands fell and held her firmly above the elbows, pushing back her arms as their lips met with a burning which would have stifled any protest even if such protest had formed only in Karen's mind.

Their lips separated for a moment but Sonia's grip remained on her.

'You know what curiosity did don't you my dear?'

Karen did not reply even when she felt the gown loosening about her body and Sonia's breath like the caress of a secret flame upon her neck. She closed her eyes as the robe fell away and firm, cool hands played and teased about her breasts and nipples. Electric fingers arced down her spine pushing under her gossamer briefs, into the cleavage of her behind, making her draw in her breath suddenly.

'Don't move, my dear, stay just as you are,' came the voice close to her ear, and so she remained with her eyes closed, knowing that Sonia had left her, and crossed over to the other side of the room.

'No,' she breathed to herself, 'no, I mustn't let it happen again.'

With the effects of the drink, and the turmoil in her mind because of the last few minutes, she was unaware of how much, or how little time had passed by when she once more sensed movement near her. She felt a warm kiss on the side of her neck which made her shiver as her wrists were pulled back behind her. She knew from the feel and sound of the leather strap with its metal buckle what Sonia was doing, but accepted it as her wrists were secured together with the palms of her hands facing. Thinking that it was done, she started to move but again the voice ordered, 'Stay still!'

Something was slipped behind her arms just below the elbows and began to pull on them, drawing them in towards the middle of her back, pulling ever tighter, drawing back her shoulders and forcing out her breasts.

'Wait! Sonia – please!' she protested, twisting her head around.

She heard the strap end passing through the roller buckle and felt the tension increase further until her straining elbows met and the buckle was secured. The hands moved away and the two short straps held fast. Sonia moved around and placed her hands on Karen's shoulders, bringing her face closer.

'That shouldn't be too uncomfortable for you my dear – you're double jointed are you not?'

'Yes, but . . .'

Sonia's lips met hers with greater passion and, as once before, fingers slipped down her stomach and darted outrageously into the lips of her sex, this time finding her moist and inviting. But she was fast becoming aware of other forces at work within her body which she was obliged to recognise, and these came upon her now with urgency. She sought to turn her mind from that which so possessed it.

'Sonia! she gasped. 'Please, you'll have to let me go!'

'Will I now?' breathed Sonia, looking into her eyes.

'Please, it's all that wine – I can't help it – I need to . . .'

Sonia laughed gently but showed no sign of undoing her

arms, instead she turned her towards the door just beyond the kitchen entrance.

'This way my dear, you ought to know where it is,' she said, moving Karen onwards.

'Yes, of course, but how am I going to . . . I mean, how can I . . .?'

By now they had reached the bathroom entrance. Sonia pressed the light switch, then guided her inside towards the bidet.

'Here we are, let's sit you astride it,' she said, tugging down the blue panties.

Karen twisted around and looked at her in alarm.

'Sonia, please – I can't go like this – I won't . . . I won't do it!'

She twisted about but her arms remained rigidly trussed and useless.

'I don't think you have much choice my dear,' replied Sonia, turning on the bidet taps so that the water splashed and circled about the blue porcelain bowl, the sound raising Karen's need from urgent to desperate. For a moment she stood hesitating, her face a mask of indecision. After a few agonising seconds she could wait no longer. She moved to the bidet and would have sat down facing the wall with her back to Sonia. But Sonia took her by the shoulders and forced her around to face outwards, pushing her down with her legs spread open astride the bowl. Karen sought to hold herself back until Sonia had turned away, but Sonia did not intend to turn away. Instead, she moved around to her side and, resting one foot on the bowl edge with Karen's bound arms against her leg, she circled the girl's body with her arms until her hands slid under the out-thrust breasts and her lips brushed Karen's neck and cheek. Karen gasped, felt herself suddenly lose control and began to relieve herself into the bowl beneath her in an inexhorable and copious stream. Sonia's hand slipped down Karen's stomach and her fingers squeezed either side of her sex as she continued to discharge her reservoir of pale amber liquid.

When eventually she stopped, Karen felt warm water splashed between her legs for a few moments until Sonia's fingers began once more their unstoppable drama at the core of her sensuality. She had learned that there was no point struggling and, spread astride the basin as she was, Sonia could reach her most intimate places and do, indeed was doing, just as she pleased. Nor could Karen hide her own excitement from those cool, exploring fingers. She knew that from the fire in her sex, the fire spreading through her body, that it must have been very obvious how aroused she was.

It was the second time Sonia had manipulated her this way, but this time, even with the humiliation of being forced to urinate in full view of her as part of the game, Karen felt her rising lust unencumbered by the same degree of fear and guilt which was present on that first occasion. Indeed, she threw back her head, her breath rasping hoarsely, and forced her lips back against Sonia's with wanton passion. Sonia spread and entered her sex deeper, quickening the fire into a consuming blaze until her cries rang about the small room as one in passionate despair.

As Karen's breathing became more regular, she opened her eyes and again felt the water rinsed about her loins. Sonia's arm was still about her shoulder, keeping her steady but now that same arm helped her to rise up from the bidet whilst the other applied a soft towel to her wet thighs and behind.

'You are very sensual my dear,' came Sonia's voice close to her ear. 'I think your guilt about yourself has been keeping the tide back for too long. Now the sea is coming in.'

Sonia replaced the towel and Karen, feeling discomfort in her shoulders, looked at herself reflected in the large mirror and saw, as well as felt, how strictly Sonia had pinned back her arms and rendered her helpless with those two short straps. As if reading her thoughts, Sonia released the elbow strap and then freed her wrists.

'Your arms must ache. Some people couldn't stand that for more than a few minutes you know.'

'Oh,' was all Karen could say in reply.

Sonia kissed her and even then she knew that the turmoil within was not abated and that the spirit of voluptuousness was not laid low by what had just passed.

She found herself alone for a few seconds, then Sonia reappeared with her bathrobe, helping her to put it on over limbs which were stiff and aching.

'You do so like to be in control Sonia, don't you?' she said doing up the belt about her waist.

'I always have my dear – complete control. Does it worry you?'

'Worry me?' answered Karen, following her into the main room. 'I . . . I don't know. When I feel I can't help myself, it's like being a passenger when someone is driving a car too fast. You have no control, you feel frightened, and yet . . .'

'And I want to be the driver,' interrupted Sonia. 'I want to bring out of other people what they try to hide. I want to cut through the pretence, make them say who they are and what they want!'

'But there are other ways.'

'Yes, my dear, of course. But here it's what brings us the creature comforts and puts a decent bottle of champagne in the cupboard, as you are aware.'

'Yes, of course,' Karen whispered, looking into Sonia's eyes. Sonia stroked her cheeks and smiled, 'You asked about my rooms earlier. Perhaps now you would like to see the inner sanctum?'

Her face came closer until Karen felt her warm breath.

'Would you? Would you dare?'

She felt Sonia's lips on her neck and shuddered, guessing darkly what the implications of a 'yes' might be.

'Sit down for a while and think. I have to get changed and I had as much to drink as you. It gets difficult to ignore after a bit.'

She squeezed Karen's arm and turned saying, 'If you've gone when I get back, I will understand, but I hope you have not.'

Sonia disappeared into the bathroom. Karen sat in the green leather chair in the warm half light. She heard Sonia re-enter the room and remove keys from one of her desk drawers and heard the keys being used. She did not turn to look but knew only one door to this room was kept locked, and that door was now being opened.

'Darling,' came the voice from behind.

'Yes.'

Sonia appeared from the corner of her vision and Karen was aware that she hesitated momentarily to watch her before continuing around into full view. Karen arose from the chair and regarded her with surprise.

'Oh Sonia, you ... you're ...'

'Different?' cut in Sonia.

Sonia had about her body a vivid, red and black kimono. Gone was the Victorian bun hairstyle, for now her long raven hair fell wild and gypsy-like about her shoulders, framing her dark eyes and red lips, making her a portrait of dark intensity. She saw as well, from below the kimono, the long, tight leather boots with their high stiletto heels which made Sonia more commanding still.

'Sonia you look beautiful – I never imagined anyone could transform themselves the way you have.'

'When I'm alone it's the way I like to be, and sometimes with my closest friends.'

She looked, unblinking at Karen for a few moments then walked over to her. She knew Sonia was going to kiss her and met her kiss with the same enthusiasm. She wondered if Sonia burned inside when their lips met, as she did. Somehow her emotions could not be the same, but Karen didn't any longer care.

'Shall we go?'

She turned and Karen followed towards the mysterious door, seeing it ajar now for the first time.

She was aware of the unsteadying effects of the wine and how rapidly her heart was beginning to beat as she entered this secret place. The lights were on, but like those in other parts of the house, they were kept turned down warm and low, to give the room a sense of private intimacy. The room which opened before her was, like so much of the house, luxurious. But here was not designer luxury, pre-conceived and executed to order. This room conveyed a sense of modernist simplicity, combined with traditional oriental colour. The plain walls contrasted with the rich, patterned carpet and about the plain black leather seating were scattered big plush cushions in rich and vivid patterns. A plainly fashioned pine bed stood against one wall, its surface covered in a spread of warm and intricate colours. This room was a world within a world. It presented two sides, as did Sonia herself. Karen knew, if not consciously up until now, how their roles had become established – the dominant and the submissive. It was not what she had been through physically with Sonia on a previous visit as well as a short time ago, although that was proof enough. No, their respective roles had been established long before they even met. Karen needed the security of a dominant just as Sonia needed to prove her superiority over others by being in control at every level whenever possible. She knew that in this relationship, Sonia was going to want complete control of her, perhaps mentally as well as physically. Yet, dark and menacing as the lure was, it remained still a lure. She could have turned her back on it of course as Angela had pointed out. If she had declined the visit this evening, she was sure that Sonia would have continued to treat her with courtesy and affection, just as she was sure in accepting the invitation, she would have to also accept the implications and the consequences.

A voice cut through her thoughts.

'Do you like my room?'

'Oh yes, it's very ... very welcoming, very inviting.'

'Very consuming,' smiled Sonia.

'What do you mean?'

'It's just the way I feel about it.'

'Where do they lead to?' asked Karen, indicating towards two plain wooden doors situated some three metres apart over to her left.

'The one to the right,' answered Sonia, 'is a bathroom. The other is something I'm quite sure you have never seen before.'

She smiled at Karen and said, softly, 'I'll show you if you like, my dear, shall we go and look?'

They walked across the rich, deep carpet. Sonia unlocked and pulled open the door, reached inside and switched on the lights. She was right, of course, Karen had never seen anything like it before. At first, she was bewildered by the appearance of the chrome and black leather furniture, the hanging straps and devices, but the use to which they could be put gradually became evident to her.

'I see,' she breathed.

'That door at the far end,' said Sonia, 'leads to the beauty parlour. Not directly, but through a walk-in cupboard opposite their shower room; it's convenient for some of our guests.'

Karen backed away a little from the doorway but stopped as she felt Sonia's arm slip about her waist and push her forwards again until she entered the room, full of its sinister fascination. Then Sonia pulled her around and kissed her full on the lips as she had done earlier, and as before, Karen felt the surge of dark excitement welling up inside as she clasped Sonia's waist. In the subdued light of this bizarre room, an unspoken message passed between them. Sonia loosened Karen's bathrobe and slipped the garment from her, so that for the second time that evening she stood naked before her. Sonia left her and stepped over to a wall cupboard. This time, there was no order to stand still, though Karen did not turn to watch but remained staring ahead, silent and trembling.

When she returned, Sonia carried something black and ominous in her hands. Karen lost sight of it as Sonia moved behind her. Sonia's voice whispered by her ear, 'Let me put this on, I'm not going to hurt you.'

Both her arms were pushed outwards and the smell of leather entered her nose as something cool and almost rigid was passed about her body. The first impression Karen had was of a corset but immediately she saw what was attached to it and tried to pull away.

'Wait – no!' she protested. 'What are you putting on me?'

Sonia did not reply but pulled hard from behind, almost overbalancing her. She felt and heard the straps being buckled up and the corset tightened ever more, constricting about her waist.

'Sonia, please! Why this? You know I'll stay! There's no need to make me . . .'

'There is!' cut in the voice at her back. 'We have our roles to play, my dear.'

Within a few more seconds, the corset was tight and assertive about her body, from her slim waist up to her breasts, which were squeezed prominently up by the two small, stiff cups which held and supported, but did not conceal. That which had alarmed her came next. Swinging from metal 'D' rings, riveted by plates into the thick leather, were two smooth steel cuffs, some twenty or more centimetres apart. Sonia reached around her, and taking each arm in turn, forced the cuffs onto her wrists with a soft click so that she was held firm but not too tightly by the steel bands. Short but wide straps hung from the corset at each side. Sonia took those and fastened one about each of her arms, just above the elbow, pinning her upper arms rigidly against her sides and pulling her wrists apart against the cuffs so that her hands were immobilised too.

'There,' breathed Sonia, 'it's done.'

She walked around and looked into Karen's eyes, brushed the hair gently away from them, and slowly moved her hands down over the girl's shoulders and over her breasts.

'I do hope you are comfortable,' she said softly. 'You look very sweet in that little corset; it's a perfect fit.'

'Yes, it's comfortable . . . it . . . I've never seen things like these before – I never knew they existed until . . .'

'Until you came here. No, I don't expect you did, but all of them have their place and people do get used to them.

What you are wearing now, my dear, can be kept on for quite a long time without any problem, you'll see.'

Karen's eyes widened and she squirmed visibly against the restraints.

'Wh . . . what do you mean – how long am I going to be wearing this?'

'We;ll have to see, won't we, but you'll have plenty of time to get used to it.'

She took Karen's pinned arm and led her towards the side of the room. She resisted at once when she saw the steel cage standing before her.

'No Sonia! I don't want to – you're not putting me into that!'

Sonia's grip on her arm tightened and her other hand took Karen's waist.

'Don't make it difficult. You won't be here long, I promise you, but I have things to do and I don't want you walking around and bumping into anything or tripping up – do you understand?'

The door of the cage was open and waiting. Karen glanced about in apprehension as she was half guided, half pushed into the enclosed space. The area of the cage was little over a metre square but when the door slammed shut with a metallic ring, the space seemed to contract and close in on her. Sonia withdrew the key and walked back to the bedroom door. At the door she turned, and with a smile said, 'If anyone comes through from the beauty parlour, do tell them I'm not to be disturbed won't you?'

'What? No! . . . Sonia! I don't want anyone to see me like this! Sonia! Sonia!'

But the door closed and Karen was left alone with the echo of her own protests.

She stood still and listened, listened for the dreaded sound of another's voice or the sound of the far door opening. What if Val or Kim, or even worse, Jackie came through and saw her? The thought of Pauline entered her mind. That would be unbearable. She couldn't hide or cover herself. Even after her experience in the beauty parlour, she did not want to be seen involved with anything like this.

The silence deepened, and in the warm light she heard her own breath but nothing more. She looked down at the manacles, partly hidden by her own breasts, and at the straps about her arms. There was nothing she could do. Above her, some half a metre or more away, was the roof of the cage, its steel bars were hung with bright metal cuffs, as were the bars at the sides below her. She wondered who had occupied it previously and who had put him, or her, into it. She doubted that Sonia would have been involved directly even though her room was close by.

Behind her, flat against the wall was a small, hinged seat. Karen regarded this for a few moments and wondered how it could be pulled down into position so that she could at least sit. She bent her legs and eased herself down, leaning against the cold bars and stretching out her fingers to obtain a hold on the edge of the seat. It would not move. She saw there was a small catch under the lower edge and tried to reach that too, but it soon became obvious that the restraints she was wearing would not allow her to press the catch and pull the seat down at the same time.

She sighed and stood up, looking about the room at its various fittings and furnishings, trying not, but being unable to prevent herself, from imagining some of the things which took place here and upstairs. What if she was ... what if she was as she found herself now, but with the others – with Rodolfo or Mike there as well. But was she not already involved from the day she walked into the beauty parlour, or the night of the party, with Sonia before; and now, bound and trapped inside the cage, waiting for – what? What was the difference between her and the others?

The difference was everything. They did it deliberately and with planning. They did it for money and they didn't care who saw the results afterwards. She wasn't like that. She could never be like that. She couldn't help what had happened to her earlier, and this was secret, between two people who had become very close to each other and who had something to share. There was the difference.

There was a sound, but from where? She looked about the room. Then the door to her right swung open and Sonia appeared, still in the red and black kimono, a key held in her hand.

'So my little bird hasn't flown away,' she said, approaching the cage with a hint of a smile upon her face.

Karen remained silent as the key turned in the lock and the door swung open with a muted creak. Sonia looked even more striking than she remembered from even a short time ago, with her dark hair thrown about her shoulders and her dark eyes glistening. She led Karen across the room and Karen smelled her body, heavy with musk.

When they entered the bedroom, something was different, different with the bed, and there were several items on the table by the wall which she was sure were not there before. Sonia turned her around and sat her on the edge of the bed – then she saw, and drew in her breath.

On the table, in the warm half light, lay two dildos. One consisted of a large male organ with a smaller version of the same thing protruding out underneath it. Attached to it was a pink nylon harness with white plastic buckles. By it lay another of different design. This had two male members, back to back and curving away from each other. This had no harness, nor, she realised, did it need one. By them was a small jar of some cream-like substance. Karen, her mouth open, looked around. There, attached to each end of the headboard next to her, was a leather cuff with its glinting buckle hanging below. She felt a stirring, electric tremor inside as she realised how, if she lay on her back in the middle of the bed, these cuffs might be used to hold and restrain her. Sonia watched her expression and waited for her to speak. Karen began to do so but no words left her mouth. Sonia undid the belt of her kimono and let the garment slip away from her body. She stood before Karen quite naked except for her long, soft boots, and Karen saw that she had a small triangle of short, dark pubic hair. Her figure was slim and youthful, her breasts well formed and firm though not as large as Karen's.

She sat down next to Karen on the bed and looked into her eyes, moving her face closer until their lips joined. Karen closed her eyes, feeling the hand squeezing her breasts and nipples, then moving down over the leather corset to stroke her thigh.

'My dear,' whispered Sonia, slipping from the bed and onto her knees on the soft carpet. Karen felt her legs being parted and a hand gently pushing her until she gave way and sank onto her back. She caught her breath and began to tremble, feeling Sonia's mouth brush along her thigh and gently kiss the lips of her sex.

Sonia could see the state of her arousal just as she was beginning to feel her own and so allowed her tongue to give so much ecstasy and no more before she arose. She pulled Karen further onto the bed and then around until she lay in the centre with her head close to the headboard. Karen felt Sonia move down, then the warm breath and lips below the corset, moving slowly and voluptuously down the shaved flesh. A hand took her ankle and began to lift it.

It was to be a long evening and Karen knew she was to be sacrificed many times upon the altar of lust. Sonia knew too, that she had awakened in her, her deepest and darkest desires, and that having tasted of the nectar, she could only but want to return again and again into the bosom of that dark flower.

# Epilogue

Karen sat facing Sonia at the desk in the main office on one of the green leather chairs. They faced each other as they had done at that first interview, in a remote time and a distant place, when the rain beat hard against the window and the sky was darkening.

By the door stood two small suitcases, over one of which was draped her fawn raincoat. The desk in the small office was cleared and the empty chair pushed up against it. Karen, wearing her blue suit, with the skirt cut just above the knees, gazed down at her clasped hands where they rested in front of her on the edge of the desk.

'I promise you, my dear,' said Sonia, 'I'll see no one else until I hear from you to say that you won't be coming back. That office and your room can wait for as long as you need to decide.'

'Sonia ... I ... I don't know what to say. I'm ever so grateful that you understand, but I do need to get myself sorted out once and for all. I'll probably stay with my parents for a few days, then go and call on one or two of my old friends.'

'But you'll write to me as soon as you get to England won't you; or better still, phone me?'

'Yes, of course I will – you know I will.'

'Karen, there's something I want to give you.'

Sonia reached into her desk drawer and produced an engraved, oval silver locket on a fine silver chain. She regarded it for a moment, then looking at Karen, held the locket out to her.

'Keep this with you. I've had it since I was a child. It's never been out of my possession before.'

'Sonia ... I can't ... it must be valuable; I don't mean just worth a lot of money, I mean precious to you.'

Sonia leaned forward, bringing the locket closer.

'It's because it's precious to me that I wish you to take it and keep it, and then, perhaps, it will bring you back.'

Karen reached out and took the locket, carefully opening the clasp and placing the chain about her neck.

'I will keep it, I promise. Whatever happens, I will always keep it.'

'My dear, that's all I ask you to do, all I want you to say.'

A car horn sounded outside.

'I'll have to go, my flight is at three o'clock. I don't have a lot of time.'

They arose and Sonia followed her to the office door.

'Perhaps we should say goodbye here,' said Sonia, 'I don't want to come out to the entrance.'

Karen turned and saw that her dark eyes were glistening with tears.

'You should have told the others you know; they'll wonder why you didn't say anything.'

'No,' replied Karen, 'there's only Angie and you. I didn't want to go through all that, it would make it seem too final.'

They kissed, and as before, Karen experienced the burning in her lips and a flood of passion coursing through her body. Sonia opened the door and there stood Kim, waiting to help carry the cases to her car. Karen gave Sonia a final glance and a smile, seeing only those dark eyes, then the office door closed. She walked to the door, then hesitated, bending down to tickle the ear of the snoozing ginger form just inside the entrance.

'Goodbye, Pancake,' she smiled.

As they drove past the swimming pool, Karen saw Annette and Jackie in the sun by the pool edge and beyond them, someone sitting with a magazine at one of the tables. Further along, towards the woods, Mike was strolling with a spade over his shoulder, looking as though he had not a care in the world.

'You're not going to be away for long are you?' asked Kim, as their car approached the end of the driveway and the gate which led out onto the road. 'Where are you off to, Paris?'

Karen looked at her smiling face for a few moments. 'I'm going back to England,' she answered.

'Back to . . .! Whatever for?'

'Oh, I've a few things to deal with, that's all.'

'So you'll be returning in a week or so?'

'A week or so . . . I . . . I can't say . . . I don't know if . . .'

'Never mind, I'm sure you'll miss everything around here so much you won't be able to stay over there for long. And we'll still be around, Val and I, so as soon as you're back, you'll come and see us. We'll get you all warm and relaxed. We'll give you a real welcome home treat!' They moved away from the driveway and along the road.

Some minutes passed by in silence then Karen looked back over her shoulder. She glimpsed the sunlit house in the distance, through the trees and across the vineyards as they reached the cross-roads. Moments later, it was lost from view.

# NEW BOOKS

## Coming up from Nexus and Black Lace

*Sherrie* by Evelyn Culber
May 1995   Price: £4.99   ISBN: 0 352 32996 3
Chairman of an important but ailing company, Sir James is having trouble relaxing. But in Sherrie, seductive hostess on his business flight, he has found someone who might be able to help. After one of her eye-opening spanking stories and a little practical demonstration, money worries are the last thing on Sir James's mind.

*House of Angels* by Yvonne Strickland
May 1995   Price: £4.99   ISBN: 0 352 32995 5
In a sumptuous villa in the south of France, Sonia runs a very exclusive service. With her troupe of gorgeous and highly skilled girls, and rooms fitted out to cater for every taste, she fulfils sexual fantasies. Sonia finds herself in need of a new recruit, and the beautiful Karen seems ideal – providing she can shed a few of her inhibitions.

*One Week in the Private House* by Esme Ombreux
June 1995   Price: £4.99   ISBN: 0 352 32788 X
Jem, Lucy and Julia are new recruits to the Private House – a dark, secluded place gripped by an atmosphere of decadence and stringent discipline. Highly sexual but very different people, the three women enjoy welcomes that are varied but equally erotic.

*Return to the Manor* by Barbra Baron
June 1995   Price: £4.99   ISBN: 0 352 32989 0
At Chalmers Finishing School for Young Ladies, the tyrannical headmistress still has her beady eye on her pretty charges; the girls still enjoy receiving their punishment just as much as Miss Petty enjoys dispensing it; and Lord Brexford still watches breathless from the manor across the moor. But now there's a whole new intake for Miss Petty to break in.

### *The Devil Inside* by Portia da Costa
May 1995   Price: £4.99   ISBN: 0 352 32993 9
Psychic sexual intuition is a very special gift. Those who possess it can perceive other people's sexual fantasies – and are usually keen to indulge them. But as Alexa Lavelle discovers, it is a power that needs help to master. Fortunately, the doctors at her exclusive medical practice are more than willing to offer their services.

### *The Lure of Satyria* by Cheryl Mildenhall
May 1995   Price: £4.99   ISBN: 0 352 32994 7
Welcome to Satyria: a land of debauchery and excess, where few men bother with courtship and fewer maidens deserve it. But even here, none is so bold as Princess Hedra, whose quest for sexual gratification takes her beyond the confines of her castle and deep into the wild, enchanted forest ...

### *The Seductress* by Vivienne LaFay
June 1995   Price: £4.99   ISBN: 0 352 32997 1
Rejected by her husband, Lady Emma is free to practise her prurient skills on the rest of 1890s society. Starting with her cousin's innocent fiancé and moving on to Paris, she embarks on a campaign of seduction that sets hearts racing all across Europe.

### *Healing Passion* by Sylvie Ouellette
June 1995   Price: £4.99   ISBN: 0 352 32998 X
The staff of the exclusive Dorchester clinic have some rather strange ideas about therapy. When they're not pandering to the sexual demands of their patients, they're satisfying each other's healthy libidos. Which all comes as rather a shock to fresh-faced nurse Judith on her first day.

# NEXUS BACKLIST

All books are priced £4.99 unless another price is given. If a date is supplied, the book in question will not be available until that month in 1995.

## CONTEMPORARY EROTICA

|  |  | |
|---|---|---|
| THE ACADEMY | Arabella Knight | |
| CONDUCT UNBECOMING | Arabella Knight | Jul |
| CONTOURS OF DARKNESS | Marco Vassi | |
| THE DEVIL'S ADVOCATE | Anonymous | |
| DIFFERENT STROKES | Sarah Veitch | Aug |
| THE DOMINO TATTOO | Cyrian Amberlake | |
| THE DOMINO ENIGMA | Cyrian Amberlake | |
| THE DOMINO QUEEN | Cyrian Amberlake | |
| ELAINE | Stephen Ferris | |
| EMMA'S SECRET WORLD | Hilary James | |
| EMMA ENSLAVED | Hilary James | |
| EMMA'S SECRET DIARIES | Hilary James | |
| FALLEN ANGELS | Kendal Grahame | |
| THE FANTASIES OF JOSEPHINE SCOTT | Josephine Scott | |
| THE GENTLE DEGENERATES | Marco Vassi | |
| HEART OF DESIRE | Maria del Rey | |
| HELEN – A MODERN ODALISQUE | Larry Stern | |
| HIS MISTRESS'S VOICE | G. C. Scott | |
| HOUSE OF ANGELS | Yvonne Strickland | May |
| THE HOUSE OF MALDONA | Yolanda Celbridge | |
| THE IMAGE | Jean de Berg | Jul |
| THE INSTITUTE | Maria del Rey | |
| SISTERHOOD OF THE INSTITUTE | Maria del Rey | |

| Title | Author | Month |
|---|---|---|
| JENNIFER'S INSTRUCTION | Cyrian Amberlake | |
| LETTERS TO CHLOE | Stefan Gerrard | Aug |
| LINGERING LESSONS | Sarah Veitch | Apr |
| A MATTER OF POSSESSION | G. C. Scott | Sep |
| MELINDA AND THE MASTER | Susanna Hughes | |
| MELINDA AND ESMERALDA | Susanna Hughes | |
| MELINDA AND THE COUNTESS | Susanna Hughes | |
| MELINDA AND THE ROMAN | Susanna Hughes | |
| MIND BLOWER | Marco Vassi | |
| MS DEEDES ON PARADISE ISLAND | Carole Andrews | |
| THE NEW STORY OF O | Anonymous | |
| OBSESSION | Maria del Rey | |
| ONE WEEK IN THE PRIVATE HOUSE | Esme Ombreux | Jun |
| THE PALACE OF SWEETHEARTS | Delver Maddingley | |
| THE PALACE OF FANTASIES | Delver Maddingley | |
| THE PALACE OF HONEYMOONS | Delver Maddingley | |
| THE PALACE OF EROS | Delver Maddingley | |
| PARADISE BAY | Maria del Rey | |
| THE PASSIVE VOICE | G. C. Scott | |
| THE SALINE SOLUTION | Marco Vassi | |
| SHERRIE | Evelyn Culber | May |
| STEPHANIE | Susanna Hughes | |
| STEPHANIE'S CASTLE | Susanna Hughes | |
| STEPHANIE'S REVENGE | Susanna Hughes | |
| STEPHANIE'S DOMAIN | Susanna Hughes | |
| STEPHANIE'S TRIAL | Susanna Hughes | |
| STEPHANIE'S PLEASURE | Susanna Hughes | |
| THE TEACHING OF FAITH | Elizabeth Bruce | |
| THE TRAINING GROUNDS | Sarah Veitch | |
| UNDERWORLD | Maria del Rey | |

**EROTIC SCIENCE FICTION**

|  |  | |
|---|---|---|
| ADVENTURES IN THE PLEASUREZONE | Delaney Silver | |
| RETURN TO THE PLEASUREZONE | Delaney Silver | |

|  |  | |
|---|---|---|
| FANTASYWORLD | Larry Stern | |
| WANTON | Andrea Arven | |

## ANCIENT & FANTASY SETTINGS

|  |  | |
|---|---|---|
| CHAMPIONS OF LOVE | Anonymous | |
| CHAMPIONS OF PLEASURE | Anonymous | |
| CHAMPIONS OF DESIRE | Anonymous | |
| THE CLOAK OF APHRODITE | Kendal Grahame | |
| THE HANDMAIDENS | Aran Ashe | |
| THE SLAVE OF LIDIR | Aran Ashe | |
| THE DUNGEONS OF LIDIR | Aran Ashe | |
| THE FOREST OF BONDAGE | Aran Ashe | |
| PLEASURE ISLAND | Aran Ashe | |
| WITCH QUEEN OF VIXANIA | Morgana Baron | |

## EDWARDIAN, VICTORIAN & OLDER EROTICA

|  |  | |
|---|---|---|
| ANNIE | Evelyn Culber | |
| ANNIE AND THE SOCIETY | Evelyn Culber | |
| THE AWAKENING OF LYDIA | Philippa Masters | Apr |
| BEATRICE | Anonymous | |
| CHOOSING LOVERS FOR JUSTINE | Aran Ashe | |
| GARDENS OF DESIRE | Roger Rougiere | |
| THE LASCIVIOUS MONK | Anonymous | |
| LURE OF THE MANOR | Barbra Baron | |
| RETURN TO THE MANOR | Barbra Baron | Jun |
| MAN WITH A MAID 1 | Anonymous | |
| MAN WITH A MAID 2 | Anonymous | |
| MAN WITH A MAID 3 | Anonymous | |
| MEMOIRS OF A CORNISH GOVERNESS | Yolanda Celbridge | |
| THE GOVERNESS AT ST AGATHA'S | Yolanda Celbridge | |
| TIME OF HER LIFE | Josephine Scott | |
| VIOLETTE | Anonymous | |

## THE JAZZ AGE

|  |  | |
|---|---|---|
| BLUE ANGEL NIGHTS | Margarete von Falkensee | |
| BLUE ANGEL DAYS | Margarete von Falkensee | |

| | | |
|---|---|---|
| BLUE ANGEL SECRETS | Margarete von Falkensee | |
| CONFESSIONS OF AN ENGLISH MAID | Anonymous | |
| PLAISIR D'AMOUR | Anne-Marie Villefranche | |
| FOLIES D'AMOUR | Anne-Marie Villefranche | |
| JOIE D'AMOUR | Anne-Marie Villefranche | |
| MYSTERE D'AMOUR | Anne-Marie Villefranche | |
| SECRETS D'AMOUR | Anne-Marie Villefranche | |
| SOUVENIR D'AMOUR | Anne-Marie Villefranche | |

**SAMPLERS & COLLECTIONS**

| | | |
|---|---|---|
| EROTICON 1 | ed. J-P Spencer | |
| EROTICON 2 | ed. J-P Spencer | |
| EROTICON 3 | ed. J-P Spencer | |
| EROTICON 4 | ed. J-P Spencer | |
| NEW EROTICA 1 | ed. Esme Ombreux | |
| NEW EROTICA 2 | ed. Esme Ombreux | |
| THE FIESTA LETTERS | ed. Chris Lloyd | £4.50 |

**NON-FICTION**

| | |
|---|---|
| HOW TO DRIVE YOUR MAN WILD IN BED | Graham Masterton |
| HOW TO DRIVE YOUR WOMAN WILD IN BED | Graham Masterton |
| LETTERS TO LINZI | Linzi Drew |
| LINZI DREW'S PLEASURE GUIDE | Linzi Drew |

------------------------------

Please send me the books I have ticked above.

Name ...........................................

Address ...........................................

...........................................

...........................................

...................Post code ..............

Send to: **Cash Sales, Nexus Books, 332 Ladbroke Grove, London W10 5AH**.

Please enclose a cheque or postal order, made payable to **Nexus Books**, to the value of the books you have ordered plus postage and packing costs as follows:

UK and BFPO – £1.00 for the first book, 50p for each subsequent book.

Overseas (including Republic of Ireland) – £2.00 for the first book, £1.00 for the second book, and 50p for each subsequent book.

If you would prefer to pay by VISA or ACCESS/MASTERCARD, please write your card number and expiry date here:

...................................................

Please allow up to 28 days for delivery.

**Signature** ...........................................

------------------------------